SHE WOLF

Praise for Sheri Lewis Wohl

Scarlet Revenge

"Vampire stories have been written by hundreds of authors, but this is probably one of the few times that you will actually see one who works at the Library of Congress...With the setting of the story, it almost gives the feel of *National Treasure* meets paranormal."—*American Library Association's GLBT Round Table*

Vermilion Justice

"It's probably impossible to read this book and not come across a character who reminds you of someone you actually know. Wohl takes something as fictional as vampires and makes them feel real. Highly recommended."—*American Library Association's GLBT Round Table*

Necromantia

"This is one of the most sensational and thrilling books I have read in a long time. From the stirring opening scenes to the dramatic and exhilarating conclusion, this novel keeps the reader completely engrossed."—*Inked Rainbow Reviews*

By the Author

Crimson Vengeance

Burgundy Betrayal

Scarlet Revenge

Vermilion Justice

Twisted Echoes

Twisted Whispers

Twisted Screams

Necromantia

She Wolf

Visit us at www.boldstrokesbooks.com

SHE WOLF

by

Sheri Lewis Wohl

2017

SHE WOLF
© 2017 By Sheri Lewis Wohl. All Rights Reserved.

ISBN 13: 978-1-62639-741-5

This Trade Paperback Original Is Published By
Bold Strokes Books, Inc.
P.O. Box 249
Valley Falls, NY 12185

First Edition: January 2017

Credits
Editor: Shelley Thrasher
Production Design: Stacia Seaman
Cover Design by Melody Pond

Through pride we are ever
deceiving ourselves.
But deep down below the surface
of the average conscience
a still, small voice says to us,
something is out of tune.

—Carl Jung

PROLOGUE

Danzig, 1588

Snow was falling outside the window of Lily's bedchamber, making the world appear shadowy and white. It had arrived early this year, though she wondered if it came as an omen to what was to happen on the morrow. She was no different from her sisters or any other young woman of her class. That she felt like a woman drowning in the waters of the swiftly flowing river just beyond the forest trees was of no matter. It was to be done, and her heart was of no concern.

The young lord her father had chosen for her was as brutish as he was ugly. At least her sister, Sophia, had been blessed by God with a kind and handsome man who truly seemed to love her. How Lily longed for a match of the heart.

It could not be, for any nobleman her father chose her would fail to capture her heart. She would never find love, and she would always be an empty vessel. It was the way for those like her. It was not spoken of her kind and would not ever pass her lips. Only in her thoughts could she find solace. Only in her dreams would the touch she longed for come to her.

Soft hands, tender lips, and rounded flesh. Just the thought made her heart race. Fulfillment of that desire was not to be. Not for her. It was to be a hard hand and muscled flesh that took what she had guarded so carefully. Mother had sternly instructed her in the duties expected of a wife, and she knew of what awaited once her hand was joined with that of her husband. What details Mother thought too delicate to voice were shared by her sisters. They did not fill her head with pretty words and matrimonial joy. They used words of truth and brutal honesty. They tried to ready her and, in doing so, to protect her. She shivered at the thought of what she would be forced to endure and reminded herself to do as she must. Her family would not be shamed. Not by her.

Aldrich Adelmene was coarse and dreadful, but he was of noble blood and his family one of great wealth and standing. He was as powerful and well respected as he was crude and repulsive. All applauded the match between the great beauty and the great warrior. She would want for nothing, except for the love of the one she really desired.

As if bidden by the mere thought of her, Alexia floated into her room, followed by Taria. The very sight of Alexia made her breath catch in her throat. In her best gown of dark blue festooned with a string of pearls at her neck, Alexia was the most beautiful woman Lily had ever seen. It took effort not to rush forward and pull her into her arms. To kiss her as though her life was in peril, which, indeed, it felt as though it was.

It would not do to act upon her desire. Alexia had no idea how Lily felt about her, and she would keep her secret until her dying day. It was not proper, not in their world, and Alexia herself was bound to a nobleman by the contract made between her father and yet another groom's family. It was simply the way of the society into which they were born. Within a month of her own wedding, Alexia too would be the wife of a soon-to-be king and far away from the mountains and the forests of the lands where they had grown to the bloom of womanhood. When that day arrived, she would be helpless to stop the storm of tears that would befall her. Her heart was breaking a little more with each passing day.

Taria, unlike Alexia, was plain and almost man-like in her movements. She was as unexceptional as Alexia was exceptional. Despite their physical differences, they were all as close as if they were blood sisters. The three of them had grown up together, their families living within a horse-ride of each other. While Lily and Alexia were soon to be married, Taria's hand in marriage had not yet been sworn. Perhaps it was that she was so plain and so often failed to act like the lady she was raised to be. Lily had lost count of the times she had witnessed her dear friend acting contrary. Growing up, Taria could be found in sword-play with her brothers more often than in the manor house learning the ways of a lady. Her unbecoming behavior did not appear to alarm her family. Rather, they smiled and encouraged her willful ways. Lily often envied her powerful will. She just was not strong enough to defy her father and mother. She did as she was told. Always.

She turned and tried to give her friends the brightest smile she could summon forth. It was very hard for she did not feel gay or happy. What she most dearly wanted to do was to run away and be lost in the forest beyond. There she could dream of the freedom that would be denied to her.

Alexia came into the room, her gown sweeping, and gave Lily a kiss on the cheek. "You look so pale, my dearest. You must have some color when you join with your husband. He must witness the full glory of your beauty in order that he understand how he must cherish you."

Taria shook her head as she stomped in behind Alexia. Her gown was simple and dark, with very little adornment. Likewise, her hair was in a single braid and hanging down her back. Lily would have needed to run like the wind from her own home in order to be able to present herself looking so, for her father and mother would not have allowed her to be out in such disarray. Once more she envied Taria's freedom to be the woman she wished to be. How she would love to shed this heavy ornate gown and to pull every pin from the hair piled on top of her head. She would give anything to toss aside the heavy necklace at her throat, a wedding gift from Aldrich, and run with abandon.

Taria snorted. "She looks very well, Alexia, and why does she have to be primped for this man? What difference will it make if we put another pearl in her hair or add another gold chain around her neck? Her father has already sold her to the swine. The bargain has been sealed."

"Taria!" Alexia put her hand on her hips and stared at her in disapproval. "You must not speak of her father in that way. Someone might hear you. Must you always be so contrary?"

Lily sat on the edge of her bed and sighed. Her head felt heavy from the burden of her braided and jeweled hair. "Let her be, Alexia. It matters not, and if we are to speak true, she is correct. I have been sold to the highest bidder." She shivered at the thought of what awaited her on the morrow, and tears pooled in her eyes.

"See," Taria huffed. "I speak true. You, Alexia, my fine, pretty lady, are the one who does not. You live in the fairy tales our nursemaids told us when we were but babes. I do not live in that world of dreams and make-believe. I am here with my friend in the world of what truly is."

"Stop." Lily put her hands to her ears and tried not to let her tears spill. It was a difficult time, and she did not wish for it to become even more difficult. She longed only to spend a few hours with her lifelong friends before leaving her home forever. To walk out of the doors of her childhood home remembering how it was when they were young and carefree.

Taria and Alexia looked at each other. Taria spoke first as she knelt before Lily and put her hands on her face. "My apologies, dearest Lily. I did not mean to cause you pain. My heart is hurting at the thought of you leaving with that oaf…that man…and my sorrow falls to you and Alexia. It is not proper and I beg your forgiveness. I only long for tomorrow to never come and for the three of us to be together forever just as we always have been."

Alexia looked sad, tears forming in her beautiful eyes. "It is true. Our lives will change when the sun rises again, and we will never be the same. We always knew the day would come, and now it has."

Lily sighed and for a moment closed her eyes. She did not want to give in to sobs, for it would be of no help. Slowly she opened her eyes and stared at her friends, their faces so beloved. "Indeed it has, my sisters of the heart." How she wished she could sit here forever with the fire blazing and her two finest friends at her side.

"I have something for both of you," Alexia said, a light returning to her eyes. "Hold out your hands."

Lily and Taria both did as Alexia instructed. They always did as she told them. Though they were of the same age, it always seemed as though Alexia were the eldest. Their hands held out with palms up, Alexia pulled a small velvet pouch from her beaded bag. From it she produced three necklaces made of finely crafted gold links and sparkling rubies. She put one in each of their palms and continued to hold the third one in her hand.

"Our fathers and mothers may not be the same, but we are blood sisters just as though we shared blood," she told them. "These rubies will forever seal our pact as sisters. We may be taken away to far-off lands to live with men we do not love, but we will have these rubies to remind us that we will always be in each other's hearts."

Lily's tears could no longer be held back. She put her arms around her two dearest friends and held on tight. They both returned the embrace, and Taria, tough, boy-like Taria, kissed away her tears.

When it was time for them to leave, Lily kissed Taria on the cheek. Her embrace of Alexia went on a breath too long, and she knew it. If Alexia looked at her questioningly when she released her and stepped back, she paid it no mind. Her heart was breaking when the one she wished to spend her life with walked out of her chambers for the very last time.

Later that evening, Lily stood alone at the window of her bedchamber staring out into the night. A full moon rose high, and its bright golden light spilled over the beautiful snow-covered land. She wondered how a place so lovely could feel so much like the donjon of Rheinfels Castle. In the distance, the howl of a wolf cut through the night air. At least the wolf could run with abandon. She envied him.

Her room felt stifling and so she opened the window, though she knew her mother would disapprove. It allowed far too much cold air into her chambers, and Mother did not want her beautiful daughter to fall ill. At least not until after the wedding. After she and Aldrich became man and wife, her mother would be free to turn her full attention to Lily's brothers. They were the true children of her mother's heart. She was, and always had been, a burden to the cold woman who gave birth to her.

Resting her palms against the stone windowsill, she leaned out and breathed in the cold, fresh air. It smelled wonderful, and she closed her eyes to let it all wash over her. It brought her a moment of peace, and for that she was grateful. She heard the movement only a moment before she felt teeth against the fine skin of her neck. Roughly she was yanked from the window, and before she knew what was happening to her, she was tumbling through the air, falling down as the ground rushed up. She hit with a painful thump, the snow icy against her back and soaking through the thin cotton of her nightgown. She wanted to jump up and run, but she could not. Her arms and legs did not seem to want to obey her. The wolf that stood over her still body stared at her with eyes that somehow seemed familiar to Lily, though she could not imagine how that could be. As her vision began to fade to black, she wondered why her neck felt so warm and wet.

CHAPTER ONE

Colville, Washington, present day

Lily stood alongside the highway with her cell phone pressed to her ear. An amazing amount of traffic passed by, and considering where she was, she found it interesting. The breeze stirred up by the highway traffic whipped her hair around her face. She used one hand to hold it back. "You're sure this is where the problem is?" It really was hard to believe there was a preternatural issue clear out here that required her area of expertise. Of course, just as the volume of traffic coming this far out of the way surprised her, the preternatural activity did too.

On the other end of the call, her handler, Senn Heiserman, was halfway across the world sitting in his nice warm office and his nice comfortable chair. Undoubtedly he was scanning the graphs and reports his supercomputer generated on a daily basis. "Yes, our reports have been verified. You need to connect with the sheriff. What's her name?" She could hear the click of the keys on his keyboard. Just as she suspected, he was one with his computer. Some things were very consistent. "Oh yes, here it is, Jayne Quarles."

The name didn't mean anything to her. "Is she a friendly?" The long trip out here had made her weary, and she wasn't up to explanations or political correctness. Frankly, she didn't think she was up to this trip at all. Lately she'd been grumpy and discontented. Not shocking, considering how many years she'd been playing this game. It was way past time for a vacation. A really long vacation. She was going to have a heart-to-heart with Senn as soon as she was done here, and she was going to take, as they liked to say these days, some "me" time.

If Senn had any clue as to her current mood, he didn't let on. He continued talking without a pause. "I told you before you left, she's not 210-friendly. It won't be the first time you've had to deal with this, so stop stalling and get to work. I know you're not thrilled to be there, but the quicker you get on it, the quicker you can get back home."

Easy for him to say. He hadn't been out in the field in eons. Quite the opposite for her. She'd been out in the field for years. A lot of years. "Have you seen this place?"

The keys were clicking again. "Can't say I've ever been to Colville. Eastern Washington isn't a place I've visited, so no."

Hunted is what he really meant. Like her, Senn had traveled to hunt, not to vacation. Holiday was not something hunters like her or Senn ever had the time to enjoy. Except his decision to be the brains of the organization was a lot closer to time off than what she got. "Like you ever leave your little fortress. Give me a break."

It was true; Senn rarely ever left the sanctuary of his three-hundred-year-old home in Gydnia, Poland, any longer. Granted, it was a beautiful old house on the edge of the Baltic Sea that began its life as a humble little village dwelling in 1789 and eventually evolved into the impressive manor house it was today, but the man needed to get out more than he did. Ever since he'd returned from his last hunt in Quebec he seemed to isolate himself a little more every year. Something had happened there that so far he'd been unwilling to talk about. Whether he realized it or not, she was here for him and would do what she could to heal whatever wound had opened in Canada. He was like a father to her, the only one she'd had in five centuries. She'd always have his back.

That was why if she had to be out here kicking ass, he could haul his butt out once in a while too. Once he would have been right next to her, and she missed those days. Truth was she felt alone these days, or was it lonely?

"I get out." To her ears, his protest sounded like a pretty weak effort.

The wise thing to do would be to let it go. Then again, when had she ever let anything go? That wasn't her style. "When was the last time, Senn? When have you packed your bag and hunted? I'm traveling all over the world, and I could use some support of the Senn variety."

The clicking stopped and she could almost see his hands pause as they hovered over the keyboard. His head would be up, and he'd be staring out the big window that looked over the great expanse of grass outside. His beautiful green eyes would be focused on some faraway spot. After a moment of silence, he said, "We are not talking about me right now, Lily. We need to focus on the mission."

The expected response made her smile, and though she would like to continue screwing with him, he had a point. She didn't need to stand here on the side of the highway arguing about his growing agoraphobia. It wasn't going to change today, and he wasn't going to meet her here in the Pacific Northwest so they could hunt together. She was on her own, and her jabs weren't going to make any difference.

Besides, the truth was, there appeared to be a werewolf running amok up here in the mountains of eastern Washington, and she was here to stop it. It was what she did. It was what she'd been doing for almost five hundred years. She was good at hunting anything of preternatural ilk: vampires, gargoyles, witches, warlocks, and werewolves. Especially werewolves.

As the old saying went, takes one to know one.

Kyle Miller gripped the steering wheel and stared through the fog. This stretch of I-90 was a big pain in the ass, as it were. Though in pea-soup-thick fog it was more than a pain; it was a nightmare. Four hours ago, he'd hit Seattle after driving up from San Luis Obispo. That part of the trip had been awesome. The weather was great, and at the end of the rainbow, Ava had been waiting for him. She'd taken a cross-country flight from New Haven to Seattle, and he'd picked her up at the Seattle/Tacoma airport, known as SeaTac to the locals. Seeing her face as he pulled through the traffic and up to the curb had made his heart pound.

He was always up for a hunt. A hunt with Ava was the best. The powers that be didn't have to ask him more than once, even though it was about a nineteen-hour drive just to pick her up and then another six hours, give or take, to get where they needed to be. That was okay. He'd have driven across country to New Haven, if need be, just to pick up Ava. Now they were heading from western Washington to the small northeast Washington town of Colville. It would be his first trip here, though not the first time in the area. He had family in Spokane and had been there many times.

This stretch of freeway that went by the rural farming community of Ritzville was flat and, in his opinion, boring even under the best of circumstances. It was no reflection on the area. It could be pretty impressive when the crops were ripe and the wheat fields were swaying in the wind like a massive golden ocean. No, it was more that his tastes ran toward ocean views and warm breezes. He loved the smell of salt water, the sight of sailboats putting out to sea, and the feel of the ocean spray on his face. He felt alive and grounded when his feet were covered in damp sand and the sun was warm on his skin. Up this way, it was flat farmland and four seasons. Nice place to visit but he wouldn't want to live here.

This afternoon, shrouded in thick fog, the drive across the state was killing him. They'd made it over Snoqualmie Pass in the daylight, and that was good. Gassed up in Ellensburg just to be able to stretch their legs and grab a couple coffees. It was always a stirring sight coming down the final few miles of the Vantage hill and setting eyes on the massive Columbia River. It didn't fail him today either, except that bit of excitement had been over an hour ago. Now it was just mile after mile of flatlands. The most interesting part was the little signs on the fences describing the type of crop growing in each field. Damn, he was ready to get out of the car, except they still had a couple hours of driving before they hit Colville.

While it was true he might be sick and tired of being cooped up in the car, he wasn't sick and tired of his present company. He glanced over at Ava and couldn't keep the smile from his face. She was asleep, her head resting against the folded jacket shoved between the window and the back of the passenger seat. Her flight out of New Haven had been at the inhuman hour of six in the morning, which would have made it three here on the West Coast. Understandably she was exhausted. It didn't bother him to drive in silence. Time with Ava was good time as far as he was concerned, regardless of whether she was awake or asleep.

A fool he wasn't, and it hadn't taken a whole lot of brains cells to figure out he was in love with her. Seriously, though, who wouldn't fall in love with Ava? She was smart, beautiful, strong, and coolest of all, a witch. If he didn't know better he might believe she'd used her powers to cast a love spell on him. She didn't, and his feelings were the good old-fashioned kind that required no assistance whatsoever. As far as he knew, she wasn't aware of the depth of his feelings, and that was probably just as well, at least for the time being. He wasn't quite ready to 'fess up to the true nature of them. Not quite yet anyway. It was enough to be Jägers with her and to be sent out on a mission together.

When the Jägers recruited him it was like finding a home at last. Being a necromancer, even in the somewhat enlightened society they now lived in, wasn't exactly popular. On those rare occasions when people discovered what he could do, ultimately they turned out to be afraid of him or, if he was being honest, more like terrified of him. On some level, they could handle the idea that in their world existed werewolves and vampires, but somebody who could raise the dead creeped them out. More than once he thought about joining the dead he could so easily raise. Being different was okay. Being his kind of different was, at times, a burden.

At least until he met the Jägers. Four years two hundred and thirty-seven days ago, and not once since had he considered bailing on his odd life. For the first time in his thirty-one years he felt useful and, more important, necessary. As he struggled to come to grips with being the guy who reached across the barrier separating the living from the dead, it never occurred to him that there would actually be a place for him in either world. Yet here he was, trained, tough, and, dare he say it, cool. He was a preternatural ninja hunter straight out of an awesome graphic novel. It didn't get much cooler than that.

He held on to that thought as he worked to stay nonchalant during their drive toward the meeting in Colville. It was hard to do, being this close to Ava. He'd met her on his first field mission and was a goner right then and there. He didn't even know witches were real until he met her. Then again, most people didn't realize necromancers really existed either, so he figured that made them about even. She was more than just a witch, though; she was a hereditary witch. At first he didn't even know what that meant or why it was important. He might have been born a necromancer but he was like most people, oblivious to the reality of the other preternatural beings that walked through the world blending in with the majority who were plain old human. He learned that, like him, Ava was born to what she was. It made her one of the strong and powerful ones. It made her extraordinary. She was an awesome partner when it came to fighting the creatures of the night that didn't want to share the world with humans but rather rule the universe and destroy the humans. It was their job to stop them and to keep the peaceful balance between preternatural and human.

That's what it appeared they were up against now, something that was trying to upset the balance. He was excited that once again he was paired with Ava. The minute he got the call and found out who he was to pick up at SeaTac, he was off and racing north like he was running from the law.

The excitement he felt wasn't solely because he was being paired with Ava. It was to be his first werewolf hunt and his first hunt with the legendary Lily Avergne. Everyone in the Jägers knew about Lily, the sixteenth-century Prussian noblewoman attacked by a werewolf on the eve of her spectacular wedding. She was seventeen years old on the night she was attacked, and word had it that in the almost five centuries since, she still didn't look much older than thirty. Man, he wished he had some of that juju. Or not. It was weird enough to be a guy who could raise the dead. Being a five-hundred-year-old werewolf just might be even weirder. Just the same, he wouldn't mind staying young and buff for a couple of centuries.

"Where are we?" a sleepy Ava asked. She sat up and ran both hands through her hair. It was a long, tangled auburn mess and absolutely gorgeous. He had the urge to reach over and run his hands through it as well. He kept them firmly on the steering wheel.

"We just passed Sprague Lake." A few miles east of Ritzville, Sprague Lake popped up seemingly out of nowhere, the long body of water with the unique housing-free shorelines. Every time he drove past the lake he wondered why it was still as nature made it, and someday he was going to take the time to find out. Not this day, however. He was pressing on. The lake was a sign they weren't too far away from Spokane.

She squinted, cupped her hands around her eyes, and stared out the side window. "How can you tell? The fog is so thick I can't see much of anything."

It was true that the fog wasn't giving up its hold. All around them stretched a blanket of misty white. He recognized the stretch of road even if the lake was hard to make out in the shroud created by the fog. After his time in the Jägers, he looked at everything a little differently and wondered as he continued driving down the freeway if this was fog or something more sinister. He was hoping for the former.

"It's over to your right," he told her.

"If you say so." She dropped her hands and leaned her head against the headrest. "I still can't make out much in this soup."

As he passed the rest stop at the top of the hill outside the small town of Sprague, it meant they were less than an hour from Spokane and, he hoped, less than an hour from clear skies. It was going to get dark before they made it to Colville, and he'd prefer to drive that stretch in as much daylight as possible. Without the fog wouldn't be unwelcome either.

Silence fell again, and as he focused on the freeway stretching out ahead of him in the fog, he thought about what awaited them up north. He glanced over at Ava and asked, "Have you ever worked with her before?" Being one of the newer Jägers recruits, Ava had him by a couple of years so there was a chance she'd been on a team with her. Despite his preoccupation with Ava, the closer they came to their destination, the more curious he got about the renowned Lily. If even a fraction of what he'd heard about her was true, he was in for the hunt of his life, and he couldn't wait.

Ava glanced over at him and smiled. "Yes, once. We tracked down a wereleopard in West Africa. It was my first experience with a wereleopard and my first time meeting Lily. You'll like her, Kyle. She's pretty intense and pretty amazing. I learned a lot from her during that trip."

It was just as he suspected. They weren't like other people, not a single one of them. If they were, the Jägers wouldn't need them and surely wouldn't scour the globe recruiting them for their unique talents. Not only did they all possess something that set them apart from the rest of the world, but also they saw things that defied rational explanation. Without already possessing their very special traits, it would be difficult, if not impossible, to make sense of the beings they searched for. Someone who had been at this as long as Lily had to be incredible to watch. He was pretty excited to get a shot at working with and learning from the best. "That's what I thought. Pretty good-looking too, or that's what I hear." Now why on earth would he say that? Jesus. Nothing like sounding like a male chauvinist.

Ava was shaking her head, a small smile on her face. "She is beautiful, no question there. Don't get any ideas. From what I hear, you're not her type."

He could feel the rush of blood to his cheeks and hoped she didn't notice. His coolness factor would be trashed if she caught him blushing. "That's not what I meant."

If Ava knew what was in his heart, she'd realize how true that statement was. He was fascinated by everything he'd heard about Lily, but it was Ava that made his blood run hot.

"Of course not." She put a hand on his arm and gave it a pat. Her hand was warm where it met bare skin, and he hoped she didn't move it away. Ever.

"No, really." He turned and flashed her a smile. "I'm not into older women."

He caught the sparkle in her eyes as her fingers squeezed his arm gently. "I'm going to tell her you said that."

He and his big mouth. Some day he was going to learn to think before he spoke, or not. Probably not. "Oh, God, no. Please don't. I don't want her thinking I'm a jerk the first time she meets me. It usually takes people a couple of meetings before they get there."

This time Ava laughed so hard it brought tears to her eyes. She let go of his arm and wiped tears from her cheeks. "Anybody ever tell you that you're easy?"

Lord help him, but even when she was laughing at him, he loved it. "Only you and, by the way, that was mean."

"Yeah, it was but oh so much fun." She was still smiling, her green eyes glittering.

His heart felt so much lighter now. "You know I'm pretty handsome. She might just fall for me." He was into her game now.

"Oh sweetie, you are so naïve. Like I said, you're not her type."

"She doesn't like tall, dark, and handsomely buff."

"In her friends, sure."

The tone in her voice finally caught his attention, though it took a beat before he started to catch a clue. Then he felt a little stupid. "Oh," he said. "I hadn't heard that."

Ava put her hand back on his arm. "She'd go for me before you, but I don't think I'm her type either."

You're my type is what he thought. What he said was, "Seriously, though, what's she like?"

Ava turned her green eyes on him and looked thoughtful. "She's amazing. She's tiny, and yet I've never met anyone so powerful. She's strong and quick, and sees everything in a glance. I can only hope that someday I might be even a fraction as good as she is."

"We won't have as much time to hone our skills."

"True, but we can learn a lot from her in the time we do have."

"In a couple more hours, we're going to get our chance to start learning." He really hoped the hunt wasn't too quick. He wanted to spend as much time with Ava as possible. He did realize, of course, his unspoken wish was a double-edged sword. The longer the hunt went on, the longer the werewolf had to kill. That sort of went against the Jägers code.

He cut a glance over to Ava. He was just going to have to make the most of the trip. Do his job, learn from the rock star Lily, and impress the hell out of Ava. Yeah, that shouldn't be too difficult.

CHAPTER TWO

Sheriff Jayne Quarles stared down at what was once a human being and shuddered. What in the hell was going on in her town? When she'd come back home and taken over the Colville Sheriff's Department, she'd been under the apparently mistaken impression that things would be different. Back in the day, life had been pretty quiet around here. That was part of the reason she'd left in the first place and a whole lot of the reason she came back.

Well, that and the fact that being interested in other women didn't exactly set her up for happily ever after in these parts. Not that people were cruel to her. On the contrary, most were good folks who treated her pretty well. She'd been happy enough growing up around here. Plenty of friends and lots of activities to interest her. No, the real problem had been that the dating pool was awfully small. When she left high school she decided to go away to college and swim in a bigger pond.

Of course it seemed that those best-laid plans always came with a hitch. The University of Washington had been a great fit for her, and she'd found a good career with the U.S. Marshals Service. In short, she'd embraced that bigger pond and for quite a while had a grand time. A broken heart followed by her brother losing his battle with cancer brought her back home. She left the marshals service, sold her condo, and returned to Colville.

So here she was, ten years later, standing here staring down at yet another dead body and wondering why she ever left Seattle. If she'd wanted to investigate homicide after homicide, she could have stayed there. It wasn't supposed to be like this here.

"Sheriff?" Deputy Sam Azzalino was looking a little green.

She brought her attention back to the body, or what was left of the body. "Yeah."

"What's going around here, Sheriff?"

Now that was the million-dollar question, wasn't it? The people who contacted her yesterday had their theory and based on that were sending in a team of hunters. Though she was aware of the Jägers, she'd never had to work with them and didn't want to now. They were an open secret in law-enforcement circles, but she'd managed to avoid their actual presence in any of her investigations. Something odd was happening here, and one didn't have to be a genius to figure that one out. Odd didn't require the services of an organization that operated on the fringes of the rational world.

She also got that there were things in the world that once upon a time were relegated to folk legends and fairy tales and that were now understood to be reality. It still didn't mean she needed anyone outside of her own organization. They were smart, capable, and skilled, even if they were from a small, rural area. That didn't equate to hick cops. She and her department were anything but hicks. She had faith in her own skills and faith in her people.

"I don't know, Sam, but I'm damned well going to find out."

"Kinda looks like an animal attack."

"Perhaps."

"You know, Sheriff, I've lived here all my life, except for when I went to college, and I've seen my share of animals that have been attacked by other animals."

"Your point?"

"I have never seen anything like this. If this was done by an animal, it was rabid or sick or something. Nothing around here kills like that."

As much as she hated to admit it, she agreed with him. This went beyond a cougar or a bear or any other animal that could potentially attack a human. Or at least the types of animals they were accustomed to dealing with. This was not a native, so all they had to do was figure out what it was and stop it. Did it fall into the category of paranormal? She doubted it. That's why she believed they could handle this and was growing more and more irritated by the thought of the paranormal hunters on the way to her town.

❖

Her plan was a good one, yet right at the moment, everything appeared to be in complete disarray. Bellona stared at the inside of the barn and shook her head. What a distressing mess. After all the years of being alone, it was nice to have a family again, yet this family could be trying. She would never create such havoc.

Her own fault really. She'd let her lust overcome good sense. She'd been so enthralled by the beauty, and well, yes, the wealth of her precious Little Wolf that she let herself be blinded to her failings. She was exciting and willing and all the things she hoped for. She was also rash and filled with a bloodlust that was going to get them in trouble if Bellona didn't get her under control quickly.

Not that she wanted to take all of Little Wolf's fun away. That wouldn't be fair. She'd earned the right to hunt. No, the real problem was, she had to tutor her student better. The blame had to fall on her shoulders. She was older, wiser, and far more experienced. All she needed to do was spend more time with her, and she would get it. If she was honest, Bellona would have to admit that when she first came into her true being, she'd been just as rash and enthusiastic as Little Wolf was now. The difference was she had family to guide her and show her the way. Years of practicing what she'd been taught had brought her to where she was today.

Right now, however, she had a mess to clean up. Exposure was dangerous, and so she really had no choice, not if she wanted to stay here, and she did. A movement to the left caught her eye, and Bellona jerked back in surprise. Well, well, well. Now wasn't this a surprising turn of events? She studied the young man sprawled across the pile of hay, his naked body smeared with blood, his long hair tangled.

"He's pretty sweet, isn't he?"

Little Wolf stood in the open barn door staring at the man, her eyes bright and her smile even brighter. She was undeniably proud of her guest. Bellona shook her head, a wry smile on her face, and, with one arm, pulled Little Wolf to her side. She kissed her on the cheek.

"You made a mess, you know." An understatement if there was one.

Little Wolf's eyes swept the disarray that covered the open barn floor and shrugged. "I didn't mean to. It just got away from me. I mean, I'm having so much fun I can't seem to rein it in. And then I saw him…" A smile spread across her face.

Even in the condition he was in right at the moment, Bellona could see why Little Wolf was drawn to him. She had the urge to go over and breathe in his scent, trace her fingertips across his muscular chest, and run her tongue over his full lips. Men weren't her first choice, but every now and again, they could be fun. She saw potential in this one. "He is handsome."

"He's fucking hot," Little Wolf said confidently. "I want to keep him. Can I? You told me not to turn anyone, but come on. Just look at him. How could I kill him? It would be a waste."

Was there anything she would refuse this precious one? Not really. She'd searched a long time to find a place like this and a woman who made her feel again, or as much as anyone could, given that no one would ever measure up to the one she'd loved with all her heart. Together she and Little Wolf could create their own utopia. From the doorway she studied the man and thought about what it would mean to bring him into the fold. It wasn't a good idea, and yet sometimes the bad ideas turned out to be the most fun. In truth, she believed there was plenty of room for the young and, as Little Wolf described, the fucking hot man.

She allowed a rare smile to turn up the corners of her mouth. "Of course you can keep him."

Little Wolf kissed her hard, her tongue pushing between her lips and skimming over her tongue. "You won't be sorry," she said against her lips.

Bellona leaned back, took Little Wolf's head in her hands, and said, "I hope not, and now, this mess has to be taken care of."

Little Wolf smiled broadly and raised one eyebrow. "I'll clean up hottie."

Bellona pointed to the shredded body in the middle of the floor. From where she stood, she wasn't sure if it had once been a man or a woman. "How about that?"

Pulling her close again, Little Wolf kissed her hard. "Can you take care of her, pretty please?"

She wanted to say no and make her do it herself, but as her father had always taught her, if she wanted something done right, do it herself. She sighed, patted Little Wolf on the cheek, and said, "Of course."

Chapter Three

L ily rolled her head and listened to the cracks in her neck. She would complain about getting old if it were not for the fact she was not just old but rather what some would classify as ancient. A few cracks here and there were not a big deal, given how many years she had been walking the earth. Or more accurately, running from continent to continent. "Okay, Senn. I'll quit giving you a hard time and get to work."

"Very well. You can dig into my troubled psyche when you find this werewolf and stop him. Until then, I'm not the problem."

The werewolf. She hated hunting werewolves for what she considered were obvious reasons. Oh yes, she understood them all too well, which was one of the reasons she was always sent in when one was causing havoc. Understanding them didn't make it any easier to hunt and destroy them. It was a little like looking in the mirror and pulling the trigger. No matter how many times she did it, she never walked away with a good feeling.

"Deal. Now, about this sheriff…"

"Jayne Quarles."

"Yes, right, Jayne Quarles. Where do I meet her? At the police station or somewhere more covert? If she is not happy to see me, I do not necessarily want to barge into her office uninvited. I have the sense she's already pissed off, so I don't need to rile her up even more."

Those who were 210-friendly were still in the minority despite how things had evolved across the globe. The term *evolved* came from the time of the first written records of the Jägers to a day two hundred and ten years later, when they came out of the shadows and experienced the first official acknowledgment of their presence. Times had changed over the last few centuries, and no longer did the Jägers exist as something whispered about but never seen. Slowly over time, they had become a resource when all traditional methods failed. In law-enforcement circles they were relegated to a status similar to that of psychics: cops didn't really believe and they really didn't disbelieve. When there was nothing else to try, they called in the Jägers. In this instance, law enforcement had not called them in. They'd called themselves in after reports of the recent deaths made their way to Senn's office. A discreet inquiry with a 210-friendly town council member and they were on their way. When they were certain a preternatural problem existed, they came on scene to assist whether they were invited or not. The reality was traditional law enforcement wasn't equipped to deal with the kinds of creatures she hunted.

She and Senn talked for a few more minutes and came to a joint conclusion: covert it was to be. Once they'd confirmed the details of when and where, she put the cell phone in her pocket and stood for a moment longer staring at the town spreading out just down the highway. Despite the fact it was halfway across the world, in many ways it reminded her of home. A light dusting of snow made it look as though powdered sugar had been sprinkled across everything. In the distance, mountains rose, their peaks capped with white. The air was chilly though fresh and clear. It did, indeed, remind her of home.

Lily's mind flashed back to another time when the air was cool and the mountains were capped in snow. It was to have been the start of a new life for her. The term *was to have been* wasn't exactly correct. It most certainly was the start of a new life, just not the one so carefully orchestrated by her father. Everything about her life had changed that night, and nothing had been the same since. She wasn't the same either. The young, idealistic woman was long gone. In all ways that counted, she had ceased to exist that very night. Who she was these days wasn't quite clear. What she was did not suffer from the same identity crisis.

Back in the car, she covered the last couple of miles into Colville in less than ten minutes. She didn't stop in town. Instead, following the directions Senn sent to her phone, she drove past stores, the post office, and the town park until she located Onion Creek Road. A few miles down, she pulled up in the front drive of the large log home and whistled. This, according to Senn, was the home of Sheriff Quarles, who, as she'd suspected, was not in favor of meeting her at the police station.

Lily's first thought as she sat staring at the massive home was that being sheriff in this northern rural county must pay pretty well. Her second thought was that if all the places around here looked like this, she could easily live here. The rustic appearance of the large log home again gave her that wistful feeling of being home, though in another time and in another land.

Her appreciation of the home and lush landscape was interrupted when a woman came striding out the front door. She was medium height with short, sandy-blond hair that had an intriguing curl to it and crystal-blue eyes that caught the rays of sunshine as she walked toward the edge of the porch that ran the entire length of the house. The tan, long-sleeved sheriff's uniform with a full belt at her waist fit her well, emphasizing her powerful build and toned body. One long-fingered hand rested on the big black gun in her holster. Her lips were set in a thin line, her eyes narrow as she stared at Lily. Translation: one unhappy woman who was not pleased to see a senior hunter of the Jägers walking up to her porch. Even frowning and unhappy, Sheriff Jayne Quarles was, in Lily's opinion, kind of hot. Perhaps it was the fitted uniform. She always was a sucker for a woman in a uniform, and this woman wore it really well. Could also be that it had been a long dry spell for her, and she was simply reacting, as anyone would, to a good-looking woman. On the other hand, it might be time for a date.

Except she did not have time to go out for dinner or anything else, for that matter. In fact, she could not even remember the last time she went out with a woman on a real live date. There had been a couple of hookups over the last few years, one-night stands that scratched an itch without her having to get emotionally involved. Those nights had been actually pretty nice, and the women, exciting and fun. If she'd given them a chance, perhaps there could have been more. She didn't even try to find out. One night and that was it. Safer that way.

My, as she thought about that, it occurred to her in many ways she was just like Senn. He chose to hide away in his home, and she chose to hide away inside her own skin. Not a whole lot of difference between the two of them, although she intended to keep that observation to herself. She returned her attention to the woman standing just a step above her.

"Sheriff," Lily said as she held out a hand. "I am Lily—"

She cut her off and not very politely either. "Lily Aver...how the hell do you even pronounce your name?"

So it was going to be like that was it? "Aver Neen." She was accustomed to people having trouble with her name. For centuries, she had been patiently giving out the correct pronunciation. Most of the time no one paid attention anyway, so overall it was rarely worth the effort. She did it anyway because, while there was little left of the young woman she'd once been, she still had her name.

"Ms. Avergne." Now that was pretty impressive. She might be grumpy, but her pronunciation was pitch perfect. It wasn't often someone got the right tone when they repeated her name. Made her wonder if perhaps she and Jayne Quarles might have some common Prussian ancestry. That would be nice. It had been quite a long time since she was around others from her homeland, even many generations removed, which logically was the most she could hope for. The sheriff even had the directness that reminded her so much of her father when she declared, "Let's understand each other right from the get-go. I do not want you here."

Not exactly a news flash in that statement. Lily suspected Jayne might not be aware that she gave off a get-the-hell-out-here vibe. Or maybe she was, because somehow Lily had the impression this woman was hyperaware of where she was, who she was, and what she meant to say. She was strong and decisive, and Lily could respect that. Didn't mean she agreed with her attitude, only that she could respect her style.

Lily had her own manner, and it was as confident and forceful as that of the woman she faced. What the good sheriff didn't know was that she'd had a lot more time to hone her confidence and assertiveness. While she might look like a small, delicate woman, it didn't mean she was one. The reality was quite the opposite. She was small in stature and iron strong in body and spirit. Appearances in her case were most deceiving, and more than one had made the fatal mistake of underestimating her.

In this instance it also meant that getting everything out in the open right from the beginning was a very good idea. They were on the same side and their end goal was the same: stop the killer. Whether she liked it or not, Quarles was going to have to work with her. There were powers far above her head that backed Lily and Jägers, and they wanted her and her team here. They weren't going to leave until the threat in this area was neutralized, and that job would be finished a lot quicker if they came together as a cohesive unit.

Lily let her hand drop. So be it if she refused common courtesies. Rude was nothing new to Lily. She turned her gaze on Jayne and gave her curt nod. "I understand where you're coming from, Sheriff. I get that you don't want me or my team on your turf. To make certain we're crystal clear, please understand that I don't give a good goddamn what you want."

❖

In Deer Park, Kyle pulled into the service station and stopped next to one of the pumps. As soon as he turned the car off, Ava got out and stretched her arms over her head. She still looked tired though she'd slept off and on for miles. "You want some coffee or something to drink?" They weren't that far from Colville but still had a good fifty miles to go. It was going to be well past sunset before they hit the town limits. Coffee sounded pretty good to him.

Ava looked over at the convenience store and wrinkled her nose. She stuffed her hands into her pockets and looked at him with a crooked smile. "I appreciate the offer, but honestly black-tar coffee from a c-store doesn't hold a great deal of appeal."

Looking around he had to admit she was right. It wasn't like they were out in the middle of nowhere and their options limited. He had a hunch that this little town might have more to offer than gas-station drinks. "Let's find a coffee stand."

She pointed a finger at him and winked. "Now you're talking, my friend."

He finished fueling the car, punched the button for a receipt, and then crawled back behind the wheel. Ava was already buckled into the passenger seat. They only had to wait for one car before pulling out on the main street into Deer Park. One roundabout and a quarter mile later they were second in line at a nice little drive-through coffee stand. He loved it when a plan came together.

Once they were back on the highway headed north, he grabbed the tall paper cup and sipped through the two narrow straws. Oh yeah, Ava was right. Way better than coffee out of one those do-it-all machines inside the gas station. This was dark, rich, and brewed just right. He could almost feel the energy flowing through his veins. "Your latte good?" She had opted for steamed milk and espresso.

Ava closed her eyes and a dreamy expression crossed her face. "Heavenly."

"I don't know about you, but I needed both the stop and the coffee. Even though we're not that far away now, I was getting twitchy. I've been in this car way too many hours."

She nodded as she put a hand on his arm. It was becoming a habit he didn't want her to break. "I totally agree. I'll be glad when we get there. I'm a bit tired of traveling right now."

"I'll bet you are." It was a long haul from New Haven to Colville. It was bad enough just trying to get from New Haven to Seattle, and then to throw in the road trip from Seattle to Colville would stretch anyone to the breaking point.

His observation after a few minutes was the latte seemed to be helping her as much as the coffee was reviving his flagging energy. Color had come back into her face, and she appeared relaxed. In some ways, he'd be sorry when they reached Colville. He liked this time alone together with her in the confines of the car. Once they arrived at their destination, he was going to have to share her. As selfish as it was, he liked having her all to himself.

All of a sudden Ava stiffened, and the hand holding her latte started to tremble. He jerked the wheel to his right and almost drove off into the gravel before straightening the car. "What's wrong?"

"The air's changed," she said as her eyes scanned the horizon. A whisper of concern in her voice captured his immediate attention. "Something is out there."

He took a deep breath and tried to pick up on whatever she was sensing. Didn't smell any different to him, and it sure didn't feel any different. "I'm not getting it." Not that he really expected to. He might be able to raise the dead, but beyond that he was pretty much a regular guy.

She was shaking her head. "It's not like that. It smacked me like a wave or a blast of power that sent every nerve in my body buzzing. I've only had that happen a couple of times before."

Whatever it was that touched her so powerfully blew right over him because he didn't feel any different than he did a mile ago. They were getting closer to Colville and the day was fading. Dusk was settling in and pushing out the light, making the trees on the side of the road dark and ominous. He glanced over at Ava and believed what she was telling him even if he didn't feel it. The shadows he could see in her eyes hadn't been there a moment before, and the color in her cheeks was long gone. Something had hit at her at a very deep, instinctual level. This was a development he didn't much like.

Kyle took another deep breath and still couldn't distinguish any difference in the air. To him it was plain old fresh air of the type he didn't often experience in the larger California cities he often found himself in. "Tell me what it is because I'm not feeling anything odd, and nothing is making the nerves in my body buzz." Now she was making his body buzz, not that he thought it was a good idea to tell her that right at the moment. He figured there'd be time enough for that later.

Her head was moving right and left as she scanned the landscape outside the car window. "I don't know," she told him. "I can't seem to pinpoint what it is or where it's coming from. Ever experienced a feeling like someone was running a feather up your spine?" She didn't wait for him to answer. "That's what it feels like. An ice-cold feather whispering across my nerves. I don't like it."

"I'm thinking it's not a good thing." He was, in fact, starting to get a bad feeling about this. What he knew from working with Ava before was that she was incredibly sensitive to the environment around her. If she said she was sensing something odd, then she was, and it meant whatever they were about to face was pretty darned powerful. He was even more grateful that their team lead was Lily.

Ava turned her face toward him, her eyes dark and serious. It was nice to see a little of the color returning to her face, even if her words were grim. "I think it's a very bad omen. Kyle, how quick can you find where we're supposed to be? I need to talk to Lily."

Glancing up at the navigator mounted on the dash, he told her, "I say we're fifteen minutes out, give or take a few."

"It's waning," she said almost absently as she turned around to peer out the back window and the terrain fading behind them. She turned back around in her seat and put her hand on his arm again. "I still think the sooner we meet up with Lily the better. This is pretty unusual."

She sounded calm, yet the tone of her voice made him jumpy. "On it." He glanced in the rearview mirror and glimpsed what could have been the flash of a tail disappearing into the trees. "Did you see that?"

She shifted in her seat and once more stared out the back window. "What?"

"I could have sworn it was a coyote running into the trees." Or a wolf, he didn't add. But then again, it could have been his imagination. He'd wait and see.

CHAPTER FOUR

Despite the appearance of the Jägers hunter on her doorstep, Jayne was still far from convinced that her killer was of the preternatural variety. That the bastard was anything except ordinary old flesh and blood was going to be a hard sell. This person was, without question, an evil soul, only in her experience it would probably turn out to be one who was very human. She'd spent her entire professional career dealing with people who were cold-blooded and could harm others without so much as blinking an eye. This wasn't much different than cases she'd run up against in the cities across the country where she'd been sent in to stop criminals.

Okay, maybe this was a little different. Actually, things around town had been off lately. Everything had been oddly quiet. Not that Colville was exactly a hotspot for activity. It was, however, a typical small town that happened to also be the county seat, and under normal circumstances, it sort of buzzed with low-key activity. People stopped and talked to each other, and gossip flowed like water. For whatever reason, the last couple of weeks had been hushed. She attributed the change to the suspicious deaths, and she didn't blame folks for being cautious and sticking close to home. These kinds of things were upsetting even in the big cities. Here it hit the residents even harder. She figured once the killer was apprehended and locked up, everyone would wander back out and life would get back to normal.

The fact that the city council had called in the Jägers and couldn't wait for her to do her investigation grated on her big-time. If the meddling sons of bitches would just let her do her job, she'd get this thing handled. But no, their dear sheriff needed outside help to bring down the big, bad killer. She'd like to think it was just because they were afraid the perpetrator was not completely human. Deep in her heart she knew it was more complicated than that simple explanation. It really came down to the fact that she was a woman, as in the first woman sheriff ever elected in this county, and they didn't believe she had the balls to do the job right.

To be fair, not everyone held her gender against her, and she had a lot of support throughout the county. If she didn't, she'd have never been able to beat Phil Redman in the election…twice. So, the last thing she should have to deal with right now was being second-guessed, yet all it took was a cranky few who still believed in the good-old-boys system to convince the entire council to take the call that pissed her off.

Damn it anyway, she didn't need that kind of help, and if she did require assistance, she still had friends in the marshals service, not to mention the Washington State Patrol, the FBI, and a couple other agencies with nifty initials that she was comfortable calling. So-called paranormal hunters were nothing she needed at the moment or ever, for that matter. Nope, she sure as hell didn't.

Now this little sprite of a thing with long black hair and dressed in blue jeans, a black sweater, and a leather jacket was not just coming into her town to show her up but also basically telling her to go to hell. Righteous indignation was hers to own. The problem was she hated herself just a little for finding this Lily and her attitude rather fascinating. She wanted to despise her outright and not feel a little zing of attraction.

After being informed that the Jägers were sending in someone to assist, she'd imagined the kind of person who would show up. In her head she'd pictured a brute of a man who would stomp in and declare that he was here to save the day with his lightsaber or something equally ridiculous. It was most definitely not a beautiful woman with an intense stare and more than a touch of attitude. This could possibly be a far more interesting experience than she'd first envisioned, and she could hardly wait to see the looks on the council members' faces when they got their first peek at the hunter sent by the infamous Jägers. No good old boy here, and that actually made her want to smile. She didn't, though, because it would send the wrong message to this Lily Avergne. Regardless of any tickle of attraction, Jayne still didn't want her here.

"You're in my town," she said. Avergne might be cute, but she was also full of shit, and that Jayne didn't have time for. There was enough shit going down around her lately. She didn't need it imported too.

Lily squared her shoulders. "I don't mean to be rude or disrespectful, Sheriff, I really don't. You just need to understand that I am very, very good at my job, and I intend to do what I came here to do. I would prefer to work with you, but I will hunt this monster down and stop it with or without your assistance."

She was irritating before, but now she was really getting on Jayne's nerves. "Look, Ms. Avergne…"

"Lily."

Jayne couldn't help it. She rolled her eyes. Enough already. "Lily. I don't need your help to stop this killer. I don't know what you've been told, but this isn't my first rodeo." Not ever having met Jayne, Lily certainly had no idea that she'd spent over ten years as a deputy U.S. marshal before being elected sheriff in this county five years ago. Lacking law-enforcement skills was not how she showed up for her first day at work. She'd been involved in some big and messy cases and cleared them all. When she'd left the U.S. Marshals Service to come back to Colville she had a clean record. As far as she was concerned, she planned to maintain that record here, and she was perfectly capable of doing it without this particular kind of help.

"Exactly how many werewolves have you tracked down, Sheriff?" Lily had her hands folded in front of her and her expression was neutral, though her dark eyes almost sparkled. Her voice was like that of a teacher trying to get a point across to a particularly dense student.

Frankly, Jayne was sick and tired of people throwing around the word "werewolf." It had been bandied about at the council meeting as well, and it was annoying as hell. How exactly had their society evolved from fairy tales and folk legends to believing it was all real? Yes, she did understand there were some things beyond the realm of what she considered reality. Werewolves and vampires and other such creatures were not, and to her, they were still simply fictional creatures. "That would be zero because there are no such things as werewolves."

Something flashed in Lily's eyes that Jayne couldn't quite define. Up close her eyes were so dark they were almost black, and they were most definitely hypnotic. In the back of her mind she suspected Lily knew that and used it to get her way. Wasn't going to work on her. She wasn't the kind to bend her principles on account of long lashes and pretty eyes.

"I tell you what, Sheriff." Lily didn't bat her eyes or flutter her lashes. She stared into Jayne's eyes with a directness that was bold and daring. "Despite your obvious unhappiness with my presence, I'm not leaving, so how about you do your investigation your way and I'll do mine my way. When it all shakes out, we'll check to see where you stand on that belief."

God, how many ways did she have to spell it out to this woman? Were all of them from the mysterious organization this bullheaded? "I don't need you interfering with my investigation. You'll only be a liability and get in my way."

Lily broke the stare by shaking her head. "The way I see it, you don't have any choice, and as far as anyone becoming a liability there's far more chance of you being one than me."

Christ, talk about pissing her off. First, because it was true that she had no choice, and second, because Lily had the gall to throw it in her face. It was beginning to be very clear to Jayne that Lily was as beautiful as she was irritating. She hoped to hell she caught this killer soon so she could send this little spitfire back to whatever dark corner of the earth she'd emerged out of. Biting back what she really wanted to say, she said instead, "No. I don't have a choice about your being here, so we'll do what we have to do, and then you can hop back up on the horse you rode in on and get the hell of out of my town."

Lily nodded. "Fair enough. Now that we understand each other, I'll go back to town and get a hotel room. The rest of my team should be showing up before long, and I want to get them briefed as soon as possible on how we'll be working with law enforcement."

"Great," she muttered. "More of you."

"Indeed, and they should be here anytime. Kyle sent me a text when they pulled out of Deer Park."

Jayne really did want to scream now. "Fucking A, like I need more people in my house."

"We'll be staying at a hotel in town."

She might not have any choice about these people being here, but that didn't mean she was completely powerless. There were some things she could still control. "No, you won't. You're here, and I can't do anything about that. I can make sure you're not out running around town and causing problems I don't need. You and your team will be staying right here. Welcome to Hotel Quarles."

❖

Bellona stood on the deck and looked out over the river. The water was blue and incredibly smooth today. It was nice to wake up to this kind of view, and it was one of the reasons the idea of staying here for a while had appealed to her. The landscape was a little like where she grew up, with mountains and forests and fresh air. Sometimes she missed her childhood home. Not very often but every once in a while.

For a change she wasn't feeling the overwhelming urge to move away, even though she'd been here for a few months. Strangely, she liked it here, and not just because it reminded her of home. It had been a long time since she'd met someone who was so enthusiastic about joining her lifestyle. Most of the time people were frightened of her if and when they learned of her closely held secret. Not Little Wolf. She'd been fascinated, and Bellona was not immune to the feelings of flattery that brought up. When Little Wolf had suggested creating a makeshift family, at first she'd thought no way, and then when she'd pondered it a bit more, it became invigorating. To say it was refreshing was an understatement. As much as she loved what she was and how she lived her life, especially these days, there were times when she was quite lonely. She missed her friends and the feeling of being connected. Lately she was remembering that feeling, and she liked it.

Standing out here with the fresh air filling her lungs, her body buzzed and it made her smile. It always happened this way. The closer the full moon got, the more her nerves tingled with anticipation. The excitement built for days before the night when the moon rose full and golden. Those were glorious nights, and she soared as she absorbed the energy that poured forth from the power of the moonlight. The thought of sharing the full moon with Little Wolf made it even more special.

As if she'd said her name out loud, Little Wolf came walking across the expansive lawn, a coffee cup in her hand. The sight made her smile grow. She loved the way she moved, her long strides and confident manner. It was what had drawn her to Little Wolf in the first place. Every so often she came across someone with the swagger and attitude that matched her own. At least for a while, she would enjoy their company before moving on to her next horizon. This time, the itch to move evaporated, and she knew a lot of it had to do with Little Wolf's embrace of the lifestyle. She loved it. She loved her.

"Coffee?" Little Wolf offered her the large mug she held in her hands. "It's cold but it still tastes great."

Bellona shook her head. Coffee was a beverage she'd never developed a taste for. It had not been something that was part of her formative years, and in fact she hadn't even been exposed to it until many years later. Excellent tea, now that was a different matter altogether. She rarely turned down a good cup of tea. Her roots showed when it came to her drink of choice.

"No, thank you, love, but I'll join you for a cup of tea."

Little Wolf took her hand as she came up to meet her on the deck. She kissed Bellona and then said, "It was so beautiful this afternoon that I had to go for a walk. You were still sleeping so I left you and went out alone. I never noticed how lovely the woods are and how fantastic they smell until you came along. You've made everything more interesting and intense."

She understood what she meant. Most people only noticed things on a superficial level until she gave them what they needed to go deeper. Only then could they appreciate what had been there in front of them all the time. The sights, the sounds, and the smells, all joined together to create a world with depth and flavor.

Her mind turned back to a night long ago. She'd hoped to share the wonders of her world with the woman of her heart, only it ended badly. She'd never quite gotten over what had happened, though she'd learned some valuable lessons that night. Not once in the years since had she made a similar misstep. Now, Little Wolf, on the other hand, was going to have to be watched. She recognized the same sort of recklessness in her that Bellona herself had embodied in her younger days.

"Did you take your boy-toy with you on your walk?" The last time Bellona had seen him, he'd still been in the barn and Little Wolf was doing her best to clean him up.

Little Wolf shook her head and a frown darkened her face. "He's sleeping in the cell. Typical guy. It's like he has a hangover and needs to sleep it off. Hot as some guys can be, they can also be lazy bastards."

The cell was a locked room-sized gun safe in the basement of the large house that Bellona had used to contain Little Wolf until she had mastered at least some control over her change. It was actually well thought out for her to have placed their newest member of the family in there. She'd seen it before with men. The change was brutal when it hit them, and well, as far as she was concerned, they often took it far harder than women. Whoever said males were the tougher sex had never been around a man going through the change. Oh, he'd be fine in a day or two, but in the meantime, the cell was a very good place for him.

"Good idea. You'll need to keep an eye on him, although he should sleep for at least another twelve hours or so if history is any indication."

"He was out cold last time I checked. Come on." Little Wolf held out her hand. "I'll make you a cup of your favorite tea. I picked up a fresh supply when I went into Spokane yesterday."

"You know," she said as they turned and began to walk inside, hand in hand. "I have a better idea. Let's skip the coffee and tea and open a bottle of wine instead. We can sit out here and watch the sun finish going down."

This was undoubtedly the last night it was just the two of them, and she wanted to take advantage of it. Not that she minded what was coming. On the contrary, she was experiencing rushes of excitement when she thought about what they were building here. Adam, as she dubbed their newest member, was a wonderful start to their pack.

Her reward was a big smile and a squeeze of her hand. "You always know exactly the right thing to do. My world was so boring before you came along. I can't even imagine how crazy I'd be right now if you hadn't brought me into the life. I'd heard stories of werewolves, but I never imagined them to be real. I sure as hell never imagined how incredible it was to be one. Thank you." Little Wolf kissed her on the top of the head.

Bellona pushed up on her toes and touched her lips to Little Wolf's. "Happy to help."

Chapter Five

Lily stepped back off the wide porch and started to walk in the direction of her car. Time to make haste toward town and the privacy of a hotel. "I am not going to stay *here*."

Honest to God, this was a first. She'd run up against resistance like Jayne's many times, and it was something she was well schooled in how to handle. She was a pro in many different areas. The idea she was to stay in the home of her resistor was a whole different scenario that she had no idea how to handle. It was bad enough she'd have to work with this highly combative sheriff, but spending 24/7 with her in her home was absolutely out of the question. Granted, she was cute, and that detail would make the sting a little less. But it didn't make up for her poor attitude and the clear desire to be in total control of everything. Lily needed to do her work without the distraction of someone who was obviously going to fight her every step of the way. Cute only got her so far.

The other glitch was a little more complicated. Though she only occasionally had to pull it out of her toolbox, if it became necessary she might have to change. That was not something she wanted to do in the company of strangers or, worse, unbelievers. In the safety of a group of other Jägers it was fine. In the presence of someone who truly believed and appreciated what she and others of preternatural abilities could contribute, no problem. In the house of a sheriff who thought she and others like her were crackpots and who wanted her a million miles away, changing in her presence was definitely not fine.

In short, staying in the sheriff's personal residence was quite out of the question. No way was she, or any of her team, staying here under any circumstances. They would book rooms in one of the local hotels she'd spied on her way through town, and that was that.

"You'll stay here," Jayne insisted, undeterred by Lily's insistence to the contrary. In fact, it seemed to Lily that she stood a little taller and her eyes were a little brighter. The impression Lily got was that she was hell-bent on getting her way. Oh, just let her try. This woman had no idea what she was up against. Lily might be little in stature, but she didn't back down to anyone even if they were carrying a gun.

"We will stay in town." She was equally insistent. Sheriff Quarles wasn't the first strong personality she'd run up against. For hundreds of years she'd been standing up against those in positions of so-called authority. Holding her ground wasn't a problem.

"No," Jayne said, her confidence still clear in her voice. "You won't. You don't have to like me, but on this you're going to do as I ask."

Actually now she had her less annoyed and more curious. Lily's own ability to stand tall and fierce in the face of any combatant normally worked to her advantage. Typically, she could back down the most unrelenting opposition, yet this woman wasn't yielding an inch. Had to give her props for that. "Why?" There was clearly some agenda the sheriff wasn't sharing quite yet. Time to find out what that was.

Jayne blew out a long breath as her posture relaxed. She stuffed her hands into her pockets, and the eyes so intense a moment ago lost some of their fierceness. "Look," she said in a voice that was more pleading than intense. "This is a small town and people talk a lot. I know you've probably been in places like this before, and I'm sure you understand what happens in a community this size. These are good people who live here, and they are already scared shitless over the killings. If you and your team check into a hotel, it will be all over town in about thirty seconds, and the implications of what and who you are will scare them even more. I don't want that to happen. So the reality behind my demand that you stay here is that it's really less about me and more about the people I'm here to protect."

Reason that appealed to her emotions was about the last thing she was expecting to hear. Well played, Sheriff, well played. In fact, her whole argument was pretty solid, and honestly, Lily was inclined to agree with her except for one small detail that appeared to have passed her by. "Will they not talk just as much if we stay with you?"

Jayne wasn't wrong in her observation that Lily had been in small towns before. In point of fact, she'd been in thousands of them, and she knew what happened in less time than it took to punch a number into a cell phone. Her presence, and that of her team, would be all over town in a heartbeat. One stranger was enough to attract attention. Three were guaranteed to be the number-one topic of the morning coffee group at the local cafe. In their line of work, that was never helpful.

At Lily's question, Jayne winced and said, "Yes and no. You're right in that it will spread over town in nothing flat. Strangers camped out at my house is something that will set the gossip trail on fire hot enough it will need the wildfire specialists to put it out. That said, with you staying here I can at least somewhat control the gossip because, you see, Ms. Avergne, you and your team are my friends from college." She made the last statement with a very satisfied look on her face.

Lily squinted and studied the good sheriff for at least a full minute. On the face of it, the plan sounded pretty solid and plausible. There was a little *but* in the mix, however, and it was significant enough to deflate Jayne's bubble of satisfaction. "I don't mean to undermine your great theory, but I am relatively certain that story is not going to fly."

Jayne's brow furrowed. "Why not?"

Lily gave her a small smile and inclined her head. "For starters, if we're such good friends, why won't you call me by my given name? If this ruse is going to fly, you will have to call me Lily, and I'm not sure you can do that."

"It'll work," Quarles insisted and now refused to meet her eyes.

"No, it won't." She was just as insistent as she wasn't wrong on this.

Jayne's face took on the dark cast again as she looked out somewhere over Lily's head as if someone was out there who would back her up. Her shoulders stiffened once more, and all of her earlier calmness faded. "Look. You're starting to piss me off. It's a plausible plan, so why don't you believe it will work?"

The sheriff came across as pretty darned bright, yet she was missing the obvious, at least as far as it concerned Lily. She wasn't seeing the big picture, and in this instance, it was important. "Because all three of us are, or at least look, enough younger than you that there's no way we'd be in college at the same time. Not unless my team and I were all three child prodigies."

Jayne Quarles looked to Lily to be in her late thirties or early forties, while Lily knew she appeared to be in her thirties. She'd been very young when she was turned and in the intervening years had aged very, very slowly. It was one of the advantages of being a werewolf. Ava and Kyle were likewise in their early thirties, and both of them looked it. Ava did anyway. Her opinion on Kyle's appearance was coming solely from a photo Senn had provided to her prior to making this trip.

Jayne opened her mouth and then closed it as the truth of Lily's words apparently hit her. Her gaze swept over Lily's face, and she could see the acceptance settle in. "Shit," she finally muttered. "You're right about you, at least. And if your pals look your age, you're right about them too. Damn, it sounded so good in my head."

A thought occurred to Lily, and she mulled it over for a few seconds before she decided to run it by Jayne. "How far are you willing to take the charade in order to get us to stay here with you?"

"I don't want my town upset any more than it already is."

"All right then. Tell me what this scenario does for you. What if we tell everyone you and I met on a dating site, and I'm here and staying with you because I've come to meet you face-to-face. To keep it all aboveboard, my brother and his wife have come along too."

Surprise, or was it shock, showed in Jayne's eyes. "What makes you think I go for women?" Was that a trace of outrage she heard?

Lily shrugged. "What difference does it make? It's a cover." In her mind, the details weren't all that critical. She needed to get to work, and if it meant some ruse, then so be it. For her it wasn't a deception in that she did prefer women. She didn't know where the sheriff fell on that score and honestly didn't care. It was simply a means to the end. At least it would be easier to pretend to be interested in the sheriff than it would be some big burly man. In fact, it would be entertaining to pretend interest in the sheriff, particularly if it bugged her, and Lily suspected it would.

The silence that hung between spoke volumes. The sheriff wanted to argue, Lily could see it in her eyes, yet Lily suspected she was unable to come up with an alternate plan better than what she'd just proposed. "Okay, as much as I hate to admit it, I think your grand plan could actually work. I've been single for quite a while, and more than one of the busybodies in town have been trying to find a girlfriend for me.

Most people don't even think twice about the online dating thing. Some of the old folks, sure, but to everyone else, it's the way it is anymore."

Girlfriend. So, she had inadvertently hit that nail on the head. Staying at the sheriff's house was starting to hold a lot more appeal than when she first brought it up. How Kyle and Ava were going to feel about being cast as a married couple was an unknown. During the one mission she'd worked with Ava, she'd been impressed both with her powers and her personality. Ava was smart and skilled, and she was pretty sure she'd roll with anything Lily asked of her. Kyle was more of a wild card. Never having worked with him before, she didn't have a handle on his personality or how he functioned in a team. Word came down from on high that he was a good recruit, and the Jägers felt he had a long and powerful future. That said, she hoped he would agree to their impromptu plan.

"Agreed," Lily said and stepped back toward the house until she was standing next to Jayne. "Online dating is the bar scene of the new century. I kind of liked the bar-scene style, it was always fun to watch people in the wild, but the world does move on. Now, since we are potential girlfriends, I suggest we start this all over." She smiled broadly and held out her hand. "Hello, my name is Lily Avergne, and I am very glad to meet you."

Jayne looked down at her hand for a moment and then returned Lily's smile. It did something very nice to her face. "I'm Jayne Quarles." She took Lily's hand in hers.

The shock that roared through Lily's body the moment their flesh touched made her head jerk back. The surprise she felt showed on Jayne's face as well. "Who are you?" Jayne said in a whisper. "What are you?"

❖

"Son of a bitch. How much money do you suppose they pay a sheriff in these parts?" The words passed through Kyle's lips before he could stop them, but in his defense, this place was some kind of crazy. He'd brought the car to a stop before the big log house and then just sat there staring without making a move to get out. The route Siri had taken them on didn't quite work out, and so he'd had to call Lily to finally get directions he could follow. The surprise once he got here was twofold:

first that they were sitting in front of a monster house and second that they weren't at one of the motels they'd passed going through town. Frankly, he was probably most surprised at the latter. Why Lily didn't already have their rooms booked was outside of normal protocol, but then again, she was in charge, and he'd been taught to follow their fearless leader, whoever he or she might be on a given hunt, and to do so without question. That didn't mean he couldn't question something like the salary of a county sheriff.

Ava leaned forward in her seat and stared out the windshield, her long hair swinging around her face. "No kidding. This place is amazing. How big do you think it is? Four, five thousand square feet?"

If he was to speculate, he'd say closer to five thousand. He might not be an accountant, but he was smart enough to realize there was no way this place was feasible on a county employee's salary. The taxes alone had to be huge, even in a small county like this one. There had to be a story, and he was itching to know what it was. "Maybe she has family money or a husband with a million-dollar job." Both were pretty good guesses, he thought.

Ava was still staring out the windshield. "Maybe, but good grief, who'd need to work with the kind of money it takes to own a place like this? This is worth half a mil if it's worth a dime. I sure wouldn't be putting on a uniform and heading in to work every day."

"Right there with you. I'd be a man of leisure, and I know I could do it well." He turned to look at her and wink. He didn't qualify his statement by saying he'd never give up his work for the Jägers. It was too much a part of him now and the part that made him feel almost normal. He'd be crazy to walk away from that. A regular job though, yeah, he'd give that up in a second.

"Come on," Ava said as she reached for the door handle. "Let's find out what's going on, and while we're doing that, we'll get a chance to see what this place looks like on the inside. If it's anything like the outside, I'm sure we'll be impressed."

"Yeah, let's check it out." Ava was right. The house was massive and built from gorgeous red logs. He didn't know his trees very well, but he recognized beautiful wood when he saw it. The porch ran the full length of the front of the house, and the underside of the overhang was fully finished tongue-and-groove cedar. It was pretty damned impressive. Somebody had paid a lot of money to build the house that was obviously planned down to every little detail. Even the grounds were impressive. At least an acre of grass surrounded the house and attached four-car garage. It was hard to see beyond the yard in the dark, but he'd bet the scenery beyond was as beautiful as what they could see here.

He and Ava got out and mounted the steps to the porch. Before he could knock on the wide door with the oval glass insert, it opened, and a short, beautiful woman stood holding it ajar. An introduction wasn't necessary. He'd recognize Lily Avergne anywhere. The thing that surprised him was that the pictures he'd seen didn't do her justice. She was quite beautiful, with an air about her that radiated something special. He felt an immediate draw to her.

"Kyle, Ava, come on in." She beckoned them through the door.

Pulling his attention away from his leader and to his surroundings, he let out a breath. Yup, he and Ava got it right. The inside was as incredible as the outside. They stepped into a great room with soaring ceilings, log walls, and massive windows. A huge staircase led to a second level, its banister made of beautifully carved and polished wood. Two sofas and several overstuffed chairs were clustered around a river-rock fireplace that he swore was big enough to burn half a tree. He almost whistled and then caught himself.

Another woman was in the room, though he was so caught up by the coolness factor of the house's interior he hadn't noticed her initially. Now that he did, he took stock. She was tall and blond, and his first thought was Viking. His second was sheriff. He was confident number two was the right one and fairly confident number one wasn't far from the mark either. He held out his hand. "Kyle Miller." His mother had always taught him to be polite.

She shook it. "Sheriff Jayne Quarles." Her grip was firm, her hand cool, and her expression neutral. He had a feeling she was one unflappable woman. Definitely Viking.

"Sheriff," Ava said and stepped forward. "I'm Ava Crescent."

He was carefully watching Ava's body language as she took the other woman's hand. Ava didn't flinch, and in fact a little smile flitted across her face. That was a good sign in his book. In their previous work together he'd learned that her skill in reading people was unmatched. He trusted her first impressions.

"As long as you're here, please call me Jayne." She released Ava's hand and stuck both of hers into the pockets of her pants. At least she didn't cross her arms over her chest.

Kyle still raised an eyebrow at her invitation. Now this was a new twist. Not once in the missions he'd been on so far had law enforcement been quite so accommodating or casual. Usually it was the polar opposite. He wasn't sure he even knew the given names of any of the deputies he'd worked with since joining the order. Off the top of his head, he couldn't think of a single one. "Okay, Jayne," he said, trying the name out on his tongue. Felt okay. She seemed like a Jayne, whatever that meant. "So you two want to bring Ava and me up to speed?"

Lily stepped in, her dark hair shining in the glow of the overhead light. She was a tiny woman whose presence came off as so much bigger. "Why don't you two have a seat. This one's going to play a little different from any of the missions you've been on thus far."

Not a big revelation at this point. This one had started out different right from the beginning. Despite his obvious delight at being paired with Ava, the configuration of the team had struck him as unusual when he'd received his orders. The pairing of a werewolf, a witch, and a necromancer was a little odd.

Toss in the casual relationship with the sheriff and it was doubly strange. Working with Ava made perfect sense, given what he could do. Her magic had the potential to strengthen his. So far, however, he'd had little experience with the preternatural hunters like Lily. Usually the order didn't pair a were-anything with a necromancer. Until now, that is.

"So what's up?" He wasn't one to wait around or stand on formality. Lily was the leader of the pack, so to speak, and that meant she always took the lead. This time around it was so different, he didn't have a problem jumping in and asking questions. Hopefully it wouldn't start his first meeting with Lily off on the wrong foot. His curiosity could only be contained so long, as anyone who was familiar with ADHD could attest.

Fortunately, it didn't seem to bother Lily. Maybe she was accustomed to being around ADHD personalities like his, or maybe she was simply ready to move forward. Either way, she was ready to rock and roll. Lily looked at him and nodded. "Here's what we're up against, and here's how we're going to handle it."

By the time she finished explaining the online dating scenario between her and the sheriff as well as the cover that he was her married brother who came with his wife, Ava, as chaperones, it was all he could do not to burst out in laughter. Nobody had to explain to him that it would have been the wrong thing to do. This was a deadly serious situation, and their solution was a serious cover. His urge to laugh was no reflection of what that meant. No, he wanted to laugh because it was like his prayers were being answered. He got to be up close and personal with the woman of his dreams, and it was all Jägers approved. It didn't get any better than that.

What he did find interesting was that Jayne was clearly not a 210-friendly. She made that very plain through the bits she added to Lily's explanation of what they were going to do. He should let it go and see where it went. Not his style. He opened his big fat mouth and voiced his observation. "So you're not 210-friendly, and by that I mean you don't believe in what we can do."

Jayne's eyes narrowed. "Anyone who's been in law enforcement for any length of time understands the 210 reference to the Jägers. I get it. It just doesn't mean I agree, believe, or that I have to like it." Apparently suggesting she might not understand the 210 reference was insulting, if he was to judge by the edge in her words.

Oops. He'd put his foot in his mouth that time. Might as well put both of them in there. "Okay, noted. Even though you don't like it, you're willing to go along with all of this?"

Jayne stared at him for a second, her blue eyes serious, before she nodded. "Yes. I suppose that sums it up fairly well."

"But you really don't want us here." As long as he had both feet in his mouth already he figured it wouldn't hurt to confirm what he was picking up as easily as though he were a psychic. If she could wish them a thousand miles away, he was pretty sure that's exactly what she'd do.

Lily jumped in before he said anything else or the sheriff had a chance to respond. "The Jägers have helped all over the world for centuries." Her words carried just as much edge as the sheriff's. *Back at ya, sister*, he thought. He was a little surprised at how insulted he felt by her obvious reluctance to acknowledge them or their skill sets. As far as he was concerned, they were all pretty damned cool, and she should be pleased they were here to help. It wasn't like they were amateurs and had no idea what they were doing. If she knew anything about them, she'd understand it was the exact opposite.

Jayne was shaking her head. "When I think of international organizations that can help in instances like this, I think of entities like Interpol, not—"

"Not necromancers," Kyle said, his irritation taking a giant leap. She didn't approve or, worse, believe. In his time with the order, he'd been fortunate to have worked with those who at least believed enough to make the hunts successful. By all indications, that wouldn't be the case here. After everything the order had accomplished over the years, it was unfair to continually have to prove themselves.

"Or witches," Ava added. He noticed that, unlike him, she remained calm and polite. She obviously had more willpower than he did. Maybe the longer he hung around her, the more it might rub off on him. His family would like that.

"No," Jayne said, and the edginess of a moment before was gone. "Not witches or necromancers." Her gaze cut to Lily as if silently asking her what she had to add. Lily said nothing, and Kyle wondered why. Everyone in the Jägers knew what she was, and the fact she was not defending the order or her own preternatural powers was puzzling. Honestly, he figured it wasn't much of a secret.

Then again, they were here because of a suspected werewolf. If he gave it more than a glancing thought, then perhaps it might not be the best idea to have everyone know that Lily was, in fact, a werewolf herself. A werewolf with drug-aided control of her powers, but a werewolf nonetheless. Even in this so-called enlightened age, a very real danger for people like Lily still existed. Not everyone believed the world was big enough for both humans and preternaturals. So, if she didn't want anyone to know, he wasn't going to be the one to spill it.

It went beyond protecting one of his team, and he knew it. Regardless of how he might justify his actions in his own head as being for the greater good, he wanted the order's number-one hunter to like him. It was something a good psychologist would absolutely be able to make a case out of, but there it was. He possessed an underlying need for approval from the mother figure, and that was really kind of funny when he looked at Lily. At thirty-one, he appeared to be a few years older than she was. In reality, she had him by a few centuries, so it was a bit of a twist that he appeared to be her elder.

"You know what?" He looked at Ava and winked. No sense in letting the sheriff's reluctance to accept them for the help they really were affect him or what he came here to do. No, he was going to look at the positive side because that's the way he rolled. "I'm on board with the plan. I can absolutely do brother and husband. It doesn't matter what any of you believe or don't believe. We're here together to do a job, and that's what we'll do even if it means pretending. We got this, and among the four of us, we'll stop this bastard before he even knows what hit him."

Ava raised her eyebrows at him and shook her head slightly. "I too can play whatever role you need me to…emphasis on playing a role. Got it, Kyle? Play the role." She patted him on the shoulder, taking a bit of the sting out of her words.

He grinned, and a surge of something indefinable washed over him. "Sure. You got it, Ava, my dear wife. I'm simply playing a role." He also got that when the universe dropped an opportunity right smack in the middle of his lap, he planned to make the best of it. Ava didn't know it yet, but he was going to be the husband she'd always dreamed of.

CHAPTER SIX

This whole thing was fucked up, and Jayne still didn't like it. It continued to rub her wrong that everyone believed she needed help. That the help came in the form of a woman who barely topped five feet tall bordered on downright insulting. She was a trained professional and perfectly capable of handling an investigation without outside help. Who knew what this *team* was really trained to do? A necromancer and a witch? Really?

Her biggest problem was that bucking up against the city council was generally a bad idea. No, that wasn't accurate. It was always a bad idea. They didn't put her in office, but given the size of her county, they could do enough damage to make it impossible to win another term. She liked being sheriff here, and as much as it galled her to do it, she was smart enough to know there were times she had to play their game. Once she'd made the decision to leave the city behind and come home, she'd found peace, and she didn't want to lose it now.

She gazed at the unlikely trio in her home and wondered how in the world they were going to make a difference in this investigation. Throughout her law-enforcement career she'd heard rumors of the Jägers, but personally she'd expended very little effort listening to any of those stories. Some of her counterparts had been and probably still were true believers. Not Jayne. She'd always considered the tales of the so-called amazing order of supernatural hunters a crock. Hard to take people seriously when they came in claiming to be vampires and werewolves. Or, in this case, a witch and a necromancer and whatever in the hell Lily was. Those folk legends made for great horror movies, and that was about it. These creatures of the night didn't really exist. Nobody was ever going to be able to convince her otherwise.

The only flaw in her personally held theory was the condition of the bodies recovered so far. During her time in federal law enforcement she'd been present at enough violent crime scenes to have a pretty strong stomach. She figured she could handle anything. She'd figured wrong. Nothing had prepared her for what she'd seen when the bodies of Clinton Bearns, Pearl Buffet, and Cheryl Tisdale were found. Vicious didn't even begin to describe what they saw. It was as if each of them had been torn apart. She wanted to believe human hands had committed the horrible deeds because she knew how to hunt down and stop a very human killer. The problem facing her now was that every time she studied the photos from the various scenes, all she could think of was that each of the victims looked as though an animal had attacked them. Ignoring that deep-down belief of what her eyes were showing her was the route she took, focusing instead on the kind of person who would do these heinous deeds.

Until she heard the medical examiner's findings she was able to keep to her stand that it was done by human hands. The report that came down indicated all three showed distinct signs of being ravaged by an animal or, as the ME hypothesized, ravaged by a wolf. His opinion came with a caveat. If it was a wolf, it would have needed to be one big-ass *Canis lupus*.

She wasn't buying his assumptions, exactly. The rational law-enforcement side of her screamed to stay in the real world and to avoid thinking of avenues outside the norm. No big-ass wolf but rather a person who tried hard to make it look as though an animal had made the kills. A part of her—a tiny part—wondered if maybe there was more going on than met the eye. She hated that little voice and wanted it to go far away.

Except it was hard for that annoying little voice to shut up when she had three people sitting in her house who all possessed something otherworldly and who had been sent here to stop a so-called werewolf. Between the ME and these three, all she heard was wolf, wolf, wolf. Made her wonder what her world was coming to.

Fighting the inevitable was futile and a waste of energy, and given what was happening of late, she didn't have time to squander. This team was here, she was stuck with them, and this rash of murders wasn't normal. The sooner she reconciled with the way this investigation was going down and got to work, the sooner she could send this trio back to wherever they came from. Now that appealed to her a lot. "What do you propose we do first?" She directed her question to Lily.

If Lily was bothered by all the back-and-forth and the irritation Jayne hadn't been able to hide, she didn't let on. Her manner was calm and unflappable, which made Jayne think she might be okay to work with after all. "I presume you have files with photographs?"

Actually that was a kind of a stupid question, or insulting if Lily thought her county was so backward they didn't even have basic crime-scene skills. She was going to give her the benefit of the doubt and go with stupid question. "Of course."

"Here?"

Jayne's gaze dropped to her hands, almost as if she might actually be holding a file, which, of course, she wasn't. Still, was it a guess, or did this woman possess some kind of extrasensory perception? It would be improper to have a second set of documents here, and that's exactly what she had sitting on top of her desk in her office here at home. Every night since the discovery of the first body she'd pored over the photographs searching for any clue she might have overlooked when on scene. She was certain she was missing something in those images that could bring this horrible nightmare to an end. Her sense was that Lily's question wasn't a guess. For a brief moment she wondered if Lily's special skill might be mind reading.

She chewed on her lip before answering, giving herself time to think through what she would share. It was tempting to keep her impropriety under wraps. Her eyes met Lily's, and she made a split-second decision. Hopefully it was the right one. "Yes."

Lily stood, and Jayne had the impression her answer pleased her. "Well, then let's take a look. It's a good place to start."

Given everything she'd done and the appearance of this strange team, it was silly to put up any kind of resistance. She did it anyway. "It's not protocol."

Lily tilted her head, her long shiny hair swinging, and raised a single eyebrow. "And neither is keeping copies of official police files at your house."

Lily had called her on it, and Jayne had to admit she had her there. "No, it's not." She waved her arm in the direction of her office. "All right, I give up. This way. Let's see what we can all come up with together."

Sometimes a person just had to give it up when they were matched wit for wit. This Lily might be pretty and tiny, but she was sharp and intuitive. Jayne was going to have to keep an eye on her.

Her office was large enough to comfortably accommodate all four of them. They pulled chairs around the round table that most of the time served as a catchall space, and she laid out the files once she'd cleared everything off the top. The room got very quiet as soon as they began poring over the files and photographs she'd brought home. It might not have been the proper thing to do, but right at the moment, it felt like a good decision. After probably twenty minutes, Lily sat back and ran her hands through her long, dark hair. Then she looked over at Kyle and Ava.

"What do you think?" Lily's question wasn't directed at her. She was talking to Kyle and Ava almost as if Jayne weren't even there.

Ava brought her gaze up to meet Lily's. "Looks like a were to me." Slowly she ran a finger across one of the photographs, her eyes narrowed as she studied it once more, then looked back up again. "Feels that way too?"

Jayne scrutinized Ava from across the table. Her black hair framed her face and made her green eyes stand out. She was one of those people others describe as striking, and it was certainly true in her case. She also seemed to radiate a power that was alluring. "What do you mean, it feels that way?"

Ava's hand hovered over three photographs she'd laid out on the table, one each of the three victims. She didn't look up at Jayne as she said, "It's what I do. Objects can sometime emit an energy I'm able to pick up on. These photographs have that kind of force even though they're only images of a tragedy. It's kind of a residual energy, if that makes sense to you."

Strangely it did, although it wasn't something she was willing to admit out loud at this point. Sometimes it felt to her as though inanimate objects retained an essence of evil. Just because she didn't believe mythical creatures were roaming the earth and creating havoc didn't mean she totally discounted bad forces. On the contrary, she believed the spirit of evil did exist, and it surrounded some people like a fog. The person out there killing in her town was that kind of individual:

all human and yet intimately evil at the same time. When they held an object in their hand, touched a thing or a person, at times that evil lingered.

Lily tapped her fingers on the table as she studied the series of photographs. Suddenly she rose to her feet and met Jayne's eyes. "I need to go to the sites where the bodies were found."

"Why?" As far as she was concerned, the photographs and the reports gave them all the information they needed. Her people had done an excellent job documenting the scene both in writing and in image. She didn't think it was necessary to go on a guided tour. "I'd prefer not. There's nothing left to see." The scene earlier in the day remained fresh in her mind, and she had no desire to relive it again so soon. She needed the distance to work through the details.

Besides, she'd already been freaked out by the electric shock she got when she touched Lily earlier. It was the strangest thing that had ever happened to her. She didn't need to sit next to her in the car and have it happen again. A little too close and a lot too confined.

"Your opinion," Lily said firmly. "The fact is I need to touch the ground they were found on, and the same goes for Ava. You have no idea what we can discern from physical contact. After that, we can let Kyle work his particular brand of magic."

Jayne ran both hands through her hair. "And his brand of magic would be?"

"I'm the necromancer we discussed earlier," Kyle said cheerfully.

"That means exactly what? I'm not up on all the terminology of your group."

Jayne didn't miss the way his gaze cut to Lily's face. She gave him a little nod before he turned back to look at Jayne. "I can raise the dead."

Bellona was restless. Even after a late-afternoon roll, it just wasn't enough. As she paced across the bedroom naked, her gaze kept straying to the windows. The acres and acres of forest land beckoned to her. A long, hard run would feel so incredible. A hunt would make it even better. Darkness was beginning to take hold, and she loved racing through the night with the stars and the moon overhead.

A run she could do and it would be safe. A hunt was quite out of the question. Too much had happened recently, and scrutiny by local law enforcement was too intense. The biggest problem was her protégée. Little Wolf was so enthralled about her new abilities that she tended to go overboard. Honestly, it didn't bother her much. In fact, she found it rather endearing. It had been so long since she'd had someone beside her who enjoyed this much as she did. She, however, had had a really long time to develop her skills and knew how to keep things nice and tidy.

Once darkness fell completely, she would run. She was anxious for the night of the full moon. The folklore that dictated the change only occurred on full moons was quite incorrect. The change was, when one was experienced, at will and not predicated on the presence of a full moon. Young ones needed time to harness their abilities, and it was always the tricky part that got them into trouble. Their joy and lust pushed them to change in inopportune times and led them to do unfortunate things. She was a patient teacher, though, and she would work with her children to create the family she envisioned. It was going to be beautiful and fill the void that had been in her heart for so long.

Full-moon nights were infused with a raw power that made her feel more alive than at any other time. They were special nights for the young too, for it was only then that they came completely into their powers. The first one was always a rite of passage and a night filled to the brim with pure joy.

For centuries Bellona had been alone, and to have someone at her side was refreshing. Her partners throughout the years had been few and many years in between. Always she searched for the one who held her heart captive, and always she came up short. She ultimately made do with those who came close, even though they were poor substitutes for the one she truly longed to be with. The only one who'd ever touched her heart had perished so many long years ago in a place on the other side of the world from here.

In this lovely area, she'd discovered a woman who was beautiful, smart, and wealthy. Not that she needed money. On the contrary, she had amassed a great deal of wealth, beginning with the legacy she inherited from her family. Back in the time when the last of her family had perished and she was the sole survivor, many had discounted her ability to manage her estate, based solely on her gender. It hadn't mattered to her, and she took their disdain in stride. Their approval had never been something she needed. Instead she worked quietly to build upon what was left to her until she reached a point of complete independence. None of it had happened by accident, and that's what none of them ever understood.

Still, it was a lonely life for her. It had been so long since her family had passed away, and the paintings tucked away in storage were the only way she could remember their faces. Friends came and went in her life like the passage of the seasons. Lovers were even more infrequent. That's why it was so nice here. She found a companion who was an exquisite lover and ultimately an enthusiastic convert. She didn't run into someone like Little Wolf often, and so when she did, she stayed to enjoy their company for as long as possible.

She leaned over and kissed her sleeping partner and then pulled the comforter up over her naked body. Their lovemaking had lulled Little Wolf into a late-afternoon nap, and she still slept soundly as the last of the daylight faded away. A bit of perfection out here in what seemed like nowhere. It was so incredibly refreshing. Made her feel a little of the old spark.

Naked, Bellona walked outside. No sense in bothering with clothes, given what she wanted to do next. The sun was slipping far below the horizon to the west, the darkening sky slashed by brilliant hues of red. The wind was picking up, and it carried with it a bit of ice. As it blew across her skin, she shivered.

She let her head drop back and breathed in deeply, filling her lungs with the clean, fresh air. Yes, it was so nice here. She felt a deep connection to the land and didn't plan to leave anytime soon. She raised her arms over her head and stretched, loving the feel of the cool air across her naked body. Yes, it was going to be a grand night. She could feel it deep in her bones.

As darkness finished pushing out the last of the light, she called the change.

CHAPTER SEVEN

L ily dropped her bag onto the floor of the spacious bedroom and swept her gaze over the large, comfortable room. It was nice, and as much as she hated to admit it, there was a better-than-average chance that staying here wouldn't be all that bad. The remote location provided them with a nice, quiet place to work without drawing too much attention, and the view out her bedroom window, well, it was flat-out incredible. Jayne's reluctance aside, this was pretty great and gave them the best chance of staying out of the public eye.

She liked keeping a low profile the best. Drawing unwanted, or for that matter any, attention was something she avoided at all costs. She'd never been one to seek interest from others, even before everything changed. Afterward, well, it was the only wise way to live. Move in the shadows, stay to herself, and do her job. Get in. Get out. The less people knew about her, the better and most definitely the safer.

At the window she stared outside. Darkness obscured detail for those with human eyes, but not for Lily. Her vision pierced the night and let her see what others could not. A river was off in the distance to the right, and to the left, massive, thick pine trees and evergreens created an impressive natural barrier. A light wind blew, making the trees sway in a silent ballet. A slice of home in a land far away, she thought. As a young lady she'd stand in her chambers and gaze out at the forest during one of the many storms that ravaged her land. She'd imagine how the wind might pick her up in its chilly embrace and sweep her away to a different life. In that room a fire was always crackling in the large stone fireplace, doing its best to push away the chill that touched both her skin and her soul. Outside her chamber doors lingered the ever-present family and servants who did their part to protect the golden goose. Night after night she dreamt of being set free. Little did she realize her dream of a new life would actually come to pass. Not that the winds picked her up and took her away from the life her father had carefully orchestrated for her. She touched her neck where the scars still marred her otherwise smooth skin.

"Settled in?"

Spinning away from the window, Lily dropped her hand from her neck. She was surprised to see Jayne leaning in the open doorway. She hadn't heard her come in, and that was simply not like Lily. She heard everything all the time. It was one of the perks of being a were. Even the serum she used to control her lycanthropy didn't suppress her senses while she was in human form. Actually, she benefited from many things that the serum didn't dampen. It did the job it was supposed to, and that granted her a superhuman type of control that had been responsible for her being here today. A bit like having the best of both worlds, human and were.

She nodded. "I am, thank you. This is a lovely home. A very comfortable room." She wasn't just saying it to be polite either. The minute she stepped inside the bedroom she felt at ease and as if she'd simply returned home, which made no sense whatsoever. Nonetheless it was how she felt, and feeling at ease would go a long way to making this hunt more productive.

Jayne's gaze moved over the room as if she were taking it in for the first time. Quietly she said, "I know. It's a little much for a county sheriff. Especially a single county sheriff who lives alone."

Lily raised her eyebrows. Interesting that she would bring up two bullet points that were of particular interest to her. Not something she was expecting from the sheriff. "Well, now that you mention it…"

Jayne's gaze came back to Lily. Her blue eyes were clear. "My brother built this place, much of it himself. He had such grand plans for making a life here. He often talked about his dream of a wife and children. Of raising goats and cattle."

There was a greater story within her brief words, and the ending of that story wasn't a happy one. Lily could feel the depth of emotion that Jayne's words hinted at. "It didn't work out as he planned."

She shook her head. "No." Deep sadness washed over her face, and tears glistened in her eyes, making them look like two pools of crystal-blue water. As tough as Jayne had been since the moment they met, it surprised Lily to see the raw emotion in the other woman. "Cancer took him before he even had a chance to truly live here. He'd barely finished it when he was diagnosed with pancreatic cancer. At the time he was single with no children. Our parents were gone, and it was just me and Sam. Now it's just me. He was gone inside of a year, and that's the reason I now live in this large and beautiful house."

Jayne's sorrow was as real to Lily as if it was her own because she had walked in her shoes. "I'm sorry." The pain of losing family was something she understood, and thus her words were not simply platitudes. The only difference between them was all of her family had been gone for more years than she could count. By now the heartache of their passing should have eased. It hadn't. She'd learned that time never took away the sadness of a loved one lost, regardless of how many years passed. Despite everything, from the arranged marriage to the way they handled her attack, she still missed her family as if they'd just left her yesterday. She would give anything to see their faces one more time.

Jayne blinked several times and the glint of tears disappeared. She was one tough woman. "Thank you. It's been almost ten years, and I still miss him every day." A ghost of a smile flickered across her lips as she once more looked over the bedroom. "This place is incredible and reminds me of him every day. I do love living here, but I would just love to have my brother back more."

Jayne's words hit so very close to home for her. "I understand more than you know."

Jayne tilted her head as her gaze locked on Lily's. Slowly she nodded. "I believe you do."

"So." Lily changed the subject. Going any further with this conversation was touching on forbidden ground. Or at least ground she'd deemed forbidden. She didn't talk about her family or the life she left behind, ever. "Can we visit the sites?"

Jayne's brow creased. "It's getting really dark outside, not to mention late. I think we'd be better served by going tomorrow." Her gaze shifted from Lily's face to the window behind her.

For that few minutes they seemed to be finding common ground and maybe even forging a tentative friendship. Then in a flash, they were back to the earlier stonewalling. Lily wanted to keep her impatience in check, but it was hard. She hadn't come all this way to sit around. Day or night didn't matter in her line of work. Getting the werewolf stopped before anyone else was hurt was more important than anything else.

This is where this particular arrangement was a little problematic. If they were at the hotel, they could have been out and on their way, with or without the sheriff's help. But being here they were pretty well stuck with the sheriff being at their side 24/7. Trying to find a way to explain to her why they needed to go now was somewhat tricky. She wasn't quite ready to reveal her own special talents to Jayne, particularly considering the issue they were here to solve. Some didn't take it well.

Picking up her jacket from where she'd tossed it across the bed, she slid her arms into the sleeves. "That's not a problem for us. You'd be surprised how much we can glean even in the dark. It's important or I wouldn't bother you."

"You realize this whole thing is a big pain in the ass to me." That tone was back in her voice.

Lily worked hard to make sure her words remained neutral and didn't carry any of her impatience. "I do, and if I could change things, trust me, I would. But whether you wish to believe it or not, you have a werewolf here, and we're the ones equipped to take care of it for you. I want to get a feel for this killer as soon as we can, and if that means we go tonight, then we go tonight."

Jayne argued. "We have a serial killer, not a werewolf. They don't exist."

"Just as the Jägers is an order of legend, we don't exist either, yet here I am."

"Werewolves don't exist," Jayne repeated. "We're tracking a serial killer. Period. End of story."

Lily had been through similar discussions more times than she could count. Even those who gave credence to the Jägers had trouble seeing the full picture. Throughout the years she'd worked through every type of obstacle imaginable, every personality that sat behind a law-enforcement desk. In days long past, it had been somewhat easier. All it took was a little money and a powerful ally. These days it was far more politics than cash or influence. She hated politics. "You do, indeed, have a serial killer. I don't disagree with that conclusion in any way. What you're failing to see is that the werewolf and the serial killer are one and the same."

❖

Kyle winged around the corner and into Ava's bedroom, where he launched himself on the big bed. It was queen sized with a dark-blue comforter and plenty of pillows. Oh yeah, he could totally make himself comfortable here on his *wife's* bed. He smiled and put his arms behind his head. The coffered ceiling was awesome.

"Nice digs," he said.

Ava leaned against the closet door and crossed her arms over her chest. "Don't make yourself comfortable, big boy. You'll be staying in your own room."

He pretended to pout. Nothing she could say would dampen his enthusiasm. "Ah, honey, is that any way to talk to your husband?"

Ava laughed, walked over to the bed, and smacked him with one of the decorative pillows. "In your dreams."

"You know me so well." He spoke only partially in jest. She was indeed in his dreams and had been since the first time he laid eyes on her. He hadn't even looked at another woman since that day. Until that fateful meeting he'd never even considered the possibly that the love-at-first-sight thing actually existed.

Though his parents had divorced when he was five years old and he spent the rest of his formative years shuttled between them, he took inspiration from his grandparents. Nana and Papa had spent fifty-three years together before a bad heart took Papa to the Great Beyond. In today's world, with so many shaky relationships and given his unique talents, wishing for something like half a century with one woman might be unrealistic. He couldn't help it. He wanted what he wanted, and he wasn't going to give it up without the old college try.

Right in front of him was the one he wanted to give it try with. His heart told him she was the proverbial one. She didn't know it yet, and it might be a while before she did. But that was okay. He was a patient guy. Nothing worth having ever came easy, or at least that's what Nana used to say to him when he became frustrated when a project didn't come together. Or when he was coming into his powers and he couldn't control them. She was always there at his side, guiding him and showing him the way. She taught him that patience did, indeed, make him stronger. She also taught him love was worth fighting for.

He rolled onto his side and propped his head on one hand. "So you can see into my dreams?"

A look crossed her face that he couldn't quite define. She was serious when she answered. "If I chose to, yes, Kyle. I could see into your dreams. Do I want to make that choice?"

Oh yeah, baby, come on in, he wanted to say. Get an eyeful of the desire that nearly burned him up. Nana's voice in the back of his head said, *Not now.* At an early age he'd learned it was a good thing to listen to her. Timing was everything, and if he was going to win the heart of this beautiful witch he was going to have to do it Nana's way. Patience, patience, patience.

"Well," he said with a sly smile. "You might not want to jump in cold turkey." He winked. She smacked him with the pillow again. He remembered that kind of move from junior high: no doubt about it, she liked him.

She sat on the edge of the bed. "Seriously, Kyle, we've got to pull off this husband-and-wife thing. I haven't had to play-act before. I've always been just me. This is a new twist."

He continued to gaze at her face. He loved the way her dark hair framed her face and lay soft and wavy against her shoulders. Her deep-green eyes seemed to sparkle with life and intelligence. He could stare into those eyes for hours. "Well, kind of a new one on me too. Can I tell you a little secret?"

She tilted her head and returned his gaze for a long, silent minute. "Sure."

He smiled. "I'm happy it's you I get to pretend with."

A slow smile crossed her face, making her green eyes light up. He took that as a good sign too. "So am I."

Oh, man, how was he supposed to take that? Did she feel the same draw that he did, or was he reading more into it than she really meant? He wanted to read the world into her statement and didn't dare. All it could mean is that she felt comfortable with him, and if he was being smart, he'd accept that right now it was enough. It was a good beginning. In fact, it was more than that; it was a great beginning.

"Good." He jumped up from the bed. "Shall we go see what our fearless leader has in store for us, my lovely bride? I think we're going to have to do some serious work to win over Sheriff Jayne. She seems a little skeptical of our skill level in this situation."

Ava tossed the pillow onto the bed. "I picked that up as well. I don't think she's very happy that we're here."

"Ava, Kyle, let's roll." Lily's voice came from the bottom of the staircase.

Kyle held out his hand. "Our fearless leader calls. I don't know about you, but I'm ready to go kick some werewolf ass."

Chapter Eight

Jayne still wasn't sure about any of this. In her opinion all they really needed to bring this killer to justice was tried and true police work. With the resources they had available to them in this day and age, bringing in outsiders was unnecessary. Outsiders from some crazy organization that had been around since before the Middle Ages racing in to save the day was absurd. To say their time had come and gone was not being disrespectful. It was simply stating the obvious truth. Besides, she was a good cop and always had been. She surrounded herself with equally good people, and so it was going to be a long time before she reconciled with the edict of the council to invite in these hunters. Damn straight, her pride was hurt.

Driving out to the site where the first body was discovered, she starting fuming all over again. For a while back at the house she began to think she could work with these three and get the job done quickly. Now she wasn't so sure. What purpose could it possibly serve to stumble around in the dark where a body had been dumped many weeks ago? There was nothing left in the woods to uncover anyway. At the time of discovery, her crew had gone over everything in minute detail. Her confidence that nothing had been missed was rock solid. They might be a small county without the money or resources of many other counties in the state, but that didn't mean they were unskilled, undermanned, or behind the times.

None of her arguments dissuaded Lily. She was more than insistent that they go tonight regardless of what time it was or the lack of daylight. Jayne had to wonder if all the team leads from this mystical, in-the-shadows organization were as stubborn as Lily. One way or the other, she was determined to visit the dump sites. Jayne quickly picked up that it meant she'd go, with or without her.

In the end, Jayne caved because she felt it was more important to be with Lily and her team than to impose her own will. Why, she wasn't really certain. It was more about a feeling in the pit of her stomach that told her to stick close to the three strangers currently in her car. That damned little voice was whispering in the back of her mind again, and it was telling her these hunters might, just might, be able to add something to her investigation. Damn it anyway, she just wanted them to go away and things to get back to normal. *Shut up, little voice.*

"Here," she said as she pulled off the road and put the car in Park. "This is the location where some hikers discovered the first body." She stared through the windshield to where the trail the hikers had started out on so optimistically disappeared into the trees and the blackness beyond. In the daylight it was beautiful and peaceful. In the shadows, it was ominous. "I'll be surprised if either one ever steps foot out here again."

She popped the lever for the trunk and then circled around to the open trunk and grabbed the large flashlight she kept inside. When she clicked the On switch it sent a flood of light across the forest floor. Trees, underbrush, and fallen branches popped out of the shadows. The spot where the body had been spread out, battered, and shredded was covered with a light layer of snow. At first glance, she saw an early winter forest scene, clean and beautiful. In her mind's eye, however, blood still soaked into the ground and scavengers circled the sky above.

As they moved from the car to the forest no one said a word. Her take was they were each using their particular brand of paranormal to see what they could sense. She didn't put much stock in that until Lily stopped exactly where the body of Clinton Bearns was found. Some might call that a coincidence. She didn't. Never believed in them and even now, when she didn't want to give any credence to her unwanted guests' self-proclaimed abilities, she couldn't quite make the leap. Though she couldn't explain how she knew, Jayne was certain it was no coincidence that Lily knew exactly where his body had been left.

Only when they stopped did she notice that Lily carried nothing with her, while Ava had a tote bag over one shoulder and Kyle carried a messenger bag across his body. She was as curious as to what Ava and Kyle carried in their bags as she was about why Lily had nothing despite being the clear leader. Surely the great Jäger hunter had some kind of tools to do her dirty work. Lily had no gun on her, no knife, no weapon of any kind beyond a cell phone in the back pocket of her jeans. So how much help was she going to be exactly?

The answer to any questions would have to wait. Lily wasn't standing around. She strode ahead and stopped in the center of Jayne's light as it fell on the spot where the body was discovered. She closed her eyes, pressed her lips together in a thin line, and tilted her head back. Her chest was rising and falling rhythmically as she took in deep, full breaths. Jayne wasn't sure if it was a calming technique like those used in yoga or if she was attempting to pick up something in the night air. If it was the latter, she figured it was a bust because nothing unusual was floating around tonight, just the scent of a forest in the snow. Or at least that was her impression. Lily appeared to have a different one, because with each breath she drew, her body seemed to quiver as if something unpleasant passed through her. Jayne felt nothing but a cool breeze carrying a hint of the moisture that brought the snow.

At last, Lily tilted her head down and turned her gaze to Jayne. "The body was here." She pointed to her feet.

Jayne nodded. She'd been correct in her initial conclusion that Lily's stopping where she did was not a coincidence. "Yes. What was left of him."

It still made her a little sick to the stomach recalling what she'd witnessed. Despite having been around a long time, what she'd seen that day came as a shock. It was the first time she'd ever witnessed the aftermath of a body ravaged in such a brutal manner. This killer went beyond warped, and the nightmares the scene gave her continued.

Lily turned a full circle slowly, her arms out and her eyes focused on something Jayne couldn't see. "He wasn't killed here."

"No," Jayne confirmed quietly. "He was not. Just as I told you back at the house, his body was dumped here. We're not sure where he was actually killed." Earlier, as they'd pored over the crime-scene photos, she'd explained what they'd learned so far, including the fact that all three victims had been killed elsewhere and dumped where they were discovered.

"He was dragged here from"—Lily turned full circle and then pointed—"from there."

A cold chill raced up Jayne's spine, and it had nothing to do with the wind that was picking up in intensity and flowing through the pines. How could she possibly know that? She spoke as if the forest floor had been sprayed with luminol, lighting up the trail of blood like a neon sign. "I'm going to ask you one more time, what are you?" As she did earlier, Jayne reached out and put a hand on Lily's shoulder. The same shot of electricity traveled from her hand up across her shoulders. "What the hell are you," she whispered.

It was both the same question and the same reaction from earlier in the day, neither of which she had received an answer to. She took hold of Lily's shoulders and turned her so they were face-to-face. Dark eyes held hers as she waited for Lily's response. This time she was going to get an answer.

"I'm a Jägers hunter," Lily said calmly, her gaze steady.

Jayne nodded and didn't look away. Two could play this game. "That still doesn't answer my question. He," she nodded in Kyle's direction, "is a necromancer and she is a witch. That leaves you. What are you?"

❖

With whispered words Bellona had called the change, and now she ran from the back deck on all fours. The pulse of the moon, so close to being full, pulled in her veins, and her body reacted. Oh yes, this was what she lived for. The ground was wet and soft beneath her paws. Winter was on its way, but for tonight, the ground still yielded.

Along the river the air was cool and sweet. She stopped and dipped her head to drink, loving the coldness and the unique taste of the water. It was far different from the waters of her home, and often when she ran she missed the smells, the trees, the mountains, and most of all, the people. Yes, the people.

As she sailed over the ground she thought of the one of her heart. So long ago lost to her and yet after all these years, the ache of it still filled her heart. Not even when the moon was full and she soared with the power it granted her did the pain of losing her ever ease. Year after year she searched for her, finding solace in the others who each fell short. That included the woman who waited back at the house for her. As lovely as she was, she too failed to measure up. They all did, and though she scoured the world trying to find another who could fill the void, she never found her.

Running along a ridgeline Bellona gloried in the way the wind ruffled her fur and the scents of the forest that were so comforting. For several miles she ran hard and fast. Her muscles screamed, and the exertion filled her with pleasure. The joy it gave her never got old.

Finally she stopped at the top near the edge. As she stood panting, a scent drifted to her on the wind. It made the hairs at the nape of her neck stand up, and every nerve ending in her body went on alert. Her mind told her it couldn't be, yet her senses screamed that it was. She brought her nose up into the air and breathed in deeply again and again. The scent was sweet and somehow familiar, like something out of a dream. She whipped her head to the right and once more began to run.

As she loped along the ridge the scent grew stronger, and then she heard the voices carried up to her sensitive ears on the wind. The sound of women's voices floated up out of the nightfall. Crouching, she slowly crept forward until she could see them through the darkness. Or rather she could see their shadows. It appeared to be three women and one man. She was less surprised about the man than she was about the familiar scent that she now placed. One who stood below was her kind, and hers was the smell that was carried up to her on the breeze. The others she wasn't quite certain about. They were *something*. She just wasn't sure what that something was. The urge to race down to them was overpowering. Her nose twitched and her muscles tensed.

Before she acted on the wolf impulse that urged her to charge, she took several steps back. The one below who also carried the wolf inside had turned her face up toward the ridgeline. It was as if she'd sensed Bellona's presence and her gaze had found the place where she stood watching in the darkness. She shouldn't be surprised. Her own senses were acutely tuned to the scents and sounds of the world, and given what she was certain the one below her was, she undoubtedly possessed the same acute senses. Just as Bellona had picked up her scent, so too would she be aware of Bellona. After a moment's hesitation, she turned and ran in the other direction. Fear, an unfamiliar emotion, sent her fleeing. It had been a long time since she'd encountered another of her kind and even longer since she'd experienced fright. Every fiber of her being screamed, *Beware!*

She raced back across the forest weaving in and out of trees, her tracks large and clear in the snow. Instead of going back to the house, she veered toward the river and ran into the water. Swimming downriver, she moved as fast as she could, and when she emerged, she was once again walking on two feet.

CHAPTER NINE

What was she? Oh, if Lily had a dime for every time she'd been asked that question she'd be rich. Not exactly accurate, considering the fact she was already rich, but it was the point. It didn't matter where the hunt was or who she was with; they always asked the same question.

And she always avoided answering if at all possible.

"I'm a hunter." Simple and to the point. True, as well. She was a hunter. What she told her wasn't a lie. Rather, she simply omitted what was need-to-know only, and the fact was, Jayne didn't need to know.

Jayne's shoulders tensed and her eyes grew hard. She'd seen that look before too. "You know what I mean."

Lily stood tall, or as tall as she could for a woman who barely made five foot, and met her gaze. "I do, and what I'm telling you is it's not relevant. I'm a hunter and I'm damned good. That's all that's important. We're not going to be around each other long enough to have to worry about life histories."

As she spoke the wind picked up and brought a scent that gave her the chills. Slowly she turned to her left, where the scent was stronger. There the elevation of the hillside began to rise until above them a ridgeline loomed in the darkness. The distinctive smell of wolf hit her with sobering familiarity, yet the scent was growing weaker as the breeze flowed down and around her.

Her first urge was to strip off her clothes and call the change. She wanted to chase the scent until she found the source. It didn't matter that she wasn't in a position to change and go forward with the chase. The wolf was retreating, and by the time she could make the top of the ridge, it would be long gone. The pursuit would be for nothing, and so she held her ground and her human form.

Something about the scent tickled a memory far back in her mind. Somewhere along the line she'd encountered this wolf before. She was a good hunter. No, she was the best hunter, and yet there were times when every hunter failed, even the very best. She was not immune to failure. The difference between her and all others: she didn't fail twice.

As she looked down at the light dusting of snow, it occurred to Lily that she could follow the tracks of the wolf, find out where it was going. The tracks would be clear as long as the temperature didn't rise. Unfortunately, it was already warming up, and instead of snow, rain was predicted. The tracks would wash away in even the lightest storm. The wolf would probably be smart enough to the hide its tracks, with or without the rain. Wolves were a smart breed. Combine that with the human factor, and werewolves were one of the most challenging creatures to track and ultimately stop.

That they were smart didn't deter Lily much. What most of them didn't understand was that she got them: how they thought, how they moved, and most especially how they hunted. She might not be predatory, but that didn't mean she was oblivious to the emotions that drove the preternatural creature.

"Bullshit."

Lily moved her gaze from the ridgeline back to Jayne's face. "No, it's not."

"Look, you want me to work with you, then cut the crap. I'm either in a hundred percent or I'm out, and so are you. I don't care what the council said when they brought you in. I'll shut you down in a New York minute."

"It won't happen like that." Her group was old, as in many, many centuries old, and they had influence that went far beyond what could be seen or heard. It went deep, and she knew that once they were here, Jayne could pull every string she had and still wouldn't succeed in running them out before the job was done. It was easier and quieter if they worked together, but it wasn't like she hadn't worked around a reluctant sheriff before. Not one quite this attractive, though, and despite the back-and-forth they kept having, she would really prefer to work with her.

Jayne stood with her feet slightly apart and one hand on her gun.

"I don't care who you've worked with before or what kind of political pull you have, I'm telling you I can make this really difficult for you, and I won't hesitate to do it if you continue to stonewall me. We either play nice together or you can consider it a declaration of war."

This was one of those moments when she had to make a call. Did she push back or bring Jayne into the inner circle? She let her gaze drift to Kyle and Ava. They were both watching her closely and waiting in silence for her lead. They wouldn't volunteer her personal information; that was just the way it worked, and for good reason. It was one thing to control magic as Ava and Kyle both could do, but it was another matter altogether to be one of the very creatures they hunted. Exposing herself could be dangerous if not outright deadly. She hadn't existed this long by being stupid.

Sometimes, however, a person just had to take a leap, and this was one of those times. It wasn't a big leap because she had a good feeling about Jayne Quarles. She'd been wrong before and had paid a heavy price for that miscalculation. Deep in her heart, she felt this was not going to be a repeat of those errors in judgment. This woman could be trusted. So, she took a breath, rolled her head from side to side, and then said calmly, "I'm a werewolf."

Kyle could have been knocked over by a feather. He'd heard lots of stories about Lily going into a hunt like a ninja. In—prey captured and destroyed—out. Easy peasy, as the saying went. As the legends went, she was a shadow who rarely revealed herself to the outside world. Her backstory was a mystery, and he wasn't sure anyone knew the truth of it. If she had shared it, only a handful of people were privy to it, and they weren't talking. The one thing he did know about her was that she kept her true nature very quiet. The other hunters of the Jägers were aware of what she was, and they also knew not to talk about it. The secret was easy to keep because she garnered so much respect even from those, like him, who had never even met her. She'd done much for the world and kept it safe without anyone ever even realizing what she'd accomplished. That she never asked for anything in return made her even more special.

That she so boldly revealed herself to this wholly human sheriff now shocked him. From the look on Ava's face he wasn't the only one feeling intense surprise at the revelation. He'd jumped at the chance to work with both Ava and Lily, believing it would be a tremendous experience both to learn from Lily and to be side by side with Ava. When he'd gotten in his car back at his home in California, he'd been clueless about how interesting this hunt was going to turn out to be. Considering they were just getting started, this could be one roller-coaster ride.

He kept his eyes on the sheriff's face, watching to see what her reaction would be to Lily's quiet announcement. Again, he was as shocked at her as he was at Lily's confession. Jayne barely reacted at all. In fact, she simply nodded and said, "Good. Then if, as you say, this monster is a werewolf, you'll be perfectly equipped to deal with him."

Lily raised an eyebrow. "Indeed."

Jesus, were they at some tea party? Judging by the stiff formality of the conversation between the two women, it was as if running into a werewolf hunter was just an interesting afternoon sidebar. It was pretty damned amazing, if you asked him. In fact everything that had happened to him since the Jägers came knocking on his door had been pretty fucking amazing. He was born for this order, and even after four years, it still made him pause in awe and wonder at the things he saw and heard. Jayne Quarles acted as though it was no big deal. As his brother would say, it was a big fucking deal.

"So," Kyle ventured, not feeling all that brave but wanting to defuse whatever the hell it was going on between the two women. "What do you think, Lily? Should Ava and I give it a go?" It might not be the thing to say because he wasn't totally sure Lily knew about his special brand of necromancy. He was unique even among the practitioners of his particular art.

The words sort of hung there for a few while Lily and Jayne continued to stare at each other. It wasn't out-and-out hostility. He didn't know what to call it. He just sensed that whatever it was, it needed to be redirected before something went kaboom.

Lily was the one to break the stare-down. She swung her gaze from Jayne's face to his, her eyes clear and intense. Though he was afraid she'd be pissed at him for interrupting, he didn't see any anger in her face. Instead of ire, he saw thoughtfulness. "I think you're up,

Kyle. The wolf that did this is gone, though I suspect not far. I'm certain it hasn't left the area and may even have been returning to the dump sites. I could smell it here, pretty strong, and I'll lay odds we run into the same thing at the next site. Anyway, give it a shot and see what you come up with. We could use some helpful intel."

Good. Maybe she had been fully briefed on what he could do, and it was nice that he wouldn't have to go into detail. His powers had manifested for him when he was a teenager. Fortunately his grandmother had been waiting and watching for the next family member to inherit the gift. He was the lucky soul, and so when it came to pass, she was there to guide him. What none of them had realized at the time was he was some kind of superhero necromancer. All of the necromancers before him had been able to raise the dead just as any good one could. Unlike his predecessors, he'd developed über skills, to put it technically. He could not only raise the dead, but he could get inside the deceased's head by simply standing on the ground where their body had fallen. Nana had been pretty impressed, though it took him a while to figure out how to make sense of the things he saw and heard. As a young man having to deal with all sorts of other normal guy issues, interacting with the dead was a complication he could have done without. The choice hadn't been his to make, and so he'd learned how to integrate what he was with his life as best he could.

When the Jägers recruited him, he'd found out they'd been watching him for years because he was the first of his kind. No necromancer before him had commanded the sort of psychic ability he seemed to possess. What he discovered much later was that his grandmother contacted the Jägers as soon as she realized how special he was. She wanted him to do something important in the world and figured out what it needed to be. So, here he was. He tried every day to make Nana proud and was pretty sure he was succeeding.

Nodding to Lily he said, "I'd be happy to give it a shot." He looked over at Ava and winked. He liked the way her eyes sparkled every time he did that.

Lily stepped away from him and moved to stand next to Jayne. For someone who seemed to be less than warm toward her, Lily was standing awfully close. And for someone who seemed to reciprocate those less-than-warm feelings, Jayne sure didn't move away. Kind of interesting to watch the dynamic between them, and he'd love to spend more time simply observing, but it was time to get down to business and the reason he was on this hunt.

Kyle moved to the spot Lily had just vacated. Setting his messenger bag on the ground, he took out the bundle of dried sage he'd wrapped with red ribbon before he left California. Red held no special significance other than it was Nana's favorite color. Each time he made one of these bundles and tied the red ribbon, it made him think of her and smile. With a lighter he pulled from his pocket, he lit the tips of the sage stalks and held the burning bundle up as he turned full circle three times. At the conclusion of the third turn, he dropped the sage to the ground and put out the fire with his boot. For a moment he stood still and breathed in the pungent scent of the burned herb. Yeah, it felt right, and so he slowly lowered himself to the ground, crossed his legs, and put his hands in his lap, fingers interlaced. He closed his eyes and concentrated on breathing in the faint, lingering scent of the sage. Easy breaths in and out, slow and even.

The first shock hit him like a hardball right between the shoulder blades, only to be followed by scorching pain throughout his body. The breath was knocked out of him, and he struggled to stay upright. Behind his closed lids it was as if a horror movie began to play in bright, vivid colors. He wasn't just seeing what happened on this spot; he was inside the victim, looking out through his eyes…his dead eyes. Strangely, it was the jaws of a wolf that filled his body with fiery pain, and yet it was two very human hands that dragged him to this lonely spot in the forest. He couldn't see her face clearly, only that it was a woman who pulled and heaved the lifeless body until it rested on the ground beneath the spot where he sat.

The man was dropped in this pine-needle-strewn patch of the forest floor without ceremony or care. Her sole intent seemed to simply find a secluded area in which to leave him. As she let go of his body and walked away, the woman didn't look back. Her posture was erect and regal, and her long, dark hair fell down her back and well past her butt—her naked butt.

His eyes snapped open and he sat still, letting emotion and sensation settle within his body. It always took a minute or two to reground himself in the here and now after being inside a dead person's mind. After seeing what too often were the horrors of their last minutes of life, he internalized their pain. Tonight was no different. His heart pounded and his eyes teared up. He could still feel the agony that had taken him to his last breath, still feel the terror that was with him as he crossed over. He hated it. Not because it hurt him but because, even with his gift, he could not take away the travesty visited upon the victims. The best he could do was to give light to the evil that tried to keep itself hidden in the dark and to bring those responsible down. The Jägers had a particular brand of justice for monsters like the naked woman he'd seen walk away, and he wanted to be there when it was meted out.

Finally, when his hands stopped trembling and the threat of tears had passed, he brought his head up and stared over at Lily. A werewolf might have killed this unfortunate man, but it was a very human woman who dragged his body to this place. It was more than just the fact she'd dragged him; it was the fact that she could. The murdered man had not been slight of stature, and yet what he'd seen said the killer was more than capable of handling him on her own. How many women of her petite size could pull that off?

Lily's face tightened as she stared at him. He hadn't uttered a word, and yet he sensed she understood everything that had gone down here. "Shit." She blew out a long breath. "Ava, can you lock this place down?"

Kyle knew she could because he'd seen her do it before. She was some kind of wicked-awesome witch, and she would cast a spell that would essentially repel anyone with evil intent. They would never step foot on this ground again. No one else would ever be left here alone and discarded as if their life hadn't mattered.

Kyle stood and picked up the blackened sage bundle. He tucked it back into his bag as Ava stepped near him and opened her own tote. The first thing she pulled out was a bottle of salt. She used it to draw a wide circle around the area where the body had been discovered. He stepped out of her way so that she could do her work without his big feet disturbing her circle. As she poured the salt, she spoke quietly. He couldn't make out the words she whispered, though he didn't need to. Specifics didn't matter. He knew what those softly uttered words could do, and God help the poor bastard who tried to break her spell once it was in place. Wouldn't happen, and he took solace in that fact.

When she was done, she put the salt, a single candle, and a bundle of mixed herbs she'd used to cast her spell back into her bag. "It's safe," she told Lily as she stepped across the salt and stopped next to him. He liked it when she stood so close he could smell the lingering scent of the herbs on her. He loved the smell.

"Now what?" Jayne's gaze took in all three of them in a single glance.

"Now we go to site number two," Lily said as she turned and hurried back toward the car. He followed close on her heels, wondering what the hell they were going to find next and trying to will away the chill coursing through his body.

CHAPTER TEN

Jayne was all for getting out of here. When she'd driven them out to this place, she'd come here as a full-blown skeptic. She'd never bought into the whole Jägers thing despite insistence from people she admired telling her they could do amazing things. As far as she'd been concerned, it was all smoke and mirrors.

Witnessing the almost transformative change in Kyle as he'd sat crossed-legged and still as stone on the ground had her rethinking her hardline stance. There were no mirrors and there was definitely no smoke. Damned if it didn't seem a hundred percent real. It was difficult to put a name to what was making her believe little by little, but it was there.

Watching Lily as she'd stood on the spot where they'd found the first body, and not just near the spot, but the exact spot without being told where it had been, was the first thing that shook her deeply. There was something otherworldly about the way she'd looked, and it couldn't be faked. Of course, boldly declaring herself to be a werewolf would pretty much explain the otherworld aspect of her appearance.

To try to picture the petite woman with the long dark hair changing into a wolf was hard to do. She was beautiful and, compared to Jayne, tiny. Wrapping her head around the idea that come a full moon she would morph into a wolf-like creature was absurd. The moon didn't have magical powers to turn humans into animals. Or did she actually need a full moon to become a wolf? She couldn't keep her folk legends straight.

No. She didn't envision it at all. The idea that Lily could suddenly transform into a hairy, four-legged dog was out there. Lily, however, had been pretty adamant, so she wasn't about to argue the point with her at the moment. She'd still have to see it to believe it, though she had her doubts about that ever happening.

Kyle was equally interesting. He was, according to Lily, a necromancer capable of raising the dead. His skills didn't end there, as apparently he had a talent for seeing through the eyes of the deceased whether they were present or not. Again, she'd have to see him raise the dead before she'd believe it. On the other hand, she'd just seen him do a little mojo out there, and the sight sent chills up her arms as his face changed and the words coming from his mouth sounded as though they came from somewhere far off. It was as if he'd been inside their victim, and again, nothing about what he did appeared to be anything beyond legitimate. Lord knows, she'd seen enough fakes in her time as a law-enforcement officer to be able to spot an imposter a mile away.

Jayne was cognizant of the fact her basic character was that of a true skeptic, and despite that, there had been two instances when she'd opened herself up to the possibility of help from psychics. She'd been up against a brick wall in a couple of cases and finally reached a point where she'd been willing to try anything, even something she truly did not believe in.

The first time she'd opened the door to alternative methods, the case was successful in that the woman, or rather the psychic, who came in actually led them to the body of their missing victim. The peace it brought to the family of the missing was immeasurable, and it was the deciding factor for why she was willing to give it a go with the second case. Lightning did not strike twice. That self-declared psychic in the next investigation had done precisely nothing, and to date the case remained unsolved, the victim still unaccounted for. Even now, she wasn't able to set that one aside. In her free time, she continued to search, unwilling to leave the case unsolved despite it belonging to another jurisdiction.

Tonight as she drove in silence the five miles to the location where they'd discovered the second body, her mind was whirling. The road into the secluded spot was rutted, the light dusting of snow camouflaging many of the holes that jarred the wheels. She concentrated on the road and tried not to think about the second victim. Pearl Buffet had been a year ahead of her in school and a bully back before they really gave a name to people like her. Jayne didn't like her, though through the years of training and experience, she'd come to understand what made her the way she was. Unfortunately, Pearl never really grew out of the personality trait that made her an outcast in school. Still, even Pearl didn't deserve what had happened to her. Nobody deserved it.

Lily put a hand on her arm, and the touch sent a spark racing along her skin. It made her heart pound. "I understand how bizarre this must seem."

"Really?" Despite Lily's reassurance, she seriously doubted she understood at all. From every appearance, this seemed to be very matter-of-fact to the three riding in her car and as though it was nothing out of the usual. Like it was a common thing to have a werewolf running through the woods killing people and dragging their bodies around like giant chew toys. Like finding a schoolmate ripped apart was something that happened to people every day. Right, and she was the pope. This kind of shit just didn't happen, especially not here.

Or so she wanted to believe. A serial killer running around her woods was easier to swallow than a werewolf raising havoc. Even a human serial killer was a stretch, given where they were. In this small county in northeast Washington State, killers were not hanging around in the trees. She'd left that kind of crap behind when she said good-bye to the cities. Here it was beautiful and unspoiled, the people hardworking and kind, the community small and tight-knit. These were not the sort of people who snapped and started running about killing their friends and neighbors.

It all sounded good in her head, but it just wasn't entirely true. Most of it was. Where it fell down was the part about someone snapping because it was clear by the sheer number of murders that someone had, indeed, gone over the proverbial edge. One of her neighbors was a killer, and no matter what she wanted to believe, the proof was impossible to ignore.

Lily squeezed her arm gently. "Oh yes, really. I promise this will all make sense."

Something about Lily's touch and her calm, reassuring words made her want to believe. "I'll hold you to that."

"Deal." Lily's hand fell away, and irrationally, she wanted to grab it back and hold on.

Jayne pulled off the main park road and onto a service road that had she not been here several times already, she never would have been able to see in the darkness. It was in even worse shape than the first road, the ruts deep and close together. After bumping along for a minute or so, she stopped. They were going to have to hike in the rest of the way. "Come on," she told them as she opened her door. "Make a believer out of me."

❖

Bellona walked through the French doors smiling, still naked and wet from her shower. She should be worried about the hunters she saw out there tonight but wasn't. By the time she got back here, her fear had dissipated and she'd figured out why they seemed so familiar: Jägers. They'd arrived a bit quicker than she thought they would, and that was quite inconvenient. It didn't mean they were a problem. She'd been dodging that group of do-gooders for so long it wasn't even a challenge anymore. Sometimes it was fun, but other times, it was simply annoying.

Still, the inconvenience and annoyance wasn't enough to keep her from smiling. Thinking of them out there trying to use their little magic to find her was amusing. Witches and warlocks, psychics and seers, they had all tried to track her down at one point or another, and they had all failed. Time and time again. She was untouchable, and that made her horny as all get-out.

Most of the time when confronted with the pesky Jägers, she simply slipped past them as she moved on to greener pastures. This time around she had a different plan because she wanted to stay here at least for a while. No hunters were going to derail those plans. It might take a little work, but she'd get them on their way posthaste. It was all in the way one played the game.

"Hey, baby. What took you so long?"

"Little Wolf," she whispered as her smile grew. This was exactly what had drawn her in and made her want to stay. Little Wolf lay stretched out on the rug in front of the fireplace, a roaring fire crackling and sparking, her black lace teddy stunning on her curvy, muscular body. She'd thought she was beautiful the first time she saw her. In the months since, her feelings had grown even deeper. She was so fun and so attractive, not to mention she had a voracious appetite for the life, both human and otherwise. That made her even sexier.

"Did you have a good run? You looked nice and sweaty when you came in earlier." She ran her tongue over her lower lip. "Are you stiff? Sore? Do you need a little massage?" Little Wolf held up her hands and wiggled her fingers.

Bellona stretched her arms over her head and rolled her shoulders. She actually felt wonderful. "Now that you mention it, yes, I am a bit sore," she lied.

Little Wolf came up to her knees and stretched out her arms. "Well, then, my beautiful wolf. Come here and let me rub all that tension away."

It wasn't necessary for her to ask twice. Bellona lowered herself on the rug next to Little Wolf and lay down on her stomach. The rug was warm and rough against her skin, the scent of the burning logs in the fireplace filling the air. Little Wolf leaned close and began to run her hands across her shoulders and down her arms. The feel of her warm hands against her cool flesh was amazing. The soft touch of her hands and the light scent of the lotion Little Wolf liked to rub all over her body did little to soothe her. On the contrary, every nerve ending in her body lit up with a fire that made her blood warm. When Little Wolf's hands smoothed over her butt, she twitched, and when her fingers smoothed between her cheeks, she nearly lost it.

Little Wolf kissed her between the shoulders and then trailed kisses across the back of her neck. She whispered in her ear as her fingers teased between her legs, "I missed you, my beautiful wolf. I missed running with you."

She couldn't stand it. She flipped over to her back and pulled Little Wolf to her. With her hands on either side of her face, she kissed her deeply, pushing her tongue between her lips. Her kiss was met with equal fire. Another thing about this woman that spoke to her soul was that she matched her stroke for stroke.

Undoubtedly the hunters were still out searching every place where bodies had been left. So be it. Let them search. She didn't care because tonight she was going to glory in the beauty of the woman whose hands made her feel alive and whose lips were sweet. This was what she longed to lose herself in, even if she could never feel and taste the one who stole her heart.

CHAPTER ELEVEN

By the time they finished with the other locations where bodies had been dropped, Lily was tired. More than that, she was exhausted. With the exception that the presence of another predator was absent, they picked up the same info at the other two spots. Kyle was able to see through the eyes of the two dead women and, as with the first victim, was able to determine that it was a woman who left their bodies on the forest floor. They were no closer to an identity because, as with the dead man, all he could see was her back as she walked away from the women's bodies. Not once did he glimpse the killer's face.

After Ava cleansed the last two drop sites as she'd done with the first one, they returned to Jayne's house. The moon was high in the sky and the countryside was quiet. The air was cool but no longer held the hint of moisture. It wouldn't be long before the trace of snow would melt. It struck her again how nice it was here and how much it was like the area where she grew up. There too snow would fall one moment, covering the ground like powdered sugar, and then the sun would come out and melt it all away. These days she rarely thought of her life before becoming a hunter. There was no point. Yet here she was for the second time in a single day remembering a time and a place long ago lost to her.

"What are you thinking? You look a thousand miles away." Jayne came outside and sat in the rocking chair next to hers. They were big wooden chairs and built to last. Comfortable, she'd been out here alone rocking back and forth while thinking over what they'd seen out there in the woods. Trying to make sense of it was driving her nuts.

She turned and looked at Jayne. In the muted glow cast by the ornate hanging light she decided that Jayne looked as tired as Lily felt. Shadows darkened her face, and dusty circles were beneath her eyes that hadn't been there when she'd first arrived. Jayne's bad attitude had been pretty consistent since the first moment they met and low-level irritating. Not that her attitude was a huge problem, considering she was accustomed to law enforcement resenting her and her hunters. What made this one different was this time with Jayne it felt much deeper than mere resentment at the intrusion of an outside organization. Instead, it had the feel of something more personally directed toward Lily, and that didn't really make sense. They'd never met before. They'd never even spoken to each other until she walked up those steps and stood before her on the wide porch. So why did she so obviously dislike her?

Lily pressed her lips together, thinking it all through, and then said with honesty and curiosity, "I can't help but wonder why here? It's so much easier to hide violence like this in a city."

Jayne nodded as she rocked slowly in the big chair, her booted feet stretched out in front of her. "I've been asking that same question since we discovered the first body. We've never had anything like this happen around these parts, and then to have it repeated two more times is astounding. Not in a good way either."

Lily did understand that. Certain werewolves had an almost pathological need to kill, but usually when they killed in multiples, they were grouped closer together. The way these were spread out was definitely atypical. "I'm certain you've been scratching your head about this one. I'll be honest with you, Jayne, it's puzzling for me too."

Jayne stopped rocking and stared at her. "I would think you'd be used to things like this, given what you do."

Nothing much rattled her, because at this point in her long life she thought she'd seen everything. This was just a step off, and it was hard to explain to someone who had lived only a fraction of her lifetime. She tried to explain, "It's that we don't typically encounter such rampant violence."

"I would have thought it was very typical of a *werewolf*."

The snap to that last word let Lily know Jayne still wasn't buying all the way in. That was all right. Give her time and she'd come around. They always did when faced with the impossible and had no earthly way to explain what was happening. "It isn't exactly what I'd expect to see with a werewolf passing through, and they're always passing through."

Jayne turned and looked at her, her eyes filled with curiosity. "So tell me, what do you usually find?"

The disbelief and defiance were fading from her words. Whether it was the weariness that surrounded her like a cloak, what she'd witnessed during their earlier expeditions, or Lily's quiet honesty, something was changing for Jayne. That too wasn't unusual, except normally she could pick out what made them converts. With Jayne, it wasn't so easy. She was a closed book that Lily dearly wanted to open.

Instead of trying to psychoanalyze the sheriff, she closed her eyes and thought about the hundreds, no thousands, of hunts she'd been on and tried to fashion an answer that would contain a common denominator. She opened her eyes and said, "Stealth." It was the best descriptor she could come up with. "The vast majority of the time the creatures we hunt are sneaky because they value self-preservation beyond anything else. They don't want us coming in and ruining their fun. They hate the Jägers and will do anything to avoid us."

"There's nothing stealthy about what's been happening here."

Lily shook her head. "No, there's not, and that's exactly my point. It's what makes this one of those rare cases I find quite strange. It's not often we have one killing so boldly and over such an extended length of time. The pattern isn't typical in any sense."

Jayne stretched her arms high over her body before resting her clasped hands on the top of her head. "You have no idea how much I want to believe it's a garden-variety serial killer."

"Who tears the bodies apart like an animal?" Devil's advocate was a role she'd been playing for centuries. Sometimes it was the only way to get people to open their minds to alternate possibilities.

Jayne ran her fingers through her hair and then put her head in her hands as her elbows rested on her knees. "A wolf pack maybe?"

"You have a lot of wolves around here?" She knew they didn't.

"No," she said slowly and sighed. "We do not."

"And have you seen the few wolves you do have tear bodies apart like that?"

Jayne sat back in the chair. "I get the point you're trying to make."

Maybe she did and maybe she didn't. "I just want you to understand why we're here."

For a moment there was silence, and then Jayne turned to stare at her with intense blue eyes. "Okay, Lily. Here's the thing. I get Kyle and I get Ava. What I don't get is you. If you are, as you say, a werewolf yourself, then why would you hunt your own kind? It seems somehow wrong."

If one only looked at the surface, it would be hard to understand. She didn't consider herself a werewolf, even as crazy as that sounded. She could change at will into a creature who could outrun the wind, yet she was never a predator. In her five centuries of existence, she had never hunted a single human. She was, quite simply, a victim in her own right, which went a long way toward explaining her life after the night that ended her previous existence.

"They are not my kind," she told her honestly and as simply as she could. "Let me ask you a question. Serial killers are human, and are you not one hundred percent human?"

Jayne looked as though her words were hitting their mark. "I think I follow where you're going here. I'm a human and yet I'm not a serial killer."

Lily nodded, glad that Jayne picked up so quickly. "Exactly. Technically, yes, I'm a werewolf. We are the same species, if you will, yet I believe we are fundamentally different just as you are different from a serial killer. I am a hunter, not a killer, and I will stop any and all who destroy life. It is who I am, and it is what I have dedicated my entire life to."

Jayne tilted her head as she continued to stare into Lily's eyes. "Why? You're what, thirty? Thirty-five tops? Why spend your young life wallowing in darkness even if you are a werewolf?"

Lily nearly laughed out loud. "Trust me, Jayne. My life was stolen more years ago than you can imagine, and it was far longer ago than a mere three and half decades. I made a promise on the night the Jägers came for me that I would spend every day that I had making sure what happened to me never happened to another soul."

❖

Kyle knocked on Ava's door, which was right next to his room. "I know it's really late and you've been on the go for a long time," he said when she invited him in. "If you're not too tired, would you want to take a walk with me? I can't seem to settle in." He knew it was imposing on her to even ask, but he couldn't stop himself. They were *married*, after all.

Ava, who'd been opening her suitcase and pulling out some jeans and shirts, stopped and turned. He immediately felt bad, for the toll of her very long day showed in the dusty shadows beneath her eyes. She laid the clothing she still held in her hands on the bed. "What's wrong?" Her face might show her fatigue, but her voice didn't.

It might not be very manly, but he was never very good at hiding how he was feeling. Yeah, he was that guy and there was no sense pretending otherwise. Ava would see right through him. "I don't know. The stuff I picked up out there got under my skin, and it's impossible to just sit still. Each time I try to close my eyes I can see them and feel their pain. I need to shake it off, and the only thing I could think of was that a walk might help me do that."

Her head tilted and she studied him. "A walk would be nice. Let me change, and I'll meet you downstairs in five minutes." She picked up a pair of jeans from the pile on the bed. "Out."

The relief that loosened his chest surprised him. Until this second he didn't realize how important it was to him that Ava go walk with him. Or maybe he really did. He'd been so excited to work with her again, and that feeling had intensified as the hours passed. What he felt for her went very deep, and he couldn't deny that truth. Given the short amount of time they'd actually spent together it wasn't reasonable, and that reality didn't seem to make a bit of difference to his heart.

Throw in the giant wash of emotion he picked up from the residue left by the murder victims, and he was a big, fat mess. It was tough enough to deal with the kind of things he did for the Jägers. To have to find a way to deal with the realization he was falling for a gorgeous witch was a little much to ask of him right now, yet here he was face-to-face with the woman who held his heart. The universe played by some pretty dirty rules.

He smiled and nodded. That she said yes took all the sting out of her kicking him out the door. "Meet you in five. Front door?"

Ava nodded and smiled. "Now, out."

Back in his room, he grabbed a jacket before he walked downstairs. As he reached the bottom of the staircase, Jayne and Lily came in the front door. Earlier he'd noticed them out on the front porch sitting in the big rockers and talking quietly. Outside, the temperature was dropping, and the cold was probably what drove them back into the warmth of the house. Being a California boy, it seemed really cold to him, and he wouldn't be surprised to see snow start falling any moment, though the weather was reported to take a turn for the better. Even though he was accustomed to warm breezes and lots of sunshine, he liked the snow and hoped the forecast was wrong. Given that they were tracking a werewolf, a nice layer of the white stuff could definitely come in handy. Follow the paw prints was an easy game to play.

"Going out for a smoke?" Jayne asked when he stopped by the big front window. A smoke was almost funny. He wouldn't touch the nasty things, and besides, he didn't think he looked—or smelled—like a smoker. Off the top of his head he couldn't even think of anyone he knew who did smoke these days. Wasn't the politically correct thing to do even if it wasn't a deadly habit.

He opened his mouth to say no and then realized she was kidding him. "Walking out the kinks," he told her. "Too much time in the car today and too much despair picked up from the victims. I need to get out and shake it off, or I won't sleep at all."

"Alone?" Did he hear a note of humor in Lily's seemingly innocent question?

He shrugged and pretended he didn't hear the bit of ribbing in her question. "No. Ava's going to walk with me. We both spent most of the day in transit with our butts in seats."

"Well," Lily drawled. "That's very nice of Ava to go out with you."

He wasn't sure how to take that. Word around the Jägers was that Lily was one dead-serious hunter. Not once had he heard anyone mention she might have a sense of humor. So, was she teasing him? That sure didn't seem to fit with the picture he had in his mind after hearing what others said about Lily. Then again, he had to consider that he was basing his assumptions on gossip. Even the best of the Jägers could fall victim to the whispers and conjectures about a legend. If he was a smart guy, he'd toss out everything he'd heard about Lily and make up his mind based on his own personal interactions. That decided, he figured he'd go with the belief she was teasing.

"Yes." He grinned at her as he leaned against the front door. "It is very nice of Ava."

"What's nice of me?" Ava came down the stairs wearing black jeans that fit very nicely and a puffy zip-up jacket. She looked beautiful.

Jayne joined in. "Keeping Kyle company. We don't want him to get lost or scared."

Yup, definitely teasing. It was a good sign. He swept his gaze over the three women. "How exactly did we get into pick-on-Kyle mode?" It was pretty clear at least two of the women in this room were having fun at his expense.

"Pick on you? Not at all. Just making casual conversation." Lily smiled, and it struck him how lovely she was. He'd wager she'd broken more than a few hearts in her time.

He cut his gaze to Jayne. "Don't believe her. She probably got a memo that said to mess with the new guy."

Jayne patted him on the shoulder. "Makes sense to me. Seen a memo or two like that in my time."

"Always happy to entertain where I can." He bowed to Jayne.

"You're a good man."

Ava held out her hand as she reached him at the door. "Come on." She gave him a wink the other two couldn't see. "I'll make sure you're safe, and I promise not to give you a hard time."

See, he thought. Ava's here for me. It was a sign that she was sticking up for him. Proved his long-held belief that the universe had a way of working things out and it was bringing them together. Besides, he knew she would never pick on him. Wasn't her way and there was that connection thing they had going. It wasn't hopeful imagination. It was real. Yeah, real.

"Be careful," Lily warned them as they reached the door. "We don't know where the wolf might be, so keep your eyes open."

"Always," he told her and held the door for Ava.

Outside, the cold air was biting. It hit him in the cheeks and almost made his eyes tear up. Yeah, it was exactly what he needed. He zipped his jacket and pulled a cap out of his pocket. His long hair smashed against his skull as he slipped the hat on his head. That was better. The wind was now refreshing more than frigid.

"You didn't bring a hat." It was the first thing that popped into his head. A brilliant conversationalist, that's what he was for sure.

She reached around her neck and pulled up the hood on her jacket. "This will work. Thanks for caring."

"I'm a caring guy."

"You are a funny, interesting, and talented guy."

"You're going to make me blush."

Ava took his hand and squeezed lightly. "How am I to know when this wind is going to make us both red as Christmas bulbs? So tell me what the problem is. Why can't you sleep?"

The surprise of her hand wrapped in his almost made him go mute. God, it felt great. Better than when Suz Belton kissed him in the sixth grade. Funny, he'd had the same reaction back then as he was having now. After a second, he found his voice and didn't consider being anything except honest.

"You understand that I don't have to actually raise those people from the grave to know what they went through."

She nodded. "I've seen you do it before."

"Tonight wasn't the same as in the past."

"Why was it different this time?"

He'd been asking himself the same question all night and still wasn't sure he figured it out. He gave her his best guess. "It was far more intense than I've ever experienced before. Energy and despair were soaked into the ground and the trees and the brush out there so heavy, it was like it had just happened. All three of the victims were terrified by what was done to them, and that strength of emotion came through like a hurricane."

She stopped, brought his hand up, and pressed it against her chest. "It hurt your heart."

It wasn't the way he thought of it at the time, but once she said it he realized that's exactly how it felt. "Yeah, it hurt my heart. I hated that they suffered so badly and were scared so much. It wasn't right. No one should have to go through what they did."

"That's why we're here." Ava patted his hand, her eyes steady on his face. "We're going to stop this monster and make sure no one else is harmed. Whoever this is has put out too much evil into the universe, and it will bring it back to them threefold. Trust me, Kyle. We will stop them."

He brought his hand away from her chest but kept hold of her hand. Once more he began to walk. With Ava beside him and combined with the fresh, cold air he already felt calmer and more focused, and they hadn't even walked a hundred yards yet. The air was crisp and clear, and their feet crunched as they walked across the snow-dusted gravel. No sounds of danger reached his ears, only the gentle murmur of the night. "You're right because we have to stop him."

"You think it's a him?"

The pronoun had slipped from his lips without conscious thought, and it was strange considering it was a woman he'd seen walking away from the victims. What was throwing him and what brought the "he" across his lips was the level of violence visited upon the victims. The intensity was so extreme it felt like the power of a male. It was a sexist fallback and he knew it. To stick with the conviction that it was a man who did these things would be easy, yet he couldn't quite make that commitment. He knew very well that women could be as brutal as men.

"I don't know," he finally admitted. "It feels that way and yet it doesn't. Something is really off about this whole thing. I think that's part of what's getting to me as well."

Ava leaned closer and took his arm, holding it against her body. "I sensed the same thing as I cleansed each piece of ground. They all had a very different feel to them, which is a little strange when you consider that the condition of each body was essentially the same. I'm pretty sure Lily felt the disturbance too. Did you see the look on her face when we were at the first site? It was as if something or someone had just slapped her. She was definitely feeling something there. We haven't even been here half a day, and already this is turning out to be a strange and puzzling hunt."

He had noticed the change in Lily out at the first stop. A person would have needed to be blind not to. Though his skills tended toward the dead, it also gave him a heightened sense of the living. While he couldn't get into their heads like he could with the dead, he still sensed turbulent emotions. The tension that brought Lily's body rigid made him think of one of Nana's favorite sayings: "Someone just walked across my grave." If Lily had been in wolf form, all the hair on the nape of her neck would have been standing up. So far Lily hadn't shared with either him or Ava whatever it was that put her on full alert. He really wanted to know and yet wasn't going to be the one to push. Better sense kept him silent and watchful. She would let them know when it was time.

"Do you think she'll tell us what was bothering her out there?" While he might not broach the subject with Lily, he didn't have the same reluctance when it came to Ava.

She nodded, her cheek resting against his shoulder as they walked. "In her own time, yes, I believe she will. You'll learn to trust her, Kyle. She really is the best and has a way of working through every hunt that manages to stop the violence while keeping her team and the innocent people she came to protect as safe as possible. I've seen her do the most amazing things."

Her words were heartfelt and at the same time tinged with some emotion he couldn't quite catch. "I hear a but in there."

Again she nodded. "Sort of. You know, she's little and mighty all at the same time. I've seen her take down monsters three times her size without breaking a sweat."

"And?"

"And, once you get past the power and the skill there's something lost about her. Solitary. She's hands down the best hunter in the order, yet my sense is she's a lonely soul. I don't know if she's ever had the chance to love someone or if she's always walked the warrior's path by herself. I hope not. It would make me sad to think she's always been alone. No one should spend their life without someone else to share the journey with them, especially if that someone is essentially immortal."

"That's a shame." He knew the kind of joy found in love. He felt it right this instant.

"It's about to change." She squeezed his arm, and he felt the warm press of her cheek against his shoulder. The light scent of her hair made him breathe in deeply.

That seemed like an odd observation, considering they'd only been here a couple of hours and pretty much the whole time had been out looking at murder sites. He stopped and turned to gaze down at her. "What do you mean it's about to change?"

She smiled as she tipped her head back so that she stared up at the velvet night sky strewn with sparkling stars. Softly she told him, "She's about to fall in love."

Chapter Twelve

Jayne's cell phone rang and startled her so badly she spilled coffee all over her hands and the table. Fortunately, she'd been sitting here holding the coffee cup long enough for it to have cooled, and instead of her hands getting burned, they were simply wet. Her thoughts had been miles away, and for good reason. Last night's excursion continued to weigh heavy on her mind.

She grabbed the still-ringing cell as it jittered on the tabletop and put it to her ear. "Quarles."

"Sheriff?" The female voice was high and trembling. Immediately she recognized it as the voice of Tess Heights. Tess worked at the popular espresso stand at the edge of town before school and on weekends. Everyone knew the outgoing teen, who took her barista duties very seriously. She could picture the young woman with her long hair that seemed to change color week by week. The last time when she'd stopped by for a coffee, it had been almost purple. She was medium height and, while not thin, wasn't heavy either. More compact is the way she'd describe her, and one heck of a pitcher on the high school's softball team.

"What's up, Tess?" She kept her question soft because she had the sense Tess was close to a meltdown.

"It's Nate." Her voice squeaked, and Jayne could hear how very close to tears she was.

"What about Nate?" A bad feeling about this call was starting to whisper down her spine. Tess could be dramatic, as could any teenage girl. That said, she wasn't one to call Jayne unless she had a good reason. While there were definitely teenage girls in town who needed an eye kept on them, Tess wasn't in that group. She was, fortunately, one Jayne didn't have to worry about.

"He's missing."

"What do you mean he's missing?" That didn't make any sense. The last she heard, Nate was away at college in Bellingham. She waited a second for Tess to continue and, when she didn't, gave her a nudge. "Tess, what do you mean Nate is missing?" One thing about conversations with teenagers, most of the time it was like pulling molars to get the story out of them.

"He came home on Friday for a long weekend." She choked back a sob. "He had dinner with me last night."

"And…" This could be a long conversation.

"And then he said he was going out for a little while. I went up to my room to do homework and fell asleep. I didn't hear him come in, but I figured it was because he was trying to be quiet so he didn't wake me up."

"He's not there?"

"No," she cried. "He never came back home."

"Maybe he left again?"

"No, no, no. You don't understand, Sheriff. His bed is still made. Nate is pretty lazy about his bed, and there's no way he would sleep all night and then get up and make the bed. He always waited for Mom to do it."

Tess made a good point and probably a very accurate one. Jayne glanced up at the clock and was surprised. Six o'clock. Geez, had she really been up for two hours already? Didn't matter how long she'd been sitting here. It was more important to calm Tess down. Nate was nineteen and a really good-looking kid. The fact he was out all night didn't shock or surprise Jayne very much. What college guy didn't stay out all night now and again? It might be a little against character to do it when he was here to stay with his sister, but given the right set of circumstances—the right persuasion from the right young lady—and he might very well have shirked that responsibility.

"He probably spent the night with a friend." Of the female variety was what she didn't add. Tess was upset enough already. No need to make her feel worse by the idea that her brother would blow her off for a better offer.

This time she could hear the tears in Tess's voice. "Sheriff, he wouldn't do that. Mom and Dad are out of town, and Nate never leaves me home all alone. Never, and he wouldn't now especially, you know?"

She did know. Not only would Tess's parents not leave a beautiful young woman at the house alone, but they wouldn't leave her alone right now. Nobody in the community would feel safe enough at the moment to do that. Nate would most definitely have come home last night, beautiful, willing girl aside. Once more a bad feeling washed over her. First thing, first, she needed to keep Tess safe. "Okay, Tess, where are you?"

"I'm at home." She sniffled.

"Alone?"

"Uh-huh."

"I'm going to call the station and have Deputy Landen come pick you up. Do you understand?" A noise made her turn. Lily had just walked into the kitchen wearing blue jeans and a cream cable-knit sweater. With her long dark hair, she looked incredible. Lily pointed to the coffee carafe, and Jayne pointed at the cupboard above it. Lily smiled, opened the cupboard door, and pulled out a mug.

"Yeah." Tess hiccupped, bringing Jayne's attention away from her beautiful houseguest and back to the terrified girl.

"All right. I want you to go with Deputy Landen, and then I'll meet you at the station in a little bit. Right now I want you to stay on the phone with my friend Lily while I call for Deputy Landen. Do me a favor and stay on the phone with Lily until the deputy arrives. Can you do that for me?" She kept her own voice calm and soothing.

"Okay. Yeah, I can do that."

"Good. Now here's my friend."

She handed the phone off to Lily, who'd been listening as she'd sipped coffee and picked up immediately on what Jayne needed her to do. God, it was great to have people around who got it. Then, she grabbed up the handset of the landline she'd never been able to part with, despite using her cell almost exclusively, and called Dana Landen as Lily continued to talk softly to Tess. She appreciated the sweet and gentle way she spoke to the frightened teenager. Not everyone could do that. This woman had more skills than she was letting on. Another thing she liked about her.

Damn it. Her hold on the righteous indignation that she'd embraced since the moment the council told her they were bringing in the Jägers was slipping away. Instead of her dislike of the interlopers growing the longer they were here, it was doing quite the opposite. This tiny, pretty woman who didn't look big enough to take on a kitten had her admiration growing every time she turned around.

She was just putting the handset back on the charger when she heard Lily say, "No, Tess don't go. Stay on the phone with me. Tess? Tess?"

Jayne whirled around to see Lily staring the phone. Her face was a mask of concern. "She hung up?"

Please don't let that be true. "She hung up?" she asked again.

Lily frowned and nodded. "She was talking with me and then said someone was there. She ended the call before I could stop her."

There was no way Dana could be there that fast. Or could she? She had been out on patrol when Jayne called, and she hadn't pinned her down on exactly how long it would take her to get to Tess. It had to be Dana...she hoped.

Jayne took back her cell from Lily and hit the button to recall the number from the last received call. It rang five times before going to voice mail. Shit. This did not bode well.

"Come on," she told Lily as she grabbed her keys and headed toward the garage door. Fortunately, even though it was early, she was fully dressed, including her gun belt. She didn't want to waste a second.

Lily didn't hesitate either. She grabbed her bag from where she'd dropped it last night and followed Jayne outside. The expression on her face was as grim as Jayne felt.

They were in her car and driving far in excess of the speed limit toward the big house where Tess and Nate lived with their parents. She didn't want to waste any time getting there, particularly after the dropped call. It made her nervous not being able to reach Tess and talk with her. She'd give anything right now to hear her voice.

"We've got to—" The ring of her cell cut off her words. "Quarles," she barked. It was Dana and relief flooded through her. Everything would be fine now that Dana was there with Tess. She lifted her foot off the gas pedal just a touch as she wrenched the steering wheel to the right. The car screeched on the gravel as it turned into the driveway. At the end of the long drive, she could see Dana's cruiser parked next to two others. Good. Her people were here in force.

"Sheriff." Her voice sounded strange, which wasn't a good sign.

Her relief was short-lived. "We have a problem." Even worse. She pulled the car next to Dana's and hit the brakes.

"Tell me." She was opening the car door as she talked, still intent on getting inside as quickly as possible.

"Tess is dead."

❖

Little Wolf was at it again. Bellona sighed as she listened to her explain what she'd done and why she'd done it. When Bellona put down her phone she simply stood there and shook her head. Not much damage control she could do for this one. Not with the sheriff now right smack in the middle of the mix. She closed her eyes and let out a long breath.

On the other hand, Little Wolf's rationale made a certain amount of sense, given the unique set of circumstances she'd been faced with. Her actions were, in their own right, a sort of damage control. She personally preferred a bit more self-control, but she'd learned over the years that things often didn't go as desired or as planned. This was one of those instances. It was going to have to play out as the universe willed.

One of the things she loved about Little Wolf was her daring and her way of thinking on her feet, whether she was standing on two or four of them. It was an asset that would serve her well over the years. If she was careful, like Bellona had always been, she could plan to use that brain for a very long time.

Despite this morning's minor setback, she still had high hopes for Little Wolf and this place. Other than the sheriff, who from everything Little Wolf had told her, was working in an environment way beneath her league, that is. Jayne Quarles, according to Little Wolf, had no business here in Stevens County. While it was her hometown, she'd been the one everyone in town knew was bigger than this place. She'd gone on to prove them all right when she rose within federal law enforcement in record time. With the exception of her brother's untimely demise, her reasons for leaving the federal life behind and returning to her hometown were not common knowledge.

Given what had happened today, Bellona really wished Quarles was back in the big city. Not that the rest of the county's law enforcement wasn't skilled or capable. It wasn't like the old days when small-town cops were hick cops. Even the smallest counties had training and resources not even considered years ago. No, it was just that Bellona suspected Quarles had more experience with violent crime and psychology expertise with respect to the mind of killers than most local officials. That sort of specialized know-how would push her to dig deeper and tap resources the others might not have developed. What it really did was make her dangerous.

If she could get rid of Quarles it would make her life much easier. From past experience, she was aware that this incident with Little Wolf wasn't likely to be the last. It was the way of the young, and she didn't blame them. Raising a new pack was a bit like raising a family. They had to grow up and mature. The decisions they made early on weren't always the best. It was to be expected.

She didn't mind the work or the energy it took to guide them. In fact, she relished it. The years had flowed by in her solitary pursuit of life, and it made her feel alive and refreshed to once more share her world with a pack of young, enthusiastic wolves. The little errors in judgment along the way were minor and something she was happy to deal with. In time, they would learn just as she had.

This blip, however, was one she had to stay far away from. The others she easily handled for Little Wolf alone and under the cover of woods and moonlight. Her confidence in her beloved was well placed as far as she was concerned. If she'd determined now the deed had to be done, then it had to be done. Better safe.

Let the sheriff do her best. Bellona would be watching from the shadows to make certain her best wasn't good enough. She'd had plenty of experience thwarting law enforcement all over the world, and ultimately, if the sheriff caused too much trouble, well, she had a solution for that as well. Avoiding that particular course of action would be her preference, and she would continue along her current path, keeping that intention in mind. Making run-of-the-mill townspeople disappear was one thing, but knocking off a sheriff. Well, that was a bit trickier.

The other slight concern was the Jägers. Today's unfortunate incident was sure to whet their appetite for a fight. They could call themselves hunters or protectors or whatever in the hell they wanted. She knew the truth about them and had known it since a very early age. They were predators no different than those they hunted. They cloaked themselves in righteousness, telling the world they came to protect the innocent. It was a lie and she would call their bluff, for she had seen them destroy the innocent too many times to buy into their sales pitch.

Not all the preternatural creatures that inhabited the world were monsters. In fact, in her opinion, few belonged in that category. Just as humans had their monsters, so too did the preternatural community. It didn't mean they were all horrible beings. Actually, she took exception to that characterization. It was true she had killed, and early in her life she had killed for sport. Each instance was the result of her youth and inexperience. It didn't make her bad then or now. She'd grown and learned only to kill when it was necessary. She would teach Little Wolf and the pack they were creating the same standards of behavior. They were not bad people, not evil werewolves. They would only do what they needed to do in order to survive.

Yet the Jägers would come after all of them if she didn't stop them first. She hoped to avoid any unnecessary violence. All she had to do was a bit of redirection for both the nosy sheriff and the interfering Jägers. Do that and they would be on their way and this little berg would be hers. She wasn't asking for much. Not after what she'd been through century after century. The universe owed her a reward and it was time to collect. Here and now.

Bellona smiled, her mind made up. They would work through this and come out on the other side victorious. Neither the sheriff nor the hunters of the Jägers were going to spoil the beauty and soul-enriching happiness she found in the small northern town. She was here to stay, one way or the other.

In the kitchen, she boiled water for tea and breathed in the lovely scent of the rich, black blend. It reminded her of the tea the servants used to bring her in the pretty little teacups—another sign that this was meant to be. She held the mug in one hand as she opened the refrigerator door and frowned. Little of substance suitable for the pack, especially their newest recruit, graced the glass shelves. Adam was bound to be starving by this time, and a bag of mixed greens and a large carton of yogurt were not going to satisfy his hunger. As much as she hated to leave her sanctuary, she needed to venture into town and to the big grocery store on the main drag. The boy had to be fed.

As if sensing she'd been thinking about him, Little Wolf's pet walked into the kitchen, his eyes sleepy and his hair standing up pleasingly on his head. He was wearing a pair of jeans that were old and soft, and they hung low on his hips. He had the body of an athlete, with broad shoulders and an impressive six-pack. Apparently, Little Wolf had left his temporary prison unlocked, not that he looked dangerous right now. Hungry, yes. Dangerous? Not so much.

The more she was around him, the more she understood why Little Wolf had been so drawn to him. What was it they liked to say in the entertainment industry? He possessed the *it factor*. Something indefinable that had the ability to draw others in like flies to honey. Yes, their newest wolf definitely had *it*. He would be an impressive addition to the pack, though the women in his college were sure to be saddened when he didn't return.

He ran his hands through his hair, which didn't make it stand up any less, and leaned against the open doorway. His voice was deep with just a hint of a growl. "Got anything to eat?"

CHAPTER THIRTEEN

The gravel drive was well-maintained and lined with aspen and lodgepole pine trees. Three cars were already parked there by the time Lily and Jayne arrived. One had to belong to Deputy Sheriff Landen, who was currently on the phone with Jayne, and another belonged to a second deputy sheriff who happened to live about a quarter mile up the country road. The families were good friends, explained a grim-faced Jayne as they walked up the large covered deck that spanned the entire back of the updated home. She also filled Lily in quickly on Deputy Landen's call, and Lily's spirits sank more with each grim word.

The lingering scent of both wolf and blood reached her the moment she opened the car door, and it hit Lily like a slap to the face that reminded her she'd been here less than twenty-four hours and was already a failure. The closer she got to the door of the house, the stronger the smell became. It provided her with a lot of information, like the fact that the wolf had been here, but only a trace of it remained strong enough for her to catch it.

Unlike last night, this time there was nothing about the wolf's scent that whispered familiar to Lily. It was a stranger's mark on this place, and that's exactly what she would expect to encounter. That fact that last night didn't feel that way still bothered her. Though she'd been searching her memory for hours to try to recall a werewolf she'd hunted and failed to stop, thus far she'd come up with nothing useful. So why, she continued to wonder, did she still feel as though the werewolf they hunted was known to her? She didn't like not knowing who.

Only now there was even more of a complication than her not being able to place the familiar scent. This one was definitely not known to her, and that bothered her a great deal too because it suggested this hunt wasn't about a loner. It told her they were up against at least two. A mated pair perhaps? Or was it possible they were about to find themselves up against a pack? It had been at least a hundred years since she'd run across one. The Jägers had become so successful at stopping werewolves, the naturally social creatures had taken to living solitary lives in order to avoid the Jägers and ultimate destruction. The thought of what they could be facing gave her chills. Senn would need to be notified as soon as she was allowed to assess the situation. This was ground the order hadn't encountered in at least a century.

As she started to enter through the back door right behind Jayne, a tall, white-faced deputy stepped up to block her entrance. "You need to stay out here." His dark eyes looked haunted. She felt for him, knowing what he'd seen here this morning would never completely leave him.

Empathy for what he was going through didn't extend to his interference. It would be easy enough to smack him right out of the way, except that wasn't how she did things. "I'm with the sheriff," she said calmly.

"You're not one of us," he returned, his voice tight. She had the sense he was holding on by a thread. This wasn't the kind of thing a deputy in this county expected to discover, and there was really no way to prepare for it.

Jayne, who'd gotten almost through the kitchen by this time, backed up and held the door open for her. "It's okay, Eddie. She's with me. Let her through."

Eddie still didn't move. "I don't think it's a good idea, Sheriff. She's not one of us."

Jayne's voice grew soft. She put a hand on his shoulder. It was clear to Lily she'd had experience with tense situations like this before. "Let her through, Eddie."

For a second he hesitated and then stepped aside without another word. He didn't glance back inside but kept his gaze focused on the fields outside. Lily went past him and through the door. The stench was so strong to her heightened senses it was almost like being physically hit with a bat. She had to take a few deeps breaths through her mouth to not be overwhelmed.

"Eddie," Jayne added. "I've got this. You can head back."

His eyes glittered. "Copy that." The order didn't have to be issued twice.

The sight that greeted them in the living room hurt Lily's heart. Guilt flooded her as she looked at what was left of the poor girl. There was no helping Tess, for she stared up at the ceiling with sightless eyes. If only she and her team had come to this place sooner, maybe they could have prevented this.

Or maybe not. The scent of the wolf that stole her life was still strong enough to let her know he or she hadn't been gone long. Probably minutes before the deputy arrived. The wolf hadn't lingered here or the scent would be stronger. That made her uneasy. Why attack the girl in this way? It wasn't a hunt for sport. It wasn't a hunt for food. This girl had been quite simply murdered, albeit by a werewolf, but murdered just the same. That left only one question in Lily's mind—why?

Jayne had stopped next to the body and squatted as she studied the unfortunate teenager. Lily could feel a muscle jumping in her jaw. Slowly she pushed back up to her feet and drew her gaze away from the body. She turned and met Lily's eyes. "A werewolf?" she asked so quietly only Lily could hear.

Lily nodded. "Most definitely."

"Why?"

She'd been asking herself the same question since the second she walked into this room. There was only one answer that came to mind, and it chilled her. "Because she knew them."

Kyle had managed to get a few hours of sleep, not that he felt overly refreshed. His walk with Ava had been great, and by rights he should have been able to rest once they returned to the house. It hadn't happened quite that way. He'd stretched out on the really nice bed and proceeded to watch the shadows dance across the ceiling for hours. He simply could not turn his mind off. Or maybe it was his spirit. Ava being here was only one piece of it. Something about this hunt had him humming in a way he'd never experienced before.

If he had decades of hunting under his belt like Lily, maybe it would make more sense to him. Or maybe it wasn't inexperience as much as it was this hunt. It felt different and not different in a good way. This werewolf wasn't a garden-variety preternatural creature; he could feel that truth all the way to the marrow. It made him question whether he was the right guy to be here. Others in the Jägers had far more experience than he and might be better choices for tracking this creature.

Except given that he was the only one, as far as anyone knew, who could do what he could do, he might be exactly the right guy for this job. He just hoped he didn't let Lily and Ava down. This quest was important in many ways, at least to him. He felt an overpowering need to prove himself to both Lily and Ava. Even more important was the need to bring this hunt to a conclusion soon. The three dead already left him feeling uneasy, as if the danger was growing, and if they didn't get a handle on the wolf soon, many more were bound to die.

As if his thoughts were a self-fulfilling prophesy, his cell phone rang. The display said it was Lily. When he'd come into the kitchen, two cold mugs had greeted him, and he had the impression they'd been left behind in haste. That didn't bode well in his book, and the ringing cell phone appeared to confirm his feeling.

"Lily?"

"We need you now," she said without preamble.

Sometimes he hated it when he was right. "Tell me where." He found a piece of paper and a pen on the end of the kitchen counter and jotted down the directions as Jayne, who Lily had handed the phone over to, rattled them off. "Got it," he told her. "I'll get Ava, and we'll be there as quickly as possible. Another death?" Stupid question, really. If someone wasn't dead, he wasn't the first guy they asked for.

"Unfortunately, yes."

"Damn."

"It's bad."

For the first time since they'd gotten here he heard something in Jayne's voice beyond irritation. She'd been pissed when they got here last night, and it didn't take a very big brain to figure that one out. It appeared something had changed while they slept because she didn't sound irritated now. She sounded scared, and that unsettled him. The simple fact she was asking for the necromancer scared him even more.

"We're on our way." His eyes met Ava's as she walked into the kitchen. She looked lovely in jeans and a Yale hoodie. He put his phone back in his pocket. "We gotta go."

"Don't tell me." Shadows crossed her face, and he was pretty certain she was picking up on his vibes. "Another death."

Ava wasn't asking him a question so he didn't bother with an answer. "You ever see anything like this before?" This place had a weird feel to it, and it was the first time he'd ever felt as though he was walking into the middle of an ongoing war. "It feels like we've entered a battle zone to me."

She surprised him when she walked over and put her arms around him. She smelled faintly of cinnamon, and he wondered if it was her shampoo or lotion. He really didn't care because he could breathe it in all day and let the warmth of it wrap around him. "No," she said softly as she rested her cheek against his chest. "This is new to me as well, and it doesn't feel good at all. People, too many people, are going to die. We have to stop her."

For a second he continued to hold her, and then her words sank in. He held her out at arm's length and studied her face. Her eyes were deep and mysterious. "Her?"

CHAPTER FOURTEEN

Jayne had to breathe through her mouth or she was afraid she'd lose it. Not that this was the first violent crime scene she'd ever been present at. Quite the opposite, actually. She'd been present at plenty of them. No, it was more about the totality of the circumstances. This shit had to stop. It was bad enough with the other three victims, but at least they were adults. When this monster started preying on kids in her town, it took her resolve to stop it to another level.

Tess was on her back, her eyes open and staring at the ceiling. Her long hair was a tangled mess and matted with fresh blood. The T-shirt she wore was likewise splattered with crimson as if she'd squeezed a tomato until it burst. Everything about the way she looked was wrong. The fact that her young life was cut so tragically short was wrong.

Jayne couldn't help but feel like she didn't do enough to help Tess. If she'd only gotten someone here a few minutes earlier she'd still be alive. Lily seemed to sense where her mind was going. As she put a hand on Jayne's arm, she said, "You couldn't have stopped this."

She didn't agree. She really believed there was more she could have done. "I should have gotten a deputy here a little quicker."

Lily shook her head. "I don't believe that would have made a difference."

"Of course it would have." Lily was missing the point. The only reason Tess was dead was because she was alone.

"I disagree. If the deputy had made it quicker, Tess and the deputy would both be dead."

Jayne's head snapped around and she stared at Lily. No, that couldn't be possible. Her deputies were armed and well-trained. They could, and would, have stopped this. She was shaking her head, but before she could say a word, Lily touched her shoulder.

"Jayne," she said quietly. "This is really unusual."

"How?" A trickle of fear whispered up her spine. As much as she'd wanted to discount Lily and her crew, with each passing minute, she was believing in them more and more. She was beginning to think perhaps they could help. Now Lily was telling her their killer was different. Just fucking great.

"This kill is all wrong."

"Every kill is wrong."

"True, but I'm just saying that this is different in more ways than one. We need to be very careful."

No shit. "That's a given."

"Of course, but with this set of circumstances…"

Lily needed to get to the point. She didn't have time to decipher her code. "What circumstances?"

"The nature of the murder."

"And that is?"

"That this was personal."

❖

Bellona was smiling as she rolled the shopping cart out to the parking lot, stopping next to her car. Undoubtedly she'd caused a stir in the grocery store. The nature of small towns was to buzz when a stranger showed up. Today it was a beautiful stranger who cruised through the store filling her cart with raw beef, liver, chicken, and pork. She'd definitely caught the attention of any self-respecting busybody within her line of sight.

She briefly wondered how many texts went flying about as she'd loaded the bags into the sleek black SUV she'd treated herself with when she left Denver. All of them would fit easily into the back. It was one of the things she admired about the vehicle. Plenty of room for whatever she happened to be doing at the time. Today it was groceries. Other days it was a different kind of cargo.

Though she'd love to know what was going on at that house, driving by wasn't an option. With the Jägers in town it was wise to keep a low profile. At least until she could spring her trap. It wouldn't take long to set up the ruse sure to lead them away from here. The pieces were almost ready. Another day, two at the most, and the game would be afoot. Not much of a game really. A little sleight of hand here, a little misdirection there, and the mighty hunters of the Jägers would be off and running in the opposite direction.

"Family dinner?"

Bellona turned and smiled at the pretty brunette who was staring at the cart full of sacks, meat bags prominent in all of them. "Friends and family," she told her, returning the smile. The woman was alluring with her short dark hair and fascinating green eyes. This tiny town was full of fun surprises.

Twirling a strand of hair around one finger she said, "I don't think I've seen you before."

Typical small-town directness. She liked it because it was something once more that reminded her of the home she'd been forced to leave behind. "That would be true as this is my first time here."

"You're staying with family?"

Bellona nodded and thought of Little Wolf and Adam. "Yes."

"Where?"

My, but she was a curious one. She should be annoyed and tell the nosy girl her to mind her own business. Instead, she found herself answering—oddly but answering nonetheless. "Well, I'm on my way to my cousin's house now, and I'm not quite sure how to get there. Can you by any chance"—she rummaged into her bag for the piece of paper she'd written Little Wolf's address on when they'd met—"help me find this address?"

Bait cast. "Oh, I can do better than that," she said as she gazed at the handwritten address. "I can take you right there." Fish on hook. She began to help Bellona load the sacks.

"Oh, that would be fantastic." Bellona put the last grocery bag into the back. "If you're not in a hurry, we could ride together. We can grab a coffee afterward. I'm Bellona." She held her hand out.

"Grace." She took Bellona's hand in hers.

CHAPTER FIFTEEN

Lily had the urge to just cry. This was awful. Death was a big part of the world she functioned in, and she accepted that as part of her reality. After all these years she normally rolled with whatever crossed her path.

Usually anyway. Sometimes, like right now, it made her want to scream. This beautiful young woman had lost her life for no damn reason. She knew something, which she probably didn't even realize she knew, and because of that she was dead. The only hope they had for getting closer to the killer's identity was to see if Kyle could come up with anything. She hoped he could.

Kyle was an interesting young man and so obviously in love with Ava. It almost made her smile, which wasn't unwelcome in this moment of deep despair. She didn't smile because it felt so very wrong. Instead she thought of the lovelorn Kyle. Senn spoke with both fondness and praise for the tall, slender man who possessed a talent that defied understanding in the rational world. She'd been around a number of necromancers in her time, but never one who could reach through death without being in the presence of the physical body. What he'd done yesterday was beyond impressive. Senn was not wrong about him. His future was both bright and important.

When Kyle came through the back door with Ava on his heels, she experienced a slight surge of excitement. While they couldn't save this young woman, maybe she could help save the lives of others. If, that is, Kyle was able to cross over into the world she now existed in. She'd seen him do it last night, and she was feeling confident he could repeat that feat today.

"Oh God," Kyle said when he stopped at the edge of the room and stared down to where Tess was sprawled in a pool of still-wet blood. "What kind of creep would do something like this?" Ava was right behind him, tears pooling in her eyes and a hand over her nose and mouth.

Lily put a hand on his arm and looked up into his face. "I'm hoping you can reach out to Tess and find out who did this to her." The faint metallic scent so unique to blood filled her senses. It was time to do what they could and get out of here. It was too close to a full moon and too long since she'd had her injection for her to be around this kind of carnage. Even she had limits.

He nodded and took a deep breath. "I'll do my best."

Jayne cleared everyone from the room, and they all marched outside grumbling as she closed and locked the doors. Not only did they not understand who the strangers were that Jayne had allowed in, but they resented not being able to monitor said strangers in the marked-off crime scene. Jayne didn't leave room for argument.

Lily looked down at Tess and then back up at Kyle. "Okay, Necromancer, the floor is yours."

As he did last night, Kyle dipped his hand in his leather bag and pulled out a small bundle of sage. Lily glanced over at Jayne, wondering if she would protest if he lit the bundle inside the house. She didn't, and soon he was circling the body with the smoking bundle. Unlike last night, he didn't sink to the ground. Instead, once the sage was out, he stood close to Tess, his hands held palm up, his head tipped back, and his eyes closed.

For a moment nothing happened; he simply stood there as still as a statue. When she thought nothing was going to happen, his body stiffened and a moan rose from deep in his throat. He swayed slightly on his feet though he remained standing. His lips moved, and Lily thought words might be passing his lips. If they were, they were too low for her to make out.

Tension in the room rose as he continued to mumble and moan. She wanted to know what he was seeing, to find out what he knew. It took effort not to reach out and grab his arm in the hopes she could see or hear whatever he was. She managed to keep her hands to herself. When someone knocked loudly on the door, all of them jumped.

"God damn it," Jayne spat out as she whirled and headed toward the door.

Kyle crumpled as if someone had just taken a shot at him. Ava rushed to catch him before he fell into the blood-soaked rug. Lily stepped forward as well, and between the two of them, they managed to help him into the large kitchen, where he sank into a chair at the table. Without saying a word, he lowered his head to his folded arms.

"Are you all right?" Lily thought he was unusually pale and had a slight tremor in his body.

"Yeah," he said, his head still down. "Just give me a sec to get my bearings. That was pretty intense."

Lily wanted to press him, to tell him they needed what he had right now. She didn't. As much as she wished to, she knew when to press and when not to, even if she didn't know him very well. Years of experience armed her with a finely tuned intuition, and it had served her well over time. She listened to it now.

Finally, Kyle raised his head, and Lily was surprised to see tears in his eyes. His voice shook as he told them, "I felt it all, the pain, the fear, the surprise."

Once more Lily put a hand on his arm as she squatted down in front of him. "I'm sorry." And she was. It had to be difficult to experience something like that. To go through it not once but four times in less than twenty four hours had to be awful. "Did you see who did this to her?"

Sadness made him look older than he was. "No. Damn it. No." His voice cracked.

She hoped she kept the disappointment from showing on her face. It was clear the failure bothered him as much as it disappointed her. "You didn't see anything?"

"All I could get is that she thought it was the deputy sheriff who was here, but she never saw the face of the person who attacked her. She was heading to the door and then took a horrible blow to the back of her head. It went downhill from there."

Kyle's heart was thudding, and it was an effort to catch his breath. The emotion that came from the young woman was overwhelming in its intensity. Perhaps her age and the way teenagers felt everything so deeply made it more powerful. He'd felt the fear and the flash of hope when she believed the deputy was on her way, he'd experienced the terror and the pain when she was attacked. He'd felt it all and yet seen nothing. Neither had Tess, for the attack came swiftly and without warning. She'd died before she ever got even a glimpse of her attacker.

Ava squeezed his hand. In a way she grounded him, and he managed to find his way out of the blackness and back to the light. Her light. As long as she was on the other side, the darkness could never hold him. He blew out a long breath and looked up at three expectant faces.

"She didn't see who killed her."

"Son of a bitch," Jayne bit out. "I thought you guys came here to help. So far you haven't given me shit."

He'd be offended except she was right. Nothing very helpful had come out of anything they'd done yet. His confidence wasn't waning, however. In fact, if anything this made him more determined to find the werewolf responsible. Tess might not have seen her attacker, but she'd felt the teeth that sank into her neck and punctured her carotid artery. No run-of-the-mill animal had made that bite. No, this was a thinking, planning beast that knew exactly where to attack to inflict a maximum fatal injury, to make certain the girl died quickly before help could arrive, like the wolf knew the deputy was on her way.

"You know," he said as he intertwined his fingers with Ava's. He didn't want to break contact with her. With his skin touching hers he felt stronger. "She didn't see her attacker, but something about the attacker struck me as odd."

"What do you mean?" Lily asked.

"She was killed very efficiently, the bite placed perfectly to end her life the quickest way possible. That tear in her artery made her bleed out in minutes. She never had a chance even with the deputy on her way."

For a long moment the three women stared at him. Jayne spoke up first. "What kind of motherfucker are we chasing?"

He couldn't have said it better himself. "The kind that doesn't hesitate to squash a young woman who was on the verge of starting her life."

"A dangerous one," Lily added. "Very dangerous."

Ava released his hand and he wanted to grab it back. "This is all horrible, and if I can do anything like cleanse this place and the poor girl, I'd like to. I want to make sure her soul is set free of the tangled mess that used to be her body. It's not much, but I can do that for her." She was right. He'd done what little he could, and now it was up to Ava to do her magic.

Lily nodded. "I think you should make sure she's free and cleanse this house. I don't want it stepping over the threshold again."

"My thoughts exactly," Ava said.

Kyle turned to Ava. "What do you need me to do?" She was there for him and he was going to be there for her.

"Just hand me my bag and I'll take it from there."

He did as he was asked and grabbed Ava's bag from where it was leaning against the still-locked back door. She took it from his hands and rummaged inside before pulling a couple of small bottles from its depths. Interestingly, she put drops of whatever was inside the bottles into the palms of her hands. He didn't know if it was because they were technically at a crime scene or not, but she didn't sprinkle any of the liquid in the bottles anywhere but on her own hands.

She stepped closer to Tess's body and then held her hands out, palms up. She murmured something so quietly he couldn't make out the words. As she did, the room grew warm and the scent of lavender filled the air as it pushed out the thick smell of blood. Her magic seemed to flow all around them, all around Tess.

What he wasn't expecting was what happened next. When a shadow rose from Tess's body he couldn't help the gasp that passed his lips. Vaguely shaped like the young woman herself, it floated up from her body and seemed to hang suspended in the air for a few seconds before disappearing. Ava continued to stand still, her eyes closed and her hands held out in front of her.

"Did you see that?" Disbelief was thick in Jayne's voice.

"It's what she does," Lily said softly. "Tess is free now, and there's nothing more we can do here. We'll leave so that your deputies can finish their work."

"Wow," Jayne said. "Just wow. I wouldn't believe it if I hadn't seen it."

Kyle was concerned because the color had drained from Ava's face. He didn't know for sure, but he suspected the effort it took to protect this house from further invasion and to make certain she could guide Tess into the light had taken everything out of her. He stepped forward, grasped her hands, and said, "Come on. Let's get out of here." He hoped he could pass along strength to her just as she'd done for him.

As he stood there holding her hand, the smell of blood once more filled the air. It made the room feel small and oppressive. Definitely time to leave. Their fingers intertwined, she followed him to the back door without a word. If he had to guess, she was too drained to even talk. At the door, he turned the deadbolt and pulled it open. They both stepped outside and let the fresh air wash over them. It felt like a heavy load was lifted off his shoulders.

"About damn time," muttered Deputy Sheriff Landen. Her face was flushed, and Kyle figured his would be too if he'd been the one to discover this scene. Even her obvious emotion was understandable. He didn't take her biting words personally.

"We're done," he told her as they stepped past her. "The sheriff says you can go back in."

Shaking her head, she started forward and then stopped at the threshold. Emotion flowed over her face, and the color that had infused her cheeks moments before faded away. The about-face was surprising until he thought about it for a second. The level of violence visited on Tess was not something she'd come up against very often in her career, and the effect on her had to be staggering.

Jayne Quarles was a different story, or so he heard. Her experience went far beyond this northern county. Given that type of background, she was the kind who could keep her cool no matter how horrible it was. Not so for this deputy sheriff. As she started to go into the house again, her skin was pale and her eyes wide. At the door, she stopped and took a step back.

"I think I'll let the sheriff handle this one." She turned and sprinted toward her patrol car like someone who was close to throwing up.

"Changed her mind in a hurry," Ava commented as they walked down the steps that led from the deck to the grass.

"Yeah, she did." He stared after the fleeing deputy and for some reason felt uneasy. Probably what he'd just been through and had nothing to do with the deputy. He shook off the feeling, got in the car, and backed out of the driveway. He wanted to get away from here as well.

Chapter Sixteen

Enough was enough; Lily needed to get out of here right now. The smell of blood was suddenly overwhelming. She had to get back to Jayne's house as soon as possible before she did something stupid. It had been a mistake to leave the house without first giving herself the injection that kept her under control. Her body was yearning to change, to roll in the blood, to run fast and wild. It was always this way when she went a little too long between injections and found herself confronted by blood and violence.

"What's wrong," Jayne asked as she preceded Lily out the door. The county coroner and assistant had arrived, and they vacated the house to let them do their work. It was more like Lily ran out to let them do their work. The crisp air outside was welcome. Hoping to vanquish the scent of blood that infused her body with desires she worked hard to suppress, she inhaled deeply. It helped, and she was able to calm herself.

"Nothing," Lily muttered and would really prefer to keep it at that. Some things were better kept close to the vest. Her expectation that Jayne wouldn't let her was not misplaced.

Jayne opened the driver's side door and slid in behind the wheel. "Bull. Something's up, so tell me what it is."

Lily sat in the passenger's seat staring out the window at the fields where the bright sun overhead was melting the dusting of snow that had been everywhere when she first arrived in town. "It's complicated." It wasn't a lie either. Trying to explain to someone who lived in the rational world about the details of her life was difficult under the best of circumstances.

"I'm a smart woman. I can probably follow."

Sarcasm wasn't swaying her or making her want to share any more than before. In her case mystery was good and no sense upsetting the tried and the true. "I've no doubt you can. We have more important things to concentrate on than my personal issues."

"I disagree. Your personal issues, as you call them, are obviously affecting my case, so spill or go home. You want me to trust you, then trust me. It goes both ways."

Share or go home…neither one of those options was likely to happen. She was just about to tell her so when Jayne reached over and put a hand on her arm. "Please."

Damn. This woman had so many sides to her, and they were all compelling. Just that one word made her *want* to tell her, and she hadn't felt that way in so long she couldn't even remember the last time. She took a deep breath and blew it out slowly. It was easier to resist when she stuck to sarcasm. "It's a long story."

Jayne squeezed lightly on her arm. "You can trust me."

"Funny thing is, Jayne Quarles, I believe you." Any resistance was fading away in a hurry.

"That's cause I'm a believable kind of person."

Again she was struck by how multi-layered Jayne was turning out to be. Humor was not something she would have guessed about Jayne. The last bit of her inner conflict evaporated, and she made her decision. Trust it was. "I'm a werewolf."

"Yes, I believe we've already established that." Jayne's eyes were on the road as she navigated country roads bordered by open fields and dotted with occasional homes, some old, some new. Presumably they were heading back to her house, although nothing looked familiar to Lily, so if they'd come this way on the trip in, she'd missed it entirely.

"True, but I'm not what is considered a hereditary werewolf. In other words, I wasn't born this way."

"You mean it can be passed down?"

That little fact had been a surprise to her too when she learned the intimate details of what she was to become. "Yes. Some families go back for generations, but not mine. My family was all too human." The sadness that washed over her as she said those words was familiar. Even after all these years, she missed her family, flaws and all. "I was attacked and this is what I became."

"So when the full moon comes, boom, you're a wolf."

Lily smiled wryly. She did so love the folk legends that sprang up around her kind. They were supremely exaggerated, even if they were based in a fair amount of fact. "The full moon is the best time for the werewolf, but it isn't the only time they change. Many other factors come into play. A mature wolf can change at will, while a young wolf has far less control and will change when confronted by blood, desire, or fear. All werewolves can lose control when in the presence of blood or when the moon is full."

"What about you? You were just in a room bathed in blood. I didn't see you turn all furry and wild."

Lily didn't admit the very real truth that she'd wanted to. The effort it had cost her not to was monumental. "It's what sets a Jägers hunter apart from the garden-variety werewolf."

"I didn't think there was such a thing as a garden-variety werewolf."

Jayne actually had a pretty good point. "Figure of speech. The Jägers saved me, and they continue to save me year after year."

"How?"

"Disivaylo."

"Disi what?"

"Disivaylo. It's the serum that has kept me sane for nearly five hundred years."

Clearly Jayne was intrigued so Lily decided to go for it. She described the serum that was given orally when she was first rescued by the Jägers. The mixture of natural ingredients stumbled upon centuries ago made life for her and others like her tolerable. It allowed her to continue living her life without becoming a predator and to harness the power of the werewolf in order to be a contributing member of the world. She told Jayne how through the centuries the formula was refined and improved so that instead of daily doses she drank with her tea, she now took an injection once a week. Jayne listened without interrupting. When Lily finished, she leaned back and thought how freeing it felt to be absolutely honest with someone.

"Now you're due, is that why you're pale and shaking?"

"It is." Had to give her credit for catching on quick.

"Let's get you back to the house then."

"Appreciate it."

The only part she didn't share was that, even with the serum, Lily retained the ability to change if she desired. What the Disivaylo did for her was grant her extreme control. She could separate the woman from the wolf so that the woman was the one who called all the shots. The wolf was never able to escape without her permission. Except, that is, as long as she didn't go too long without her injection. If she did, the wolf howled for freedom, and denying it was difficult. She was close to that right now, and it was her own fault. She didn't mention any of that to Jayne.

Back at Jayne's house, she raced to her room. By the time she unzipped the small black bag, her hands were shaking. As she filled the syringe her fingers trembled. To hit a vein without making a bloody mess, she had to really concentrate and will her hand to stay steady. It worked, and moments later she felt her body respond to the flow of what she always thought of as magic coursing through her body. This is what set her apart from those she hunted.

When she walked into the living room five minutes later, color back in her cheeks and her hands no longer trembling, Kyle, Ava, and Jayne were waiting for her. It wasn't just her appearance that had improved, but her control was back as well.

"Better?" Jayne's eyes searched hers, and she thought she detected a note of concern. It was nice to have someone care.

"Much." That was an understatement. It would be difficult to explain to anyone who wasn't a were what it was like to be at the mercy of the beast and what it meant to have control over it.

"What's our next course of action?" Kyle was looking at her expectantly. She already liked this young man who had one hand on death and the other on the joy of life. A higher power knew what it was doing when it bestowed his particular gift, for he had exactly the right temperament to be able to shoulder the responsibility that came with it and not dip into the pool of despair. Touching the dead as he could do might easily drag a lesser man down. Lily knew that Kyle would have a long and successful career with the Jägers. It was a win for him and a win for the Jägers.

To answer his question, her next course of action required the cover of darkness. The full moon was only two nights away, and she needed to scout in wolf form before it made its appearance. They had all been exhausted last night when they returned from the body dump sites, and though she would have preferred to do this last night, at the time she felt it a better decision to rest. Given this morning's tragedy, it had been the right decision. Tonight was a different story. It was imperative to get out there and to discover as much as she could as quickly as she could. The fact that darkness wouldn't fall for another few hours was frustrating. She was ready to go now.

She looked at Jayne. "Where are the bodies?"

For a second Jayne looked confused, and then her expression cleared. "Our victims?"

Lily nodded. "Yes."

"One was cremated, one was buried, and the third is still at the morgue."

Darkness might be some hours out, but that didn't mean they couldn't still work their magic while they waited. "Good. Kyle, you're up again. Are you ready?"

He nodded and his eyes were bright and alert. Senn wasn't wrong about this guy. He was smart and quick. She had no doubt he was already following her unspoken game plan. "I was born ready, boss."

❖

Kyle had been ready to charge out the door when Lily laid out what she wanted him to do, but Ava had held up her hand, and his forward momentum was halted. Not just his either. Everyone stopped and looked at her. Explaining her unease, she'd asked them to wait while she cast a protection spell around Jayne's house. At first he'd wanted to blow her off and get going. After all, she'd already helped Tess transition, and that was the important thing, given what had happened here. Glancing at Lily, he could tell by her expression that she hadn't wanted to wait around either. Still, nobody argued with Ava. Instinctively he thought each of them realized she was right when they gave it a few to think it through. It was worth taking a minute or two to let her do this correctly.

The delay hadn't taken very long. Ava had done her thing, and when she was finished, he had to admit that standing inside the circle of protection she'd cast around the house did, in fact, make him feel safer. Whatever was happening around here had the feel of something much bigger than the small community, and it didn't hurt at all to make certain things were as safe as possible. If Ava's magic could do that, then it made sense to take the time to do it.

Now after they'd covered the short distance to the coroner's office and were standing next to the stainless gurney where the body of Cheryl Tisdale was laid out, his pulse was racing and his heart beating rapidly. It was hard to look at what she'd become, but he forced his gaze to stay steady. The ravages of the attack she suffered had drastically altered her appearance. Despite that he could tell she was once a very lovely young woman. To think about what had happened to her made him sad. It wasn't fair and it wasn't right.

He couldn't undo the harm done to her, but he could help stop the monster that put her in the morgue and do his best to make sure it didn't happen to anyone else. Being a Jägers hunter meant he would spend the rest of his life face-to-face with this kind of violence. It also meant he would use what God had given him to bring justice for Cheryl and those like her. He didn't take that responsibility lightly.

Picking up the residue from a death scene was one thing. What he was going to do here was far more intense and personal. Normally it felt as though he and the dead merged their minds and bodies. People often talked about necromancers as the ones who could raise the dead and bring them, at least momentarily, back to life. That wasn't the way it was for him. No, instead of them coming back to life, it was more like he joined them in death. The experience usually left him drained and vaguely uneasy.

But it was what he did and why the Jägers had recruited him. It gave his life purpose, and no matter how it affected him personally, it was something he could never turn away from. Like right now. He'd rather be anywhere else besides in this sterile, echoing room staring down at the body of a murder victim. Cheryl's face was white and crisscrossed with red slashes that made her appear as though she were wearing a Halloween mask. Her eyelids were closed, her pale lips parted just slightly. He wanted to leave her in peace and couldn't.

Lily put a hand on his shoulder, and he appreciated the reassuring gesture. The gentle acknowledgment that he wasn't in this alone meant a great deal. He was ready. Slowly Kyle reached out and took Cheryl's lifeless hand. The moment her fingers curled around his, he was in.

"Who are you?" Cheryl's voice was soft, sweet. Her face was still

pale but no longer marred by the cuts and bruises inflicted upon her by her killer. She stood in a meadow bathed in sunlight, her eyes wide with wonder. As he'd thought when he first glimpsed her face, she was a lovely young woman.

"I'm a friend."

"I can't get away," she said as tears filled her eyes. "She'll find me."

Kyle reached out and took hold of her hands. They were cold even though they were both standing in sunlight. "Who will find you?"

"Her." Her voice trembled.

He turned his head and, as was always the case, they were alone. It was as if he shared this dimension solely with the dead. "Can you tell me who she is?"

Tears spilling down her cheeks, Cheryl shook her head. "I don't know. I didn't see her face."

"Can you tell me what happened?"

Her eyes met Kyle's, and though she was clearly frightened, she seemed to draw strength from him. "I went out for a run, even though it was close to getting dark. I got home from work late, but I'm training for a race so I had to get my miles in. Besides, it's Colville and nothing ever happens here. I can run anywhere and still be safe."

"Okay." He encouraged her. "You went out for a run and it was getting dark. What happened next?"

"It was getting pretty dark by the time I was finishing up my miles, and I decided to take a shortcut on the way back. I do it all the time, and nothing ever happens except for this time. Something came up behind me fast, and I thought maybe it was another runner, but when I turned around to take a look, I swear it was a huge dog. It hit me hard in the back and knocked me to the ground. I couldn't get my breath." Her voice grew high and tight while her body began to shake violently.

He continued to hold her hands. "I've got you, Cheryl. You don't have to be afraid. No one can hurt you anymore. I promise."

Her head turned side to side as if she was searching for danger, her hands trembling in his. "They might still be here. We need to hide."

"No one is here. It's just you and me. You're safe. Tell me about the dog." He wasn't going to let her know it was no dog that hit her.

Her hands shook even more. "It was big and it just started biting me. The pain was awful and it wouldn't stop until..."

He hated to put her through this, and if it wasn't critical, he wouldn't. "Until what?"

"Until the woman showed up and yelled at the dog. It must have run off because it was suddenly gone, and it was only me and the woman. I begged her to help me. I was bleeding really bad, and I knew I was going to die if she didn't get me to the hospital. Then she picked me up like I weighed nothing, and I thought she was going to help me, but she didn't."

He stroked her hands, hoping he could give her a sense of calm and safety. "Just a few minutes more, Cheryl. Tell me what she did to you. Please."

She closed her eyes and sighed. At first she didn't say anything, and he thought perhaps he was losing her. Then she said softly, "She carried me for a while, and then she dropped me on the ground. It was funny, you know, because I watched her walk away, and even though by then I knew I was dying, I wasn't thinking about me anymore. I kept wondering why she was out in the middle of the woods naked."

"You don't know who she is?"

Cheryl shook her head. "I've never seen her before. You won't let her hurt me anymore, will you?"

Kyle pulled her close and hugged her. "No one will ever hurt you again. You have my word. Now I need you to do one more thing for me." He held her out at arm's length. "Can you do that?"

"Yes." She appeared very calm now. The tremors in her body were fading away by the second. It was time to let her go.

"Do you see the light?"

Her eyes went somewhere beyond him, and her whole body shifted. "I see it and it's beautiful."

"You need to go to the light. Others are waiting for you, and there you'll be safe forever."

"She can't go there?" Her eyes darted to his.

"No." He touched her cheek gently. "She will never walk into the light. I promise you that."

Cheryl smiled as she stepped to his right. "Thank you," she said as she passed him. A moment later she was gone. His heart felt sad and happy all at the same time.

Chapter Seventeen

Jayne had been intrigued watching Kyle last night and expected more of the same when they reached the morgue. This was very different. She'd heard stories about necromancers and how they could raise the dead, get them to talk. It hadn't happened last night, and from what she could see right now, it wasn't happening here either, even when there was a body right in front of him.

Not exactly, anyway. No raising, no talking bodies. Something, however, was going on with Kyle. He'd taken Cheryl's lifeless hand in his, and though she noticed nothing out of the ordinary happen when he'd done it, he suddenly went stone still. In fact, he almost seemed to quiver, as if he was getting ready to disappear. His body had a translucence about it that could be a trick of the fluorescent lighting in the room or perhaps something quite different.

She felt like she should be doing something, except she didn't have the first clue what that might be, and so she simply waited. After a few minutes, Kyle once more changed and became solid again. Had to be an odd trick of the light—because really it couldn't be anything else, right? His eyes, which had been closed, snapped opened, and his expression was one of infinite sadness.

"Well," she said. If she was going to be stuck with this crew, it was time to come up with something that would get them moving forward. "Did you get through to her?"

He nodded and ran a hand through his hair. "Yeah, I did." His voice echoed the depth of emotion she could see in his face. "She was scared big-time and said it was a huge dog that knocked her down and ripped her up."

"No dog would do that." Jayne pointed to the woman's body. The severity of the injuries were far beyond anything she'd ever witnessed when a dog was involved, and she'd seen enough dog bites to know the difference.

"I think we've already established that," Lily added in a soothing voice as she laid a hand on Jayne's arm. "It was the werewolf."

"You're right, of course." Jayne sighed. "I'm sorry. I'm just so damned frustrated."

"As are we," Lily added as she patted Jayne's arm and then turned to Kyle. "Go on, Kyle. What did you learn?"

He pressed his lips together before saying, "Unfortunately, not a lot. The *dog* hit her, inflicted the mortal wounds, and then a mysterious woman showed up. This stranger yelled at what Cheryl thought was the dog that attacked her. It was the woman who carried her to where you found her body. She'd never seen her before."

"So we've accomplished nothing." To say her frustration level was sky-high was stating the obvious far too simply. She was not happy about their coming here in the first place, yet she'd let her resistance slide as she spent more time around them, especially Lily. She had a sense they were not here seeking glory for themselves or for the odd order of hunters they belonged to, but because they truly wanted to help. Through the years she'd been around enough attention hounds to know the difference. Still, she hoped for much more from them and much quicker. They weren't getting anywhere that she could tell, and instead things were sliding downhill fast. What had happened this morning had her feeling pressured.

Kyle shook his head. "I wouldn't say 'nothing.' Not at all because, you see, I sent her on her way, and that's something."

"Sent her on her way?" What the hell did that mean, and how the hell was it helping this investigation? The truth? It wasn't helping anything, and her initial inclination toward all of this being stupid was more than likely correct.

Kyle nodded, and if her tone of voice offended him, he didn't let on. "She was stuck here, grounded for some reason. Maybe she was waiting for me. Sometimes that happens. It's like the universe knows that we have to talk before they can move on, and so it holds them until I can reach them. Anyway, after we talked, I guided her to the place she was supposed to go, and now no one will ever be able to hurt her again."

"You sent her to heaven?"

"Or whatever you choose to call it, yeah. It's part of what I do."

"Okay, whatever, but how does that help us earthbound people?"

"It doesn't do anything for those of us still living," Lily broke in. "It's the balancing of the karmic scales for Cheryl."

"Karma, great." She didn't care about balancing anything. She wanted to stop this damn werewolf. Oh, crap, where did that come from? When did she buy into the werewolf theory?

"Jayne," Lily said firmly. "This was not a bust."

"Of course it is." From her standpoint, she didn't hear anything useful out of what he'd told them.

"No. We learned something important from Cheryl. She lived here all her life, right?"

Jayne nodded and stuck her hands in her pockets. "Yes." Whatever that had to do with a so-called werewolf.

"She didn't know the woman who reprimanded the wolf, and that gives us a good clue to follow up on. Even if Cheryl wasn't friends with everybody in town, would it be fair to say she'd recognize pretty much everyone who lives here?"

All of a sudden Jayne got where Lily was going with this, and she experienced the first flash of hope since they arrived. "It would indeed."

"Then we're on the lookout for a stranger in town."

Her thought exactly, and she knew just who to ask about stranger sightings, but before she could even reach for her phone to make the call, her cell began to ring. She grabbed it and put it to her ear. "Quarles."

"Hey, Sheriff, it's Jeni."

"What's up?" Jennifer Amen was the local librarian, and Jayne knew her pretty well even though Jeni had been three years behind her in school. "I'm checking to see if you've had any luck locating Willa."

Willa was Jeni's younger cousin. Developmentally challenged, Willa was a bright soul who was loved by everyone in town. While her skills were limited, she held a job as a bagger at the local grocery store. She even had her own small apartment in town, giving her a bit of independence, though between Jeni and Willa's parents, they maintained a close eye on her.

"What do you mean, located Willa?" No one had called her to say that Willa was missing.

"She didn't show up for work yesterday or today."

A bad feeling started to knot up in her stomach. Willa wasn't a no-show kind of person. In fact, keeping to a strict routine was what gave Willa the courage to live and work on her own. She wouldn't miss a shift, let alone two.

A flash of irritation made her words sharp. "Why didn't you call this in?" They should have been following up on Willa when she missed her first shift.

For a moment there was a pause. "I did call it in."

"What do you mean you did? This is the first I'm hearing of this."

"I talked to Dana yesterday when the store called and said Willa wasn't there. We checked her apartment because we thought maybe she was sick, except she wasn't at home either. That's when I called and talked to Dana."

Son of a bitch. Why in the hell hadn't Dana put a missing persons case in? It was true that for a normal person it would take longer than a single missed shift to sound the alarm, but with someone like Willa it was a completely different story. When she was late, someone should have been checking on her. They should have been checking on her.

"I'm not at my office, Jeni. Let me get back to the station and I'll call you with an update." She needed to talk to her people right away and find out what the fuck happened and why this had fallen through the cracks. Someone was going to get their ass chewed.

"Sheriff, I'm really worried."

So was she, far more than she dared share with Jeni. "I know, Jeni. I'll call you as soon as I can."

"You'll call?"

"You have my word."

Jayne ended the call and tried to come up with a good explanation for why Dana didn't follow up on Willa. Nothing came to mind, but until she talked to her and got her side of the story, she wasn't going to give in to the anger bubbling just beneath the surface.

As she studied the phone in her hand, a thought occurred to her. She raised her gaze until her eyes met Lily's. It could work. "You're a werewolf, right?"

Lily raised a single eyebrow and said softly, "Yes."

"You any good at tracking?"

Bellona couldn't have asked for a nicer place. It suited the needs of their new family perfectly. The house was big enough for all of them to have plenty of space, with room for more. She and Little Wolf called the master suite theirs, while Adam and Eve each had a room in the lower level. The big barn was perfect for those multipurpose events that she didn't feel needed to be brought into the house. Considering the youth and inexperience of her children, the barn was seeing a great deal of use. It would take time for them to hone their hunting skills so that they kept under the human radar.

Eve was a little worrisome in that respect. She was an accident, and Bellona probably should have turned her, yet something about her drew Bellona in, and she made the split-second decision to have her join their family. It seemed like such an inspired decision at the time, and to Eve's credit, she was more than willing and always listened to what Bellona told her. She obeyed without question, and that was an excellent trait to have in a student. Still, while Adam was young, strong, and smart, Eve was almost too gentle a soul. She'd turned faster than anyone Bellona had ever seen and yet lacked the instinct for survival so critical in a pack.

It was too early to make a call on Eve. Bellona felt she needed to give her time, let her learn, and let her run. Only after she had a chance to develop could Bellona pass judgment on her wisdom to allow Eve to join the pack. Besides, Eve reminded her so much of a girl from her hometown she simply didn't have the heart to end it quite yet. Just as with Eve, she had been a wonderfully tender sprite, beloved by all, rich and poor alike. This was the first time she'd run into another who touched that part of her memory and her heart. She'd been unable to end Eve's life and instead brought her into the fold. Besides, every family needed the bright sunshine that people like Eve possessed and so freely shared.

As if sensing Bellona was thinking about her, Eve came into the kitchen. "When can I run? Can I go now? I'd really like to go now."

Bellona smiled and held out her arms. Eve walked into her embrace and wrapped her arms around her waist. "Can we go now, pleeeze?"

Kissing her on the top of her head, Bellona breathed in the fresh scent of her hair. She'd obviously showered with the apple-scented shampoo Little Wolf stocked in her bathroom. "Not now, my sweet girl, but soon."

"Why can't we go now? I want to go now."

"Remember, I've told you how we must wait for darkness."

"That's stupid. You can see so much more in the daytime. Night is dumb."

"No, sweet girl, it's safe. I don't want you to be hurt."

Eve stepped out of her embrace, put her hands on her hips, and frowned. "No, it's not safe, it's stupid. We are way stronger and faster than anybody else, and nobody can hurt us, 'specially since Adam runs with us. He's nice and he's real tough. Only dummies would pick on Adam."

"Yes, he is powerful, but you still have to do this by my rules. We only run at night, and we only run together."

"Little Wolf runs alone."

"Yes, she does, but Little Wolf is older." She didn't add that Little Wolf was a handful and that while Bellona was totally infatuated with her, she wanted to throttle her about half the time because she didn't heed Bellona's warnings.

"That's a stupid, stupid reason."

Bellona kissed her on the top of the head. "Yes, it is, but sweetheart, you still can't run until tonight. We'll all go together. I promise."

Adam walked in. Eve pulled away from Bellona and ran to him. He smiled and put an arm around her shoulders. "Hey, punk, what's up?"

Eve frowned. "I want to run but she won't let me."

Adam winked at her. "Well then, since we can't run, how about we go feed the horses?"

The frown disappeared and a smile brightened Eve's face. She clapped her hands. "Yeah, let's do that."

Together they went out the door, leaving Bellona alone in the kitchen. Yes, she had high hopes for this family, this pack. Now that Adam had Eve sufficiently entertained, she turned her attention to more pressing matters. She had traps to set and Jägers to run out of town.

CHAPTER EIGHTEEN

Lily went with Jayne when they left the morgue and walked side-by-side the relatively short distance to the sheriff's department. Oddly it felt natural to be at her side, as if they'd been lifelong companions. She hadn't felt that way about anyone since she'd been part of the special trio of childhood friends. She still missed her two closest friends terribly, even after all these years.

"What are you thinking about? You're very deep in thought."

She looked over at Jayne's profile and once more thought how attractive she was. A little flutter went through her body. Given Lily was a big, tough werewolf hunter she should lie and tell her she was mulling over hunt strategies for taking down the rogue here in Jayne's county. Instead, she admitted the truth. "I was thinking about how comfortable I am around you and how much you remind me of my two best friends."

Did she imagine it, or did Jayne wince when she said "friends"? If her words bothered her, she didn't let on. "As much as I hate to admit it, you're growing on me too."

Lily laughed softly, understanding how difficult that had to have been for Jayne to confess. "I have that effect on people."

"I somehow believe that. Tell me about your friends, Lily."

Lily touched the necklace that hung around her neck, feeling the smooth stone beneath her fingers. It had been with her all these years, and the only time she didn't wear it was when it required repair. "I grew up with two special friends, Alexia and Taria. We all came from noble families and lived in fine homes by the standard of the times." She never told anyone that her family went far beyond fine, as she was born into a royal family. Her father, the duke, was distant and focused on his country, not his children, with the exception of arranging advantageous marriages. Her mother, the duchess, was kind though forever sad. Lily always believed she longed to return to her birthplace of Austria but was a prisoner in the marriage arranged by her own parents. These memories she kept locked inside. "We were so close in age and our families so intertwined in the same social circles, we were more like sisters than friends."

Jayne cut a sideways glance at her. "What happened?"

This was something she had shared with few people in her lifetime. It had cut too deep, and the scar had never really healed. She turned to study Jayne and started talking again when she made her decision. "I was to be married. My father sold me, you see…"

Jayne gasped. "Your father sold you?"

That probably wasn't fair to Father. It was, after all, the way of their world at the time. "It was an arranged marriage. The man my father chose was of noble birth and, like me, had no choice in the arrangement. It was a practice expected and normal at the time. The reality, however, is that both Aldrich and I were essentially sold by our families. We were expected to do as we were told without question. It was simply the way things were done."

"That's awful." Real emotion sounded in her voice.

In more ways than one, Lily thought. "My friends and I were together on the last night of my freedom. I was to be married the next day." The thought of what had awaited her on the night of her wedding to Aldrich still made her shiver. That bullet she'd dodged, though the price had been, and still was, very high.

"Did you marry this Aldrich?"

She shook her head. "No. After my friends returned to their homes that night, I was attacked and left for dead. At the time, I thought it was all over for me. I was in such bad shape, bloody and barely alive. Aldrich took one look at me after the attack and backed out of the marriage. My family was on the same page and gave me up for dead."

"Seriously?"

It would be hard for Jayne to understand how things were back then. Her value had been wiped out in a matter of minutes. Much had changed in the intervening centuries. "Seriously."

"You had to have been furious with them."

Another moment for decision. As the old saying went, in for a penny, in for a pound. "No. I wasn't angry at all. I was relieved."

Jayne stopped walking and turned to stare at her. "Aldrich wasn't a good guy?"

She stopped walking as well and studied her hands. "He was a fine man, as far as men went, and that was the problem." She brought her eyes up to meet Jayne's. "He was a man."

She let that hang while the implication sank in. When it did, she saw a ghost of a smile flit across Jayne's face. That little smile warmed her heart. Her instincts about Jayne didn't appear to be failing her.

"I see." Jayne didn't look away.

"My family took the attack and Aldrich's abandonment as a personal affront. The only way to save face was to let me die, and truthfully, I was happy to die. I wanted out of my life. I'd been dreading the fate that awaited me and in fact had felt dead inside. The only thing that would have changed at that point is I would have died in body as well as spirit."

"But you obviously didn't die."

"Not at all. The injuries were severe enough I could have, if not for our local priest. He contacted the Jägers, as he suspected the truth of what had happened to me. They swooped in and bundled me away to what was then the headquarters of the order. They healed my wounds, ushered me through the changes, and began giving me the serum that has kept me sane for centuries. My family and friends were told I had died, and they didn't question it. It was easier that way for them and for me."

"God, that had to be rough."

"In many ways, yes. It was difficult to say farewell to my life, even if it wasn't one I was looking forward to living."

"But it was your life." Jayne understood.

"It was my life, good or bad. One day it was there and the next it was gone. That's not something anyone can prepare for."

"What about your family?"

"It was painful to watch my family and friends from a distance, never talking to them or touching them again. Even my father, as cold as he was, I would have loved to have held his hand just once more. After my parents and my siblings were put into the ground it became so emotionally draining, I finally had to go away."

"I don't know if I'd be strong enough to do it. You know, walk away from everything. I've lost my family too, yet I find comfort here where my roots are and in the house my brother built. It makes me feel close to them."

"You might be surprised at what you can do when you have to. I know I was. The Jägers gave me a life I never would have had if not for that horrible night. I became strong and independent, able to love whomever I wanted. I've traveled the world and experienced history firsthand."

"Was it worth it?"

She'd asked herself that same question a thousand times over the years. When she thought back to her family and Alexia and Taria, the answer was a solid no, it was not. When she thought about the years she would have spent as the wife of a man she could never love and of the years she'd have spent with him with nothing to do but run a house, then her answer was the opposite. Yes, it was absolutely worth it.

She started walking in the direction of Jayne's office once more. "I'll let you know."

❖

Usually Kyle felt drained after connecting with the dead. This time he was not only drained, but he was also sick to his stomach. Everything about this trip had been a little off. A lot of what he was feeling right now probably had to do with the fact that Tess was so young. He was incredibly sad that such a young woman had been forced to die so terribly. It would take a hard soul not to feel that deeply. He ran his hands through his hair and rubbed his scalp. It didn't help.

Connecting with Cheryl had hurt his heart as well. She'd been scared and alone. Her loss was also tragic. Touching the souls of both women so close together was almost too much, but it was something that had to be done.

Ava was a sensitive person and understood what it had taken out of him when he connected with Tess and Cheryl. They'd come back to Jayne's while she and Lily went to the sheriff's office. Back at the house, Ava made a tea with some herbs and honey and who knew what else. She handed him a mug and ordered him to drink, which of course he did. He would do anything Ava told him to. The funny thing was, the tea worked beautifully so he really didn't care what she put in it. Love maybe. Hopefully.

After his stomach stopped rolling, his first inclination was to head back into town to talk with Jayne and Lily. He'd half expected to see them shortly after they'd gotten back to the house. So far, they hadn't shown up. Ava called Lily to hear what they'd discovered on the latest missing woman. So far, nothing, according to Lily, and he'd wanted to jump back in the car and follow. Lily told them to stay put. He didn't understand why because he was certain they could help. They didn't come all this way to sit around and do nothing.

Lily was, however, their team lead, and rule one of the Jägers was to follow the directions of the lead without question. She had her reasons for asking them to stay put even if she didn't share what they were with him or Ava. All he could do was to trust that it was all for the greater good.

"I hate this," he mumbled as he stood staring out the big front window while holding the warm mug of tea between two hands. A light breeze was blowing and the sun was shining. Perfect weather for a pack of werewolves to run.

Now why did he think pack? The word came to him without conscious thought, and with it came a chill not related to weather. He'd never heard of a pack hunt before. Maybe years ago before the Jägers came to full strength but not in modern times. It simply didn't happen, too dangerous for the wolves.

"We're not useless here," Ava told him as she came to stand beside him.

"What can we do?" God almighty, was that him whining? Geez, he definitely needed to man up if he wanted to impress Ava.

"I have a few tricks up my sleeve."

Oh, he wanted to see up her sleeve all right. "Really?"

She took the mug out of his hands and set it aside. Then she put her arms around him and laid her head on his chest. "Trust me, big boy."

He managed not to jump in surprise and instead wrapped his arms around her. Smoothly too, if he did say so. "You have no idea how much I trust you."

"You feel it, don't you?"

Honestly, he was afraid to answer that question. Was she talking about the odd nature of this hunt? Or was she talking about the wave of emotion that came over him every time he looked at her face? Professional question or personal question?

"Yeah, I do." Neutral answer that would work either way she was going with this.

"We have to stop this werewolf." Professional it was.

"We do."

"I've got a spell, and I'm thinking if you and I work together it might just get us closer to whoever is doing this."

"Really?" He couldn't imagine what he could do that would help her. While he could summon the dead to come to him, that was about the extent of his superpowers. He'd always admired the magic that witches could summon, partially because it was something he couldn't do. Powers he possessed. Magic, not a drop.

"Take one part witch and one part true believer, and you'd be amazed at what we can accomplish." She smiled up at him and winked. "Trust me," she said again. "I promise not to lead you astray."

He wouldn't mind her leading him astray, but he'd save that comment for another day. "You got it. Tell me what you need from me, and I'll do it."

She stepped out of his arms and tilted her head as she looked up at him, her green eyes holding his. "All right, Kyle. We'll make some magic, and after we've done that, then we have to talk about us."

Chapter Nineteen

The situation they were facing was deadly serious, and Jayne noticed how Lily had to tamp down the urge to smile each time Jayne was required to explain her being at her side. She obviously didn't have to explain to Lily how very unlikely it was for the county's sheriff to go looking for a girlfriend online. Each time she introduced Lily as just such a girlfriend, it made her twitch, and she was painfully aware that her discomfort was obvious. Her great idea for explaining Lily's presence in her life was not nearly as simple as it had sounded at the start.

Now, however, instead of being in the office fielding questions on Lily, they were standing in Willa's small apartment. Any desire to linger on her own discomfort at the façade she was forced to present faded away as very real worry invaded her thoughts concerning the sweet soul who lived here. Willa would be no match for the jaws of a powerful wolf or any other kind of predator, human or otherwise. She was a simple, sweet soul who liked and trusted everyone. She wouldn't recognize evil.

The tiny living room held a love seat and a single chair. A neon-pink fleece blanket was tossed over the love seat. A fluffy stuffed cat sat on the window sill as if watching for Willa to return, and several empty pop cans were on the kitchen counter. On the small kitchen table was a blue vase stuffed with bright-yellow silk daisies. Willa had made her little home cheerful and inviting. Jayne had a sinking feeling she wouldn't be coming back to her daisies and her sweet pink blanket.

She breathed in deeply and filled her senses with the essence of the young woman. She wondered if Lily could do the same thing and, with it, follow her to wherever she waited for someone to come.

"Well." Jayne looked over at Lily. "Anything?"

Strain was beginning to show on Lily's beautiful face. Her eyes were narrow, her lips pressed together in a hard line, and her skin was pale. Jayne wished she could ease the worry that pressed on her. She didn't know how to help Lily when she didn't even know how to help herself. "I've got her scent."

That single statement gave Jayne a surge of hope. "Can you track her?"

Lily shook her head. "Not in this form. I can tuck Willa's scent away in my human form, but to truly track her, I have to change. That is not going to happen in broad daylight. I'm sorry."

Her hopes fell. "You can't track in daylight." It didn't really make sense to her. What difference did it make if it was light or dark? Scent was scent, right?

Lily's intense eyes met hers. "I'm old, Jayne, very old, and I didn't survive this long by doing stupid things. How many people in this area have guns? How many of them in this current fearful climate would hesitate to shoot a wolf running through their property? I want to survive long enough to bring Willa home."

As much as she hated to admit it, Lily had a valid point. "I can protect you." She was the sheriff, after all, and she carried a big gun.

Lily shook her head. "No, you really can't. I know how anxious you are to find Willa, and I will help in any way I can, as soon as I can. Changing during daylight hours and risking exposure is not something I'm willing to do. It's too dangerous, plain and simple."

Jayne couldn't remember ever feeling this frustrated. Everything felt as though it was spinning out of control. "But we have to find her. You have to understand that Willa is special."

"I understand, I really do. I can feel the essence of Willa here, and I promise, I will track her tonight just as soon as it's safe for me to do so."

"But…" Her cell phone rang. She grabbed it and answered. When she heard Dana's voice, a new kind of anger rushed into her. Dana had a hell of a lot of explaining to do. Jayne ended the call and looked over at Lily. "Dana is *finally* back at the station. We're heading back."

When they'd gone to the station earlier, she been surprised and irritated to discover Dana wasn't at her desk. She'd left the crime scene before they did, so Jayne had fully expected to see her back at the office. When she'd checked with the rest of the staff and no one had seen her, she'd gone from irritated to pissed off. As she and Lily had left to head over to Willa's apartment, she'd left instructions to track Dana down and get her back to the office ASAP.

They were both quiet as they drove the short distance from Willa's apartment to the sheriff's office. As they walked through this time, they didn't have to stop every few feet and explain Lily's company, and for that she was grateful. The gossip would be all over town by dinnertime, and that was okay as long as she didn't get confronted with it every five seconds. Lily followed Jayne, who only paused at Dana's desk to say a curt, "In my office." When Lily started to sit in a chair outside, Jayne motioned her in. She was a part of this now, and Jayne figured she might as well hear it all.

Lily took a seat in the corner of Jayne's office and stayed quiet, looking a tad bit uncomfortable. She'd be worried except she was pretty sure the woman was capable of handling anything that came her way. Besides, hadn't Lily demanded right from the beginning that they be a team? Yeah, well, team it was.

She turned her attention to Dana, who walked in looking decidedly grim. Jayne wasn't sure if it was because she knew what was coming or was still shook up about being the one to discover Tess dead. Didn't matter either way. Dana had messed up big-time and had to answer for that. Her mistake could turn out to be a deadly one.

"Sheriff, I'm sorry I didn't come straight back here, but I had to get my bearings. I've never seen anything like that before. I needed a little time to process. I couldn't come back here and just pretend it was all okay."

From Jayne's point of view, she was trying to make her case before Jayne jumped on her. She sounded sincere and she might buy it, if she didn't have a funny feeling Dana was hiding something. Like Jayne, Dana had grown up here in the Colville area, but she was enough younger that she really didn't know her. Dana was already a deputy sheriff by the time Jayne took over the department. Thus far her work had been fine and her dedication to the county was solid, so there'd never been a reason to question her motives or performance. Until now.

Jayne's eyes narrowed. "I'm not worried about your less-than-straight path back to the office, Dana. Anyone would need a little breather after discovering that level of violence."

"You're not angry? Then what is it? I'll write out my report right now. I followed procedure and took notes and pictures while I was there."

She stared at Dana. "Willa."

Dana's face paled, and she began to twist her hands together. "Oh, God, I forgot about Willa."

"What do you mean, you forgot? Jeni called you yesterday. Why isn't there something on my desk?"

Running her hands over her face, Dana dropped into the chair in front of Jayne's desk. "I was going to write up something when I got off the phone with Jeni, and then I got interrupted. Besides, in all honesty she hadn't been gone long enough to be technically considered a missing person."

So far, she wasn't impressed. In their line of business, interruptions were the norm, and there were legitimate exceptions to every rule. "You and I both know that, in Willa's case, that time limit goes out the window."

Dana shrugged and had the decency to look sheepish. Her expression said she knew she'd fucked that one up.

Jayne wasn't done, however. "Explain to me what would be so interesting you'd forget something like Willa not showing up for work."

Dana turned her face away from Jayne. "My girlfriend called."

Silence hung heavy for at least a full minute. Did she just say what she thought she did? The surprises just kept coming today. Jayne sank to her chair. "Your girlfriend?"

Nodding, Dana finally looked up, a flush to her cheeks. "You have to understand, it's not something people know about."

This explanation didn't make sense. Dana was married to a man. "How about your husband?"

Dana shrugged and looked down at her feet. "He's been gone for months," she mumbled. "I didn't want people to know he left me."

How did something like that fall off the gossip trail in a town like this? Then again, she wasn't exactly on the main line, so it was possible for her to have missed it. Wasn't a great testament to her skills as a leader that she'd missed something this major for one of her staff. She looked over at Dana. "And now you have a girlfriend?"

This time Dana's eyes met hers. "I kinda thought you, of everyone here, would understand."

Of course she understood. It didn't explain anything else. "I understand many things, Dana, and who you choose to spend your time with is entirely your decision. No one else, me included, has a thing to say about it. That said, it also has no place in this office. Taking a call from your girlfriend and forgetting about a missing special-needs young woman is not just an error. It could very well be a fatal error." Life-ending for Willa and career-ending for Dana was what she didn't elaborate on.

"I'm sorry," Dana whispered. "It won't happen again."

"No, it won't."

"I'll go write the report now."

She tried to be the best leader she could, someone her staff could count on, someone the county could depend on. That meant at times having to do the hard thing. This was one of those times. "Not quite yet. First, I want your badge and your gun." She held her hand out.

"What?"

"As of this moment, you're on suspension for ten days. Write your report and then go home."

"Sheriff, that's uncalled for. I made a mistake, that's all."

"You made a mistake that could cost a young woman her life. Combine that with what you discovered this morning, and I can't trust you right now. We'll talk again in ten days." This was the only thing she could do. Unfortunately it was the worst time to be a deputy short, but allowing Dana to skate on an error of this magnitude was unthinkable as well. She had to do what she had to do.

Dana jumped up, and for a moment Jayne thought she was going to fight her decision. Dana opened her mouth and then, after staring at her for a moment, took her gun and badge and smacked them down on Jayne's desk. Without another word she stalked out. She was surprised she hadn't slammed the door on her way through.

Jayne stared down at the gun and the badge. The truth was, even when warranted, she hated doing things like this. It was, however, a necessary part of the job.

From where she still sat in the corner, Lily said, "Well, that was interesting."

Jayne looked over at Lily and shook her head. "In more ways

than one. You know, Dana's been married for years. Then she comes in here, stands in front of my desk, and announces she has a girlfriend...a girlfriend. As if things around here weren't crazy enough already."

"You mean like the sheriff meeting her girlfriend online."

This time Jayne looked up and gave her a wry smile. "Exactly."

❖

Bellona sat everyone down at the table. She was surrounded by happy faces, even Little Wolf, who had come back earlier scowling and cranky. All it took to turn her mood around was breathtaking sex and a fortifying meal, thanks to her pantry-filling trip to the grocery store. Now Little Wolf was as happy as the rest of them.

"I need you all to listen," she said. A game plan was in order, and they needed to listen and understand.

Eve was piling more beef on her plate. "Listen, listen, listen," she said in a singsong voice.

It made Bellona smile. She really did love this girl already. "Seriously, we have to be careful, and that means you, Eve. The Jägers are here..."

"Who are the Jägers?" Adam asked as he leaned back in his chair and sipped a glass of milk. He'd put away half a gallon of the stuff just in this meal.

A slight shiver raced through her body. She'd dodged them for years and survived. Even so, she respected their skill and might. None of them should be taken lightly. "They're hunters."

"I know hunters," Eve piped up, her mouth still full of food. "They're pretty nice. Joe Joseph brought me some venison sausage one time. It was good."

She put a hand on Eve's shoulder. "Not these hunters, darling. These hunters will kill you."

Eve stopped chewing and looked at her in surprise. "Why? I didn't do anything to them. That's not nice. Why aren't they nice?"

Adam put an arm around Eve's shoulders and squeezed softly. "Don't worry, little one. I'll protect you. No bad hunter is going to hurt you."

While she appreciated the way Adam looked after Eve, it was bigger than the two of them. "We will all protect each other," she said solemnly. "It's what being a family, a pack, is all about." Just saying the word "pack" filled her heart with satisfaction.

Little Wolf smiled and held up her glass of wine. "Amen to that. Our pack rules."

Bellona reached over and took Little Wolf's free hand and brought it to her lips to kiss it. "Yes, it does. However, we still need to stick together to keep all of us safe. I have a plan, and the first priority is to run the Jägers hunters out of town. We're all going to need to keep a low profile until we can redirect their efforts."

"How do you plan to do that?" Little Wolf took a sip of her wine. "I think it would be easier and quicker just to kill them."

Again she was struck by Little Wolf's lust. It was a bit of a double-edged sword. Bellona loved how fearless she was and at the same time was afraid that fearlessness could jeopardize their safety. Somehow she had to keep her in check at least until the Jägers were gone. She didn't want to lose her, but if it came down to saving her or saving the pack, she only had one choice.

"It might be easier in the short run, my sweet wolf, but we have to think of the big picture if we want to stay here to grow and flourish. This is the right time, I feel it here." Bellona tapped her chest. "If we all work together, we will make this happen."

"I'm in," Adam said as he tipped his empty milk glass toward her in a mock toast. "Just tell me what you need me to do."

"I want to run," Eve said. "Tonight."

The edginess brought on the approaching full moon was apparent in all of them. The power the moon would bring also meant her small pack would be hard to control during that time. Adam and Eve would respond even more dramatically, for the first full moon was always the most important. To deny them the opportunity to run now would further fuel the frenzy, and she wasn't going to risk it.

"You will all run tonight, together. It's important we stay together. No exceptions."

She turned and captured Little Wolf's eyes. Her wild and passionate woman was just as wild and passionate in wolf form. Difficult to control was being nice. The challenge it presented thrilled Bellona. She hadn't felt this alive in years.

Little Wolf grimaced and then said, "Got it. I'll stick close."

"No killing." Bellona swept her gaze over all three of them. "I'm serious. We can't afford the scrutiny. Priority number one is running the Jägers out of town, not your fun and games. Not right now. Your time will come if you're patient. Do I make myself clear?"

"Yes, ma'am." Adam gave her a small salute.

He was going to fit in exceptionally well. "Eve?"

"Ah-ha." She was sliding her fork around on her plate.

"You'll stick close when we run."

"I like to run with Adam."

He ruffled her hair. "And I like running with you, pretty girl."

Eve laughed and started to eat again. "I like all of you."

"Little Wolf?" Bellona squeezed her hand lightly. "For me?"

Little Wolf's smile lit her face. It was that smile that had made Bellona stop and decide to stay on the first day they met. "Just for you."

She leaned in and kissed her deeply. "I'm pretty sure I love you."

"I know I love you," Little Wolf said against her lips.

CHAPTER TWENTY

C an I watch?"
They were standing outside next to Jayne's car and Lily was only half listening. "What?"

"Can I watch you change?" Jayne clarified. "I'm still not a hundred percent on board, and I'm thinking to see is to believe."

Shaking her head, Lily said, "You are a strange person, Jayne Quarles."

Jayne shrugged. "That's not the worst thing I've been called. So can I?"

Lily wasn't sure she wanted to go there. Some time ago she'd asked Senn to video the transition so she could see it for herself. It had been a mistake. There was nothing pretty about morphing from a human into a wolf. At least the transition itself was fairly ugly. Her wolf form was not. She rather liked how she appeared: strong and sleek with a coat that shone in the moonlight. She didn't like the way she felt as well as she liked the way she appeared. In wolf form, the animal side of her warred for dominance. It took a phenomenal amount of self-control to keep that side of her at bay. Did she really want to expose all of that to Jayne?

The answer wasn't as cut-and-dried as Lily would have imagined. For whatever reason, pushing the obvious answer, no, across her lips wasn't happening. "Let me think about it."

"What's to think about? It's not like I'm going to tell anyone what you are."

Lily trusted her on that score. They'd only been acquainted for a brief time, yet something about Jayne rang true to Lily's heart. She wasn't one of those people who hid behind deception. The straight-up nature of her personality appealed to Lily. Throughout her many years, she'd run up against so many who wore masks. To say it made her weary was an understatement.

"It's not that I worry you might tell others. It's that changing is really personal. It's baring my soul at a very intimate level. I don't do it lightly or ever, if you want the truth, because it's a risk I'm not willing to take."

Jayne studied her closely. "I guess I didn't think about it like that. I suppose it could be pretty dangerous."

Lily put a hand on her arm and loved the warmth that it brought into her body. "I wouldn't expect you to see the peril involved with changing in front of others, especially since you don't really believe."

Jayne patted her hand where it lay on her arm. "You're starting to wear me down. I'm about this far," she held her thumb and forefinger about half an inch apart, "from believing it all."

Good news even if it wasn't swaying her much at the moment. Sharing the werewolf part of her took courage, and right at the moment she wanted to save every ounce of courage she possessed for finding this killer. For a second, she stopped and turned her face to the sky. Then she tilted her head down and looked at Jayne. "Is it usually this quiet on a Tuesday afternoon?"

"What?"

They were standing on the main street of town next to Jayne's vehicle, and while they'd been there, not a single car had traveled down the street. Likewise, no one had walked down the street, and the only noise she heard was a flock of birds flying overhead, presumably heading south for the winter.

"Aren't people usually out and about this time of day?" It was a small town, but it wasn't a ghost town.

What she asked appeared to sink in, and Jayne did a slow three sixty. "Okay." She drew the single word out. "It's a little quiet."

"Doesn't that strike you as odd?"

"I've got to say it does."

She'd seen this before and it rarely ended well. It was a wave of fear and panic that picked up speed and volume as it went along. It was residents barricading behind locked doors and armed with the most powerful weapons they had access to. "People are afraid."

"No shit." Jayne flinched. "Sorry. I don't blame them for being scared. This kind of thing doesn't happen around here. People don't go missing and they don't end up slaughtered. It's not that we're immune from murder. It's more that in those instances when it happens, the circumstances are usually pretty textbook. Passion or drugs and not very original. They tend to be relatively easy to solve. This is unusual and frightening. I can see people around here reacting by holing up with their arsenal."

That much was true too. She'd witnessed the same reaction in community after community. What she'd also seen happen was the erosion of faith in local law enforcement. She worried that reaction wasn't far behind the seclusion that was clearing the streets.

"We need to talk about what follows this type of behavior." Jayne wouldn't have the experience she did when it came to this scenario.

"Way ahead of you." Maybe not the experience Lily possessed but the smarts to see it through. Impressive.

Lily tilted her head and studied Jayne. "You're no dummy, are you?"

"I think that's a compliment but sort of hard to tell."

"It's a compliment." She gave her a tiny nod. "Now we need to cut off the hard cores before they rally the rest of the town."

As if their conversation had been monitored, Jayne's assistant, Ralph, came toward them walking at a hurried clip. "Sheriff, I just got a text from my wife. Jeni is arranging a community meeting at the church at five. Thought you'd want to know."

"I appreciate the heads-up. Thanks, Ralph."

"You bet." He turned around and jogged back into the building.

"Well, that's not good news," Jayne said as she slid a pair of sunglasses onto her face. "The last thing we need is the villagers storming the countryside."

Lily put her hand on the passenger's side door and pulled it open. Over the top of the car she looked at Jayne. "We're running out of time."

❖

When they retraced their path to the spot where the first victim had been discovered, Kyle was pretty impressed with himself. It had been late, they'd been on the road all day, and emotions had been running high when they'd been here before. Remembering the path they took was pretty much a miracle.

In the late-afternoon light it was beautiful and peaceful. Sad to think someone's body had been tossed away in such a wonderful place. Nobody should be treated like that, and to do it here was insulting to both the person and the place. Silently he made a promise to find who did this and stop them.

"What do you need me to do?" he asked Ava. She had a plan she hadn't shared with him quite yet. He'd followed her out here based on pure faith.

She took a deep breath and looked around as if making sure they were alone. When she blew out the breath, her face was a touch pale. Whatever she had on her mind, it was weighing heavy. "I've never done this spell before. It's difficult and not usually successful."

That explained a lot but wasn't exactly reassuring. "You think it will be this time?"

She nodded. "I do."

"Why?"

"Because of you."

He didn't want to burst her bubble of enthusiasm and knew he had to. "I don't do magic." Apparently she had some misinformation when it came to his skill set.

She put her hands on either side of his face. "You do magic every day. It's different from mine, but it's magic just the same. The two of us together can open the veil and reach through."

"The veil?" Now he was really lost. He wasn't sure where she was going with this.

"You pass through each time you reach out to the departed. It is the veil that separates the living from the dead. I'm unable to do that, but with my magic and yours combined I'm certain we'll be able to learn more. Perhaps enough to stop this madness."

In a flash the possibilities opened up to him. If they were able, as she said, to combine their strengths, maybe they could communicate at an even deeper level. It could very well be the thing they needed to bring this all to an end before anyone else was harmed. She was a smart and talented woman.

"Let's do this. Tell me what you need from me."

She handed him her bag. "Right now I want you to just sit there."

Okay, not exactly rocket science, but if that's what she needed from him, that's what he'd do. He sat cross-legged on the cold ground on the spot she pointed him to. Next to him she piled up a fair amount of pine needles before pulling the bottle of salt water that he'd watched her prepare back at the house out of the bag he held in his lap. She used it to sprinkle a circle around the two of them. Coming back to the pine needles, she laid them on top of the saltwater circle.

"Hand me the red candles, please." He dug around until he found two and handed them up to her. She placed one in the north and one in the south. "Now the white." Those were placed in the east and the west. When all four candles were lit, she sat on the ground across from him.

She completed the setup by taking a bowl from the bag and placing it on the ground between them. Into it she poured wine, milk, and honey. The surprise came when she pulled out a small knife and pricked her finger. Three drops of blood went into the bowl.

"I need your hand, Kyle." Hell, no was his first thought, and then he decided he had nothing to lose. If she was tough enough to draw blood for this, so was he.

"Be gentle," he said with a tiny smile.

She was. He hardly felt the prick that drew the blood that dropped into the bowl to join hers. Three drops. No more. No less. "We're ready," she told him and held out both hands to him.

He took her hands and listened as she softly began to speak. "We come on this night and ask that the veil between the worlds turn to mist. We join in spirit with the one who has gone before, as it was in the time of the beginning, so it is now, so shall it be."

The wind whipped up, whirling around them and making the trees sway. Surprisingly, the pine needles that made up the circle around them didn't move at all. Mist began to swirl, cloaking them in a translucent white fog. He found himself gripping Ava's hands even tighter. Pressure pushed against his chest as though it was trying to force the air from his lungs. Whatever this magic was, it was pretty mighty.

"Why am I here?"

The sound of the man's voice shocked Kyle so much he almost bolted out of the circle. He couldn't, though, because Ava still sat across from him, her eyes closed, and her hands holding his in an iron grip. He had no intention of letting go, and as tight as she was holding on, he wasn't so sure he could anyway.

"Clinton?" Didn't the sheriff tell them this guy had been cremated? If so, something was messed up because he was standing just inside the circle very much a man.

"Who are you?" He blinked as if something stung his eyes.

"My name is Kyle Miller."

"I don't know you."

"I'm here to help, Clinton."

Tears filled the man's eyes. "You can't help me. She tore me apart. I remember how it felt to die."

He wanted to tell him it was okay, except it wasn't, and regardless of the dimension he was in, his choice was to not lie. "I'm sorry, and I would change it for you if I could."

"Then why are you here?"

"I need you."

"How?"

"You can help by telling me something that could possibly save someone else. Can you do that? Can you try?"

Clinton brought both hands up and rubbed at his eyes. "I can try. What do you need from me?"

"We can start by you telling me what happened that day."

He closed his eyes and shuddered. Then he opened his eyes and his gaze met Kyle's. "That's the weird part. Nothing unusual happened. I'd decided to go out for a trail run, and I stopped at the grocery store for a sports drink first. I ran into Dana Landen and talked to her for a minute. No big deal, nothing strange until I was getting into my car, and then I noticed a woman I'd never seen before. Still didn't think much of it. Figured she was new to town, and so I waved at her, said hello when she walked by my car. She just nodded."

A stranger, just as they suspected. "Can you tell me more about the woman you said hello to?"

"Nothing much to tell. I only saw her for a minute. Not real tall and okay looking. I did notice one thing. She had a real nice necklace on. It was a ruby, I think. Pretty cool looking."

"Her face?"

"Like I said, she was okay. Wasn't a looker, if you know what I *mean, or I'd have paid a whole lot more attention. I just said hey and went on my way."*

"Tell me about the attack when you were out running."

Clouds passed over his face that was already very white. "I didn't see or hear anything. Whatever it was just hit me like a hurricane in the middle of the back. I went flying, face-first, into the dirt, and then the pain hit. More than taking a face plant into rocky ground. This was pain brought on by teeth that went into my neck. It was like my body was on fire. I've never felt anything like it before." Once more tears filled his eyes. "Everything went wrong and I knew I was dying. I was going to get married, you know."

Kyle could feel Clinton's pain as if it were his own. He couldn't imagine losing Ava, and they weren't engaged. "I'm really sorry, Clinton, I really am. I will do my best to get whoever did this to you. I give you my word."

Clinton tilted his head and appeared to be looking around him. "Hey," he said, and a note of hope crept into his voice. "Is that my grandma?"

Kyle didn't need to turn around. "It is, Clinton. She's been waiting for you so why don't you go on and join her."

And with that, Clinton Bearns was gone.

CHAPTER TWENTY-ONE

Darkness was falling by the time they got back to Jayne's house. The windows were dark, and she wondered where Ava and Kyle had gotten off to. Lily didn't know either, and that seemed to bother her. Did her pretend girlfriend have control issues?

"Can I get you something to drink?"

Lily shook her head and stood on the porch staring out toward the road. "Where did they go?"

"They didn't leave you a message?" What she'd seen since they'd been here was that Kyle and Ava didn't make a move without Lily knowing about it. Approving it, actually. Tiny as she was, Lily was the clear leader. Seemed odd to her now that Kyle and Ava would take off without letting her know what, why, and where.

"My phone never…oh, crap," she muttered as she dug the phone out of her pocket. "I turned the ringer off when we were out at the murder scene this morning and never turned it back on. Damn. Three missed calls and a voice mail." She put the phone to her ear and nodded as she listened to the voice mail.

"Well?" Jayne was pretty confident, from the look on Lily's face, that the message had been from either Kyle or Ava.

Lily kept watching the road in the distance. "Ava wanted to try a spell out where Clinton's body was dumped. She thought if she and Kyle combined their energy they might be able to bring him back so Kyle could talk with him."

That didn't make sense. If she was understanding this necromancy thing right, Kyle needed a body. "He was cremated."

This time Lily turned her head to look at her. "It's magic, Jayne. Many things are possible."

"I don't think that's possible. First, you ask me to believe a guy can talk with a dead body, and now you want me to buy that he can talk with their spirit, no body required." She could only stretch belief so far.

"Normally I would agree with you, because in my experience, necromancers need a body to actually talk to the dead. That said, what Kyle might be able to accomplish with Ava at his side remains to be seen. He's one of a kind and can do things I've never seen another necromancer accomplish."

"It's a pretty big stretch."

"We'll know soon enough because here they come."

Kyle's car was just turning off the county road and onto Jayne's long driveway. Lily hurried down the steps to meet them when the car came to a stop. Before they even got out she asked, "Any luck?"

Kyle put an arm around Ava. "Yes and no. Our witch here has some mad skills, let me tell you. She brought him back and we had quite the conversation. I'm shocked she was able to do it without a body."

So was she, although the details weren't the important thing at the moment. The fact they were able to do it all was amazing and, hopefully, helpful. "Anything we can use?"

This time a cloud crossed over his expression. "Not a lot. It was a pretty routine conversation as far as it goes with necromancy. All he could tell me was that he went to the grocery store, talked to Deputy Sheriff Landen for a minute, and said hello to a stranger. The stranger part was the only thing that felt like it had potential, except he didn't pay much attention to her so couldn't give me much. According to Clinton, she was just a regular-looking woman who happened to be wearing a pretty ruby necklace. It was the only thing that caught his attention about her."

"Damn," Lily muttered as she fingered her own necklace. "I was hoping for more. What did he say about the attack? You did ask him about that, right?"

Kyle looked offended. "Of course I did. I'm not that dense, and this isn't the first time I've done something like this."

"I'm sorry, Kyle. I didn't mean it like that."

He inclined his head slightly and his expression cleared. "Thanks.

He didn't have much about the attack because he said he was hit from behind and fangs sank into his neck. Sounded to me like that wound was quick and fatal. He never saw the wolf or anyone else when he was out in the woods. Sounds like he bled out pretty quick. All he'd wanted to do was go for a trail run."

"At least that's a little more than we had before. He ran into a woman he'd never seen around town, and we can ask around about her." Jayne was already reaching for her cell phone. She was going to put the word out ASAP and find out who the woman was. In a place this size, she'd have an answer inside of an hour.

The four of them walked into the house, and Lily turned to Jayne. "You've probably already figured this one out, but one good way to stay under the radar is to not stand out. Clinton didn't pay much attention to the woman because nothing about her was spectacular. She was a regular person doing a regular chore. Who would suspect danger in the body of a suburban soccer mom?"

Jayne nodded. More and more the two of them seemed to be thinking along the same lines. "That's why I'm putting out the word. Trust me, Lily, there are people here who keep track of everything and everyone. They see it as their busybody duty to monitor the activities and the residents of their town. They know every car, every face, everything. Somebody is sure to know who this woman is and where she's staying."

"Unless," Kyle interjected, "she just happened to be passing through and all she did was stop at the grocery store for snacks."

Kyle was right. There was that possibility. Someone on their way to Canada could very easily have passed through town and made a quick stop. The tiny lead they were jumping on might turn out to be nothing. It was, however, all they had at the moment.

Lily started up toward the stairs and her room. "I need some time," she said as she ascended without looking back.

Jayne followed, taking the stairs two at a time. "Are you all right?" Something seemed off all of a sudden, and she wasn't sure what caused the shift.

At the door to her bedroom, Lily turned. "I'll be fine. I need to prepare myself."

"What do you need? How can I help?" She felt like she should be doing something.

"Nothing." She turned to close the door and paused. "No, wait, I could use a bite to eat. Protein, if you've got it."

"I do. Give me fifteen minutes." She hurried downstairs and threw a steak on the grill. Going with a hunch she went for rare. A couple of slices of garlic toast and a glass of wine. She was back at Lily's door in the allotted fifteen minutes.

Lily opened the door when she knocked, and Jayne managed to catch the gasp before it passed her lips. Lily was dressed only in a flowing purple robe belted at the waist. Her dark hair tumbled down around her shoulders, and her dark eyes were intense. In short, she was breathtaking.

"This is wonderful." Lily took the plate from Jayne. She didn't take the wine.

Jayne stood and, in her opinion, dumbly watched as Lily made short work of the steak and toast. Finally she found her voice. "Do you want the wine?"

Shaking her head, Lily wiped her mouth with the napkin Jayne had placed on the tray. "It's not that I dislike wine. On the contrary, I appreciate a good one. It's just that I've found alcohol slows me down."

That made sense when she thought about it. Setting the glass of wine on the dresser, Jayne moved farther into the room. It was interesting being here with Lily barely dressed. Intimate. She liked it.

"What else can I do for you?" Helplessness wasn't a welcome emotion. She was accustomed to being in charge and knowing what to do in any situation. Of course, in the academy there were no classes on how to deal with preternatural hunters who changed into werewolves. No, not a single class. She was going to have to wing this one.

The clatter of silverware on the plate brought her head up. Her eyes met Lily's. "It's time," Lily said quietly. She set the tray on the bed and stood.

Outside the window, darkness had fallen. It was, indeed, time. "Do you want me to stay up here?"

Lily bit her lip and studied Jayne intently. She couldn't tell what was going on behind the blue eyes. "Do you really want to see?"

She did and she didn't. Jayne was incredibly drawn to this petite beauty despite resenting her presence so very recently. It was amazing what a few hours could do to a pissy attitude. She couldn't help but wonder if the pleasant warmth brought on by that attraction might fade if she witnessed her change from human to canine. "Yes," she finally admitted. "I do." And she meant it.

Lily gave her a single nod. "I need somebody to hold my robe."

"It would be my pleasure." It wasn't a lie. She'd hold her robe any day of the week, even if she wasn't about to change into a wolf.

Together they walked downstairs and out the back door. The last of the daylight had fled since she'd brought the food up to Lily, and now moonlight brightened the backyard and the fields that bordered the fringe of pine trees and the river beyond. The air was clear and cold, the breeze light. She shivered and crossed her arms. No taking off clothing for her. Putting another layer on was more likely.

Lily stood on the bottom step with her head tipped back. She breathed in deeply and slowly blew out the breath. For probably a full minute neither of them said a word. Jayne didn't want to disturb whatever ritual Lily was performing. The calm was over the moment Lily stripped off the robe and handed it to Jayne. She was gorgeous but, she reminded herself, for how long?

At first Lily moaned low in her throat, and as the moments passed, her moan turned into cries. Her body twisted, and it appeared to Jayne she was in severe pain. It was all she could do not to go to her and tell her to stop, that it wasn't worth the agony. Before she could say anything, Lily dropped to the ground and, like something out of a special-effects lab, ceased to be human. Instead, a wolf, lean and gorgeous, rose from the ground. Its great head came up and sniffed the air. In the blink of an eye, it was off and running into the night.

Stunned by what she'd just witnessed, Jayne stood motionless and stared. Damned if that wasn't the coolest thing she'd ever seen.

❖

Bellona's paws hit the cold ground hard, and a surge of energy roared through her entire body on contact. Behind her Little Wolf, Adam, and Eve raced, growling and rolling, their joy clear. Her wolf gloried in the beauty of the pack, relishing what had been denied to her for so many years. There was nothing that compared to running as one. Her kind was never meant to exist in the solitude forced upon her century after century.

The moon continued to rise overhead, spilling golden light on their playfield. She ran to the river and dipped her head low, savoring the sweet taste of the icy water on her tongue. Eve splashed into the shallows next to her, and she growled as she grabbed the scruff of her neck and hauled her back out of the water. Eve yipped and then dropped and rolled. Nothing, not even the reprimand of the alpha, could dampen the young wolf's enthusiasm. Eve was a joy to behold.

She turned and swept her gaze over the nearby hills and the thick trees that would afford them cover. It was only then she realized Little Wolf was gone. Again. Bellona raised her head and howled. Adam and Eve raced to her side, her call bringing them in as it should Little Wolf. Eve nuzzled her face, the worry bringing her close.

Her howl did not bring Little Wolf back. Once more she lifted her head and roared. When it had the same result, she began to run. Her paws barely touched the earth as she raced between trees, over fallen logs, and up and up until she stood on the ridge looking down upon the valley below. Adam and Eve, panting and happy, waited behind her.

Her howl from high above did not bring a different result. Little Wolf was once again running rogue. It was not pack protocol. Discipline would be forthcoming. She could not allow disobedience or chaos would result. Every pack had rules.

Likewise, obedience should be rewarded, and thus Bellona would not take away the adventure from her more compliant pack members. Adam and Eve were, as they should be, waiting for her lead. She would not disappoint them. They had earned this night, and they would have it.

She kicked with her back feet, gave a little yip, and then began to run swiftly along the ridge. Adam howled and took off running so fast he passed her, his tail straight out behind him. Eve yipped again and again, signaling what Bellona understood to be her sign that she was happy.

The cool air was refreshing, the scents of the woods as intoxicating as alcohol. The wolf in her gloried in this night and all it had to offer. Simply to run together with her new family filled her with excitement and joy, despite her unhappiness with Little Wolf for so blatantly disobeying. But she refused to allow that to taint such a glorious run. For hours, the three of them ran, jumping and rolling, and letting the night fill their hearts.

Later, Bellona stood on the back porch wrapped in a thick, warm robe. Adam and Eve, both exhausted and happy, were in their rooms asleep. The night's run had been long and energetic and exactly what they all needed. She'd hoped that somewhere along the line Little Wolf would have joined them. It didn't happen, and Little Wolf still hadn't shown up.

A flicker of movement near the barn made her groan. God, this woman was going to be the death of her. While she loved her energy and her spirit, she hadn't been joking around when she told them earlier to lay low. The Jägers were nothing to take lightly. They were dangerous and their methods deadly. They could not afford to draw attention to themselves.

She walked down the back steps and across the yard to the door of the barn. A light was on inside, and she could hear a low moan. Damn it, she'd done it again despite everything she'd dictated. "Little Wolf," she barked as she swung the door open and walked inside.

Little Wolf was sitting on a pile of straw. A woman was stretched out on the ground with her head in Little Wolf's lap. She was stroking her head and almost cooing. "It's going to be fun, my pretty one. You will be one of us soon."

"What the hell have you done?" Bellona snapped. Rage had her almost seeing red.

Little Wolf looked up and smiled. "She's so pretty. What could I do? She had to be part of the family. Look at her hair. Have you ever seen such a beautiful color?"

"Sweet Lord, did you not hear a word I said tonight?"

Shrugging, Little Wolf didn't even bother to look sheepish. "Yeah, well, I figured that speech was for Adam and Eve."

"It was for all of you."

"Hey, this is my place after all. I should be able to do what I want."

With her hands on her hips, Bellona shook her head. "It's for all of us. This kind of attention will get us killed if we're not careful."

This time Little Wolf did have the good grace to look chastised. "Sorry. I just can't help it sometimes. I get so happy, and well, I want to share this excitement. You know what I mean?"

Unfortunately she did. There was a time when she was Little Wolf, and only by the grace of a good teacher had she survived. She was trying to do the same thing for her now, only this student wasn't paying much attention to the lesson.

She kneeled down next to Little Wolf and her newest recruit. The woman's hair was a most amazing shade of strawberry blond, and she was drawn in to run a hand over the silky strands. "This has to be the last one until we can get rid of the Jägers."

"Okay." Little Wolf stroked the woman's cheek.

"I mean it."

Little Wolf looked up, smiled, and leaned in to kiss Bellona. "I'll be good. I promise."

Bellona kissed her back. "I'll hold you to that." Or, she didn't add, I'll have to kill you.

CHAPTER TWENTY-TWO

Lily often forgot how freeing it was to be the wolf. Her feet carried her across the ground as though she were running on air. It was unlike anything in the world and impossible to describe to those whose existence was completely human.

Now she searched the air and the ground for a hint of the missing woman. She'd gathered Willa's scent from her apartment and knew she would be able to catch it if it was there to be found. First she had to make her way closer to the apartment so that she had a starting point. Under the cover of darkness she benefited from a certain amount of safety. Still, it paid to be cautious so she only went as near as necessary. She didn't have to go all the way into town, just close enough to pick up Willa's scent, which she did quite quickly.

It was all around her on the outskirts of town, and that meant this was Willa's safe zone. She was comfortable in the area and moved around freely. What she had to do now was work out from the concentrated area to try to find the trail that would hopefully lead them to the killer.

Cars went down the street, and each time, she ducked behind shrubs and trees. It was frustrating and the wolf wanted to howl. She didn't dare. Too dangerous. Finally, she worked her way to the grocery store at the edge of town, where she still had the scent, though it was growing weaker as she moved. Even as it weakened, she still had it and knew that all she had to do was keep it in her nose and she'd have the wolf who took Willa.

Except it didn't work out that way. All of a sudden at the edge of the store's parking lot, the scent disappeared. One moment it was there and the next gone, as if she'd never been there at all. This time she couldn't help it. Her howl was deep though short. Even the wolf knew why: Willa had gotten into a vehicle. She cut off the howl before it drew too much attention and raced away into the darkness. She could do no more here and so she ran instead.

Over the deepening hours of the night she ran through the woods, up the hills, and around the houses that dotted the countryside. Dogs barked, cattle stomped nervously at the ground, and horses whinnied as she passed. Hopefully somewhere she would once again pick up Willa's scent. As time passed and the miles beneath her paws increased, she grew more frustrated. She picked up nothing. It was as if Willa had vanished. Finally, she made her way back to the big house where lights still shone out the windows.

For a moment she sat and panted, unwilling to shift back to her human form. It felt good to be the wolf. It felt natural, as though this was how she should always be. The draw was intoxicating and hard to resist.

But resist she did. As much as she relished these times and as much as the wolf spoke to her spirit, her soul was that of a woman and a warrior. Her job was to save those who couldn't save themselves, and that meant embracing the part of her that was human. Taking one long, last draw of the night air, she closed her eyes and let the change take over. Soon, she came up from her crouch and stood once more on two feet. Cold air washed over her skin, bringing goose bumps up on her arms and legs. The air felt good because it made her feel alive and human.

She was back.

And she knew precisely nothing.

Jayne came racing out the back door, Lily's robe in her hands. When she got to Lily, she reached both arms around her to wrap her in the warmth of the robe. Their bodies were close, Jayne's head next to hers. Instead of pulling away, Jayne drew even closer, her breath warm on Lily's cheek. Slowly, their lips met, the kiss soft and gentle.

But not for long. Lily wrapped her arms around Jayne as the robe fell to the ground. Her kiss was hot, her body even hotter.

"What did you find?" Jayne whispered against her lips. She didn't move away.

Lily sighed. As wonderful as she felt right at this moment, she wished she had something positive to share with Jayne. "I lost her trail near the edge of town. The edge of the grocery store parking lot, to be more precise."

This time it was Jayne who sighed. She kissed her again quickly on the lips and then leaned down to grab the forgotten robe. She wrapped it around Lily and then put her arm across her shoulders as they walked back toward the house. "Near the road?"

"Yes. I'm afraid so."

"She got into a car."

"That's what I'm thinking."

Inside the house, Lily ran quickly upstairs and slipped into jeans and a sweatshirt. She could say one thing about the twenty-first century, the clothes sure were more comfortable than what she'd grown up in. She'd take jeans any day over a heavy brocade gown. Back in the kitchen, Jayne waited, a bottle of wine in the middle of the table. "You want a glass of this or shall I make you some tea?"

It was, as she often heard people say, a no-brainer. "Wine, please. Now that the shift is complete, it won't interfere with anything." Besides, she could use a little numbing effect. Losing Willa's scent and not picking up anything important was a heavy burden on her heart. She was one of the best or, if she listened to Senn, the best, yet she had nothing to help bring the girl back home. That was unacceptable.

"Now you're talking." Jayne poured a generous amount into a glass and handed it to Lily.

The first sip sent a flood of warmth through her system. Not quite as pleasing as what she'd felt when Jayne wrapped her arms around her but not too bad either. After a second sip, she looked up at Jayne. "We'll find her."

A shadow flitted over Jayne's face and was gone as soon as it appeared. "We will."

Jayne's voice lacked confidence, and Lily had an urge to buoy her. Usually she worried very little about what law enforcement felt. She always came in with the intention of doing her job and leaving the area safer than when they arrived. She still wanted to leave Colville safe from the ravages of a preternatural creature who threatened the lives of those who called it home, but the way she felt about law enforcement was different. Or more specifically, how she felt about one particular law-enforcement officer.

Something about Jayne pulled at her. Yes, she excited Lily in a very primal way, and if that's all it was, she'd jump her bones and call it good. Except that wasn't it. Whatever she was feeling toward this woman went much deeper and, in a way she didn't understand, was far more exciting than simple lust. This was just about the last thing she'd expected when she drove into this pretty town. No, that wasn't right. It was very much the last thing she'd expected.

Lily looked down at the glass full of ruby wine and turned it in her hands for a moment. When she looked up, she met Jayne's eyes. "I promise you, one way or the other, we will bring Willa home. I hope we will bring her home safely, but in any event we will bring her back."

Jayne's gaze stayed on her face for a long time before she nodded. "Yes, I believe you will."

"You can take it to the bank."

That brought a smile to Jayne's face. "Somehow that just sounds funny coming from you."

"I've been around a while and have picked up every cliché ever uttered. I can rattle them all off for you, if you'd like."

Jayne held up a hand. "Not necessary. In my line of work you pretty well hear them all, along with every excuse under the sun for criminal behavior."

Lily smiled thinking about Jayne listening to criminal after criminal recite a story too fantastic to be true and yet expecting her to believe them. "Of that I have no doubt whatsoever. Hey." She paused and looked around. "What happened to Ava and Kyle?"

❖

Kyle was sprawled on his bed wearing nothing but boxer shorts featuring a popular superhero. He couldn't sleep. It bugged the crap out of him that he hadn't been able to draw out more information from Clinton. The fact that Ava was able to create a spell that let him call Clinton from beyond the grave, beyond the flames, was incredible. Until he'd seen it with his own eyes, he'd not even known it was possible.

That wasn't saying much. His experience with witches was pretty slim. Ava was the only one he'd spent any time with at all and certainly the only one he'd witnessed practicing her craft. It was all so fascinating and helpful. The protections she could weave were so powerful, no one could penetrate them. Today, she had ripped back the veil between the living and the dead, effectively supplementing his powers to a degree he didn't even realize was possible.

As if he wasn't already loving everything about Ava, she kept amazing him until he could hardly concentrate on what he was here to do. He felt like he was spinning his wheels and should be making more ground toward finding the killer. What good was he if he couldn't get any helpful information from those he brought back? He had to figure a way to pull his weight.

Maybe he should put on some pants and go downstairs. A few minutes ago he'd heard Lily come in, and it was possible she might have learned something during her run. Actually, it was more than possible; it was likely she'd discovered some piece of helpful information that would lead them to those who were missing and the werewolf causing the problems.

He didn't move. Instead, Kyle continued to lie on his back and watch the shadows as they danced across the ceiling to a silent symphony. The performance was soothing and captured his imagination. He figured if he relaxed something might come to him. So that's what he did.

When the door to his room opened, he vaulted from the bed, all traces of the hard-won relaxation gone. Shock smacked him as Ava slipped inside and shut the door behind her. Without a word, she walked over to him and sat down on the edge of his bed. He sank back onto the bed next to her and, with her hip, she nudged him. "Move over."

His voice still seemed to be down somewhere he couldn't reach. "Okay," he squeaked as he shifted on the bed. She stretched out next to him and pulled him down with her. As he lay back, she put her head on his shoulder and an arm across his bare stomach. He managed not to gasp, though he was so tense he was surprised she didn't say anything. He was so not cool.

"I couldn't sleep," she said with a sigh.

"I'm having the same problem." He didn't add that her snuggled up tight against him wasn't helping to solve the problem either. Now he was more wide awake than he'd been five minutes ago, and that was saying a great deal.

Ava let out a long, slow breath. "I feel like I should be doing more."

Man, oh, man did he understand. He'd been feeling the same way since they got here. "Oh yeah, I feel ya on that one. I just can't figure out what else to do. My powers are limited and it's frustrating."

"I know exactly what you're saying. I wish I had a fraction of the knowledge and power my grandmother did. I think then I could do so much more. I'm such a novice, I don't know why they sent me in."

Novice? He didn't think so, and he was incredibly glad they'd put her on his team. "Should we go see what Lily found out during her run?" *Please say no.*

Against his shoulder she shook her head. Her silky hair against his bare skin was almost more than he could stand. "No. I think she and Jayne need some time together."

That made him smile. "You still believe they're going to fall in love."

She patted her hand over his heart. "I don't think, I know."

"But they just met." He'd been watching them, and yeah, he could definitely pick up on the attraction. There was a distinct vibe between the two. All in all it appeared pretty normal to him. No big love-at-first-sight thing. Obviously Ava was seeing more than he was.

"Love doesn't have time limits, you know. Or any hard and fast rules. It is what it is, and it does what it does in its own time."

She had no way of knowing that he did get that all right. He'd been in love with Ava since day flipping one. Not a single thing had changed during the time they were apart, and in truth his feelings had only grown deeper since he'd picked her up at SeaTac. He was good old-fashioned crazy about Ava. "I'll trust you on that one. What do you think we should do? Go downstairs? Try another spell together?"

"I'd like to stay right here, if you don't mind." She snuggled in even closer.

He definitely didn't mind. "Not at all." It would take an earthquake—a big earthquake—to move him away from her.

"You make me feel safe."

"You make me feel great."

Her arm tightened. "I like that." She yawned. "I think I might be able to sleep now."

Kyle reached over and grabbed the spread that earlier he'd kicked off to the side. He pulled it up around them both. This was heaven. "Sleep would be nice." Not that it would come any easier for him with her, warm and fantastic, pressed against his side. He'd like to do other things besides sleep. He kissed the top of her head.

She was already asleep.

CHAPTER TWENTY-THREE

Jayne's heart was racing, and it was easy enough to blame it on the wine. If she was in denial, that is, and she wasn't. Watching Lily change earlier, seeing her come back, striding across her lawn naked and gorgeous, put her over the top. She had come into this uneasy partnership a grumpy nonbeliever. Any lingering doubts she might have had evaporated a little while ago.

She was on board with Lily and her team one hundred percent. To say it was all because of what she'd seen them do would be a lie. At least part of it was attributable to the reality that she was attracted to this woman in a way she couldn't remember ever feeling before. She'd been single a long time and had never even come close to making a lifetime commitment. Oh, her heart had been broken a time or two, but in hindsight, she could blame herself for those disappointments. Marriage had not been an option until recently, and she'd been okay with that. Her relationships had never even reached a point where that might be a discussion, and it gave her an easy out. She liked easy.

Suddenly she found herself entertaining all manner of foreign thoughts. Words like "forever," "marriage," and even "love" were floating through her mind. Unwelcome thoughts, if she was being honest. This was the absolute worst time to be thinking about a relationship of any kind. She had deaths, missing people, and, especially, Willa to worry about. Her love life was way down on that priority list.

Rationalizing any of this made not a damn bit of difference. She felt what she felt. Damn it anyway. She told herself that kiss out in the yard was going to have to be enough. Yes, it was enough. She pushed all the troubling thoughts out of her head and kept her expression neutral as she talked to Lily.

When Lily had asked about Ava and Kyle, she'd told her they'd retired about an hour ago. Actually, she was a little surprised neither of them came down when Lily got back. It was possible they were sound asleep. The strain was beginning to wear on all of them. She certainly didn't blame Kyle or Ava for trying for sleep when they could.

"What next?" God, she hoped Lily had something.

Lily ran her hands through her hair. Long, dark strands fell around her face. It was the first time Jayne had noticed how tired she looked. "I think we're done for tonight. A bit of rest would do all of us good."

A part of her wanted to protest and suggest they search tonight or, as an alternative, stay right here. She didn't want her time with Lily to end. But the practical side of her knew they both had to get some sleep. Exhaustion wouldn't help anyone.

As much as she wanted to argue against it, she capitulated. "Good idea. Let's get some sleep and hit this hard in the morning. I want to track this son of a bitch down fast. I want to find Willa. No, damn it, I need to find Willa."

She picked up the wineglasses and took them to the sink. With the cork pushed back into the top of the bottle, she set the wine on the counter. Nothing else to do here. She followed Lily in that gorgeous robe up the stairs. At Lily's door she wasn't sure exactly what to do. Walk away? Kiss her good night? What?

Lily took the decision out of her hands when she pushed up on her toes and kissed Jayne lightly on the lips. "Thank you," she said against her lips. Then she turned and went into her room.

Jayne stood there for a moment, letting the warmth of the kiss roll through her. *Wow* was all she could think. Things weren't exactly progressing in the way she'd imagined. Of course nothing in her world right now was as she believed it would be when she came back here, beginning with living in this house.

This was her brother's home. He'd built it with loving hands, intending to spend his life here. Instead, he was gone and she was rattling around pretending she didn't mind being alone. In those moments, those rare moments, when she let herself dwell on truths, she knew she was living a coward's life. Some might argue that logic, given her chosen profession. They'd be wrong. It wasn't hard to put her life on the line for others. It somehow felt right and the thing she was destined to do. Where it fell apart was when it came down to her personal life. She holed herself up in this monster house and kept herself nice and secure. If she didn't get close to anyone she didn't have to worry about losing them or getting her heart broken. It was so very safe.

It was so very lonely.

Actually it had been working pretty darn good for her until this team showed up. Kyle and Ava were young and kind and dedicated. She could sense that each of them possessed the heart of a warrior while still holding on to compassion. It was admirable. She was beginning to like them a lot.

And then there was Lily. This tiny little woman was incredibly strong and complicated. She was smart and intuitive, and everything about her appealed to something deep inside Jayne. Something that had been missing in her life for a very long time.

The typical Jayne side of her wanted to keep all of this on a strictly professional level. Danger lurked right outside the door, and as the sheriff it was her job to eliminate that danger and keep her people safe. There was no room for her to give in to desires of the heart. It would be distracting.

Except, she thought as she placed the palm of her hand on Lily's closed door, when their lips touched. How in the world could she stay focused and neutral when all she wanted to do was throw off her clothes and make love to Lily? A very good question that would most likely require the services of a very good psychologist.

Taking her hand away from the door, she moved down the hallway to her own room. Inside, she paced for a few minutes before deciding to take a shower. Perhaps the warm water would relax her muscles and calm her racing thoughts. It wasn't an idle comment when she said they could all use some rest. She was quite serious. The more rested they were, the better equipped they were to deal with the craziness that was defining the situation in Colville at the moment. She intended to get this thing done and over with tomorrow. She would figure out what was going on, and she would stop it. She would bring Willa back to her cheerful little apartment.

The shower felt wonderful, and Jayne was pretty sure it was the secret to helping her sleep. In a T-shirt and a pair of boxer-style shorts she was rubbing a towel over her wet hair when she walked out of the bathroom and back into her bedroom. Glancing over her shoulder and back into the bathroom, she lobbed the towel in the direction of the laundry basket with one hand. As the wet towel hit the intended target, she smiled. "That was a three-point shot," she declared.

"Three points?"

At the sound of Lily's voice, Jayne spun around. Stretched out on her side in Jayne's bed with her head propped on one hand, dark hair cascading like a waterfall onto the pale linen, Lily smiled. That alone was a big shock. Her heart almost stopped when she realized Lily was naked.

❖

Bellona was frustrated. First, because once again Little Wolf had openly defied her. It was hard because she truly cared about her and didn't want things to have to change. But if Little Wolf didn't stop, they were all going to be in trouble. She could only clean up so much. Once more, she would forgive her, though this time, her pet had to go.

Trying to spin a positive out of the situation, Bellona realized she could use the woman as the bait. She had to draw the Jägers out of Colville and get them focused on a different area. This woman could be the ticket. Currently, she was in the back of the SUV as Bellona drove south. She was going to take her closer to the city to make it appear as though they were on the move. That should redirect the Jägers. If it didn't, she'd have to resort to Plan B, and it had been a long time since she'd had to take that path. The last Jägers hunter she'd killed had been over a century ago. They didn't take it well when one of their own bit it, so it was always best to avoid that course if at all possible.

The other problem wasn't as much a problem as a sadness. She'd lost her ruby necklace somewhere, and she had no idea where. It wasn't that the necklace was terribly valuable in monetary terms. The value lay in sentiment. She'd had it a very long time, and it reminded her of her childhood. Or at least the part of her childhood that had been filled with happy memories.

To lose it now after all these years was a cruel joke, one that she, of course, had played on herself. She couldn't blame anyone else because it was her responsibility. The necklace was never out of her possession, except when she was in wolf form, and even then, she was careful about her things. She made sure her clothing and possessions were tidy and, when she shifted back, right where she left them.

In this instance all she could figure was that the clasp had broken, and it had fallen somewhere during her travels. She'd covered a lot of ground today, and even if she spent tomorrow retracing her every single step, realistically she had little hope of finding it. The more likely reality was that the final piece of her past was gone forever.

Driving down the highway lit only by the moon that tomorrow would be full, she tried to blink away the tears that filled her eyes. It was stupid to be so sentimental about a piece of jewelry. For that matter, if she really wanted, it would be an easy matter to have it recreated. Plenty of jewelers would be able to make it for her even better than the original. With the back of her hand she wiped away the single tear that escaped to roll down her cheek. She knew she'd never do it because it wouldn't be the same. It was as if the gods were sending her a message: let go of the past.

This time of night there was virtually no traffic on the highway this far north. The two-lane highway was mostly flat and straight, with just a few changes in elevation between Colville and Spokane. In many places the trees grew so thick on either side of the road it was a little like being in a tunnel. Or thrown back in time a few hundred years, before cities and towns wiped away the forests. She liked it because it reminded her of a time when she and her family and friends would travel by carriage surrounded only by forest and wildlife. Here, too, wildlife was something to watch for. Deer, elk, and moose were common sights and another reason she didn't prey on humans. There was no need.

In the distance was the glow of red light that grew larger as she drove. When she got close enough she could see it was another car pulled off onto the shoulder with its emergency lights blinking. Her first instinct was to swerve left in order to give it a wide berth, and then another, more intriguing thought crossed her mind. If she was trying to create a path leading the Jägers away, one body was good...two were even better. Bellona put on her blinker and pulled the SUV to the side of the road. Honestly, it was like the universe was simply handing her the tools to solve her problem.

Opening the driver's side door, she got out. Instead of heading straight to the disabled car, the head of its occupant clearly visible in the glow of her headlights, she walked around to the back of her SUV. She popped the hatch open and quickly removed her clothes. Not bothering to fold them, she tossed them into the back. She didn't plan to be gone long enough for them to even get wrinkled. Not that it mattered. Who exactly was going to see her on this trip? Well, anyone who would live to tell about it anyway.

So far the driver of the car was being cautious and staying inside. That was good. Smart, really. With a smile she leaned around the back of her SUV and waved. "Hello," she called out. "Do you need any tools? Water or snacks?" Isn't that what a Good Samaritan would ask?

The driver's side door of the disabled vehicle started to open. One leg came out and then another. A man stood next to the car. Perfect. With her head tipped to the buttery glow of the moon, Bellona called the change.

CHAPTER TWENTY-FOUR

What she was doing was crazy and completely out of character for her. Didn't matter. Lily had felt the draw to this woman in every fiber of her being. Never in all her years had she experienced such all-consuming desire. This was neither the time nor the place to give in to passion, and yet while she'd been in her own room, alone, she'd decided why the hell not?

Frankly, she was tired of always doing the right thing. She'd been the face of the Jägers for centuries. Going where Senn directed her, cooperating with people who hated her, pretending to be something she wasn't, and worst of all, always living with a secret she couldn't share. Until now, that is. For the first time she'd met someone she trusted instinctively. She had no real basis for that trust, but she knew it was real. When a person lived and walked this earth as long as she had, they knew real when they felt it.

So, why pretend she and Jayne were colleagues working together on a case and nothing more? It was a lie and she knew it, as, she suspected, did Jayne. When she'd shifted in front of Jayne, she'd harbored a bit of worry that she would be repulsed. That worry was put to rest once she'd walked naked back into the yard. It was surprising and delightful to have Jayne come to her with the robe.

It was even more delightful to feel her arms around her body and her lips pressing against Lily's. The sensation was like being wrapped in one of the bearskin blankets of her youth. For lack of a better description, she'd melted into the kiss. Once they'd gone inside, they'd made an admirable effort to pretend things were the way they'd been before. At least where she was concerned, it wasn't very successful. Nothing was the way it had been before that kiss.

That's why she'd made her way across the hall and into Jayne's room. When no one had answered her soft knock, she'd let herself in. Realizing Jayne was in the shower, Lily had decided to go for it. Her nightshift was on the ground, and she was, as Senn liked to say, commando under the covers. Instead of feeling uncomfortable or nervous, she was feeling a bone-tingling excitement. Especially when Jayne walked out of that bathroom rubbing a towel across her hair. That T-shirt and boy-shorts were a damned sexy combination on her.

"Lily?" The word came out of Jayne's mouth like a strangled cry.

Lily smiled and patted the bed next to her. "Pretending isn't my style."

"I...I..."

Lily sat up and let the sheet drop away. Cool air kissed her bare breasts, making her nipples pucker. "Tell me you're not interested, and I'll trot right back across the hall."

"I'm, ah, interested." She still didn't move from her spot near the bathroom door.

Lily smiled and winked. "Yes, I was pretty sure you were. Come on, Jayne. Like I said, pretending isn't my style. I want you and you want me. Maybe if we give our mutual desire an outlet, our rational sides might be a little clearer in the morning. What do you say? Up for that kind of experiment?"

For a long moment she thought Jayne was going to turn her down, and then a slow smile crossed her lips. She grabbed the hem of her shirt and pulled it up and over her head. She kicked off her shorts as she walked toward the bed. "You're full of surprises."

"I try." She leaned in and kissed Jayne, pushing her tongue between her lips and past her teeth. She tasted like peppermint. Jayne returned her kiss.

Lily ran her hands over Jayne's shoulders and down her arms. She was well muscled, but her skin was smooth and soft. When her hand moved to her breast, Jayne sighed against her lips. Her breasts were not large but were firm, and as she teased her nipples, they beaded against her touch.

"Where have you been all my life," Jayne whispered against her lips.

"Just waiting for you, I think."

Jayne dropped back against the pillow, and Lily lowered her head until she could take one of the hard nipples into her mouth. She sucked it, making it even harder. Jayne's hands pushed into her hair, holding it tight as her body arched into the touch of her mouth. She smelled so sweet and clean, her scent filling Lily with a rush of hot desire.

Lily slid her hand down her flat stomach and between her legs. She was warm and wet, and there was no denying her desire. Jayne's hands on her head pressed her closer, and she happily obliged by pushing her tongue inside. Good God, she tasted exquisite, and Lily felt as though she were truly alive for the first time ever. Making love to this woman made her heart sing.

Jayne moved beneath her touch, her moans low and quiet as she was aware of Kyle and Ava down the hall. Lily didn't care. All she did care about was the feel and taste of this gorgeous woman. Using her tongue to tease her clit, at the same time she slid two fingers inside, moving them in and out. Jayne's breathing became ragged, and all of a sudden her body arched as she came, convulsing over and over against her fingers.

Lily moved up until she could once more kiss Jayne. "Not bad for a small-town sheriff," she said with a smile against her lips.

"Oh, sister, I'll show you small town." And she flipped Lily over on her back and proceeded to make good on her threat.

❖

Kyle slowly came to wakefulness, warmth flowing over him that tried to drag him back into sleep. Everything felt wonderful. His arms were still around Ava as she slept with her head on his chest, and he was incredibly relaxed. He could easily get used to this. It was the best way in the world to wake up.

Only something was off in his bubble of bliss. At first he couldn't figure out what it was. Drowsiness kept him from connecting the dots. When he finally did, his heart hammered. Carefully, he slid away from Ava. She made a sound and turned away, her head finding the pillow. She didn't wake, and for that he was grateful.

Swinging his legs over the bed, he stared at the woman standing near the window. In the moonlight that came through she was nearly transparent. She was also clearly dead.

"What do you want?" he whispered. His heart was still pounding, and it seemed so loud to him he wondered why it didn't wake Ava. Not once since his gift had manifested had the dead come to him unbidden. Always, he was the one who went looking for them. He could call them at will, and his skill had helped many along the way. The comfort level he'd attained through years of coming to understand his gift was solid. Until a minute ago. Now, everything he believed he knew went up in flames.

It was her voice that had drawn him out of the comfortable sleep he was enjoying as he stretched out next to Ava. It was this woman who shattered his world. He wished he could close his eyes and pretend this wasn't happening. Unfortunately, he wasn't the kind of guy who could do that. He was Jägers for more reasons than just because he could raise the dead.

"Help me," she whispered. "I'm so cold, and I don't like it out here."

"Where are you?" The fact that she was a shadowy figure wasn't the whole reason he knew she was dead. The wounds that colored her neck crimson were a pretty good indicator too.

She turned her head back and forth as if she was looking around. "I don't know. Next to a car on the side of the highway, I think. She hurt me and then I was here. It's all mixed up in my head."

The side of the highway didn't give him much to go on. Highway 2 stretched all the way to Canada in one direction and into Spokane on the other. Lots of miles in between for cars to pull off. "Can you see mountains?" He'd noticed that the closer they got to Colville, the more he could see the mountains to the north.

She shook her head. "Lots of trees and the sky. It's dark. Really, really dark. That's all. Please help me. I'm very cold."

That actually gave him an idea. If all she could see was trees, then most likely she was somewhere along the highway headed south toward Spokane. At least he hoped his hunch was right. It was the best he could come up with at the moment.

"I'll come for you."

"You promise?"

"Yes, I promise. Do you know who hurt you?"

Again she shook her head. "It was a wolf who hurt me, and I thought the woman who picked me up was going to help me, but she didn't. Why would someone do this to me? I don't want to die."

He didn't have the heart to tell her she was already dead. It happened that way sometimes. He would call them back from the world beyond, and they wouldn't know they'd already lost their life. It always made him feel bad, though he also tried to guide them toward the light that was usually waiting for them. A couple of times there had only been darkness, and those were the people that made his heart turn to ice. He helped them make that journey too.

"What's your name?"

"What?" Ava stirred behind him and came up to a sitting position. "Who are you talking to?"

He turned his head to look at her, nodding in the direction of the lost soul who'd come to him here in the bedroom of Jayne's beautiful home.

"Who?" The confusion in her voice made him turn his head back toward the window. The woman was gone.

CHAPTER TWENTY-FIVE

Jayne decided this was probably her best decision ever. As a general rule she wasn't a hook-up kind of woman. Too many unknowns, and that wasn't something she was ever comfortable with. Before she went to bed with anyone she wanted to know them, and more importantly, she wanted to like them. Love wasn't a precursor but like was.

With Lily everything went right out the window. The woman made her feel things so deeply it was frightening if she thought about it too much, so she didn't. *Don't think. Don't worry. Just feel.*

And goodness, did she feel fantastic. She'd even managed some sleep. As she stretched, her body ached in all the right places. It had been so long since she'd done this, she'd forgotten what it felt like. Only she couldn't recall it ever feeling quite like this. If not for what awaited her outside the bedroom door, she could stay here for hours. Soon enough, she'd have to leave this cocoon of warmth and satisfaction to face the real world.

A knock on the bedroom door made that reality hit sooner rather than later. "Jayne." It was Kyle, his voice urgent. "Jayne, we need you."

Lily rolled out of the bed with a motion that was smooth and natural. This obviously wasn't the first time she'd been awakened out of a deep sleep. She was fully dressed before Jayne got her shirt on. Well, if you considered that robe fully dressed.

"I can take care of this," she whispered to Lily. "He doesn't have to know you're here."

Lily actually smiled. "I'm a big girl, Jayne, and while I appreciate the sentiment, protecting my reputation isn't necessary."

Even though her words were admirable, Jayne still didn't want to wing open the door and expose their tryst. Not that she was ashamed. On the contrary, she had an uncharacteristic urge to shout out. "I agree, but it might be better to keep this between you and me."

Lily came over as Jayne pushed her arms through the sleeves of her T-shirt, pushed up on her toes, and kissed her on the lips. It wasn't the passion from before. Instead it was kind and tender. "It's all right. We're together on this. All of us." She turned and walked to the door.

"Hey, Lily." Not a trace of surprise sounded in Kyle's voice.

"What's up?" She was all business.

Kyle might not be surprised, but Jayne sure as hell was, by everything, especially by what had happened with Lily and now the unremarkable greeting as if Lily answering a knock on her bedroom door was nothing out of the norm. Did Lily do this so often it didn't faze her team? The thought sent chills through her. As if sensing her thoughts, Lily turned and caught her gaze.

"No, I don't," she whispered so softly that only Jayne heard her.

"I…" Jayne felt a flush in her cheeks.

Lily winked and turned back to Kyle. "Is there a problem?"

Kyle looked at Jayne. "Can you check with your deputies about a dead woman somewhere along the highway?"

Did she hear him correctly? "A dead woman?"

Lily stared at him. "Kyle, how do you know that?"

Ava came around from behind him. "This is pretty wild, even for the wonder boy."

Kyle blew out a breath. "She came to me in the bedroom. Let's just say my necromancy skills have morphed up to a level I didn't even know was possible."

"Actually," Ava stepped into the bedroom to join them, "I have a thought on that one. I'm leaning toward the idea that the spell we did together yesterday opened something inside Kyle. He not only calls the dead, but now it appears they also have the ability to come to him."

Jayne was having a hard time wrapping her head around any of this. Too much had happened in a short amount of time. "Let's back up a little. You think there's a woman dead somewhere along the highway, right? Do you know where?"

Kyle was nodding. "I don't *think* there's a dead woman along the highway somewhere. I know she's there. I'm not a hundred percent sure on where exactly, but given what she described, I believe we'll find her southbound toward Spokane."

Despite the fact that it all sounded a little crazy, Jayne realized she believed him. Without hesitating, she picked up her cell phone from where she'd put it on the nightstand next to the bed and called it in. Dispatch told her there was a deputy just south of Chewelah. That was good because it wouldn't take him too long to run that stretch down to the Spokane County limits.

After she made the call, Kyle and Ava followed her downstairs while Lily zipped across the hall to put on clothes. Jayne put the coffee on and leaned against the counter with her arms folded over her chest. Lily joined them in less than five minutes, and they all stood silently watching the coffee drip into the carafe. The wait for a return call wasn't as long as Jayne thought it might be. She'd just poured herself a mug of coffee when her cell went off.

"Quarles." Her heart dropped as she listened. The fact that Kyle was right about the dead woman wasn't the worst thing she heard. When she ended the call, she slowly put the phone in the holder at her waist.

"What?" Lily asked, as if sensing there was much more to the call than anyone knew.

When Jayne looked up, she included all three of them in her gaze. "They found a dead woman next to a car just south of Chewelah."

Ava looked at Kyle. "So he was right."

"Yes and no."

"What else?" Lily put a hand on her arm.

"First, it wasn't her car. Second, the Spokane County Sheriff's office discovered the body of a man just off Highway 2 a little north of Riverside. He appears to have been mauled by some kind of animal, and it was his car the woman's body was next to. It appears our killer is on the move."

Lily's hand dropped away and she seemed to mull over the news. "Yes, it would appear that way, wouldn't it?"

Something in the way she said it made Jayne look at her. "You don't think so?"

For a second Lily bit her lip. "I think someone wants us to think so."

❖

Bellona sipped her tea and watched the sun come up. Truth to be told, she was pretty darn happy with herself. Last night went really well, all things considered. They'd all had fun; she'd turned around what could have been a tragic situation and made it work to their advantage. She was back home and in bed before the darkness faded.

All she needed was a few hours of sleep, and she would be ready to face the new day. Ever since she was very young she'd been able to get by on very little sleep. It was a helpful trait.

Today was going to be a great one. Tonight the moon would be full and her new little family would be able to run free and wild beneath it. If all went well, they'd be able to do it without worrying about law enforcement or the Jägers tracking them. She could hardly wait for the night to come. She deserved this and so did her pack.

Little Wolf stretched as she came into the living room, where Bellona was gazing out the window. "Still can't believe you took her away from me," she complained.

Honestly, the woman should show a little more gratitude. What she'd done could have ended very badly. Instead, Bellona had turned it into a positive, and Little Wolf of all people should be able to understand that.

Some of the blame had to rest on her own shoulders. This wasn't the first time she'd made a slight miscalculation in a convert. Not that she was upset with Little Wolf. That wasn't it. No, it was more that she'd believed she would ultimately be more obedient. Mistakes in the beginning weren't uncommon. Little Wolf was going far beyond beginning. Every once in a while, she'd try for a companion, only to discover they were wild cards. As it appeared to be turning out, Little Wolf was just such a willful cohort.

When she thought of Adam and Eve, she smiled. Now those two were entertaining, and the fact that Little Wolf was the one to bring them into the fold weighed in her favor. In the old days, she'd have simply killed Little Wolf at the first sign of trouble and eliminated the risk. Easy solution. For the moment, she was going to avoid that particular path. No harm had come to any of them yet, and if her plan worked, they would all be safe.

"Remember the part about keeping a low profile?"

Little Wolf shrugged. "I've lived here all my life and have a pretty good idea of how far I can go."

Bellona narrowed her eyes as she put her hands on her hips. "And you don't think killing three people and turning Adam was taking it a little far? You don't think dragging that woman here last night was going too far?"

Again Little Wolf shrugged. "Those first three were accidents. I didn't mean to kill any of them. I just got carried away with the bloodlust. Adam had to be part of our family. You had an instinct about me, and I had the same kind of instinct about him. And while you're pointing a finger at me, don't forget you're the one who brought Eve into the fold. I didn't do that so it's on you."

All of what she said was true, and Bellona had nothing to argue with where Adam and Eve were concerned, regardless of which one of them turned them. They were an integral part of their new family. "What about last night?"

This time Little Wolf laughed. "I'll admit that was more of a whim. But damn, she was cute and would have been fun to have around. If we play this right, we'll be able to turn everyone we like in this stupid town. Instead of being the boring hick town it's been all my life, this place will rock. You know I'm right. The potential is huge."

It was what they'd been talking about since she realized she'd found a kindred soul in Little Wolf. Her ideas on how to make it happen contrasted slightly from Little Wolf's, however. Then again, she'd had many more years to learn patience than had her sexy companion. In time she would learn patience, but for now, it was up to Bellona to keep her reined in and to make sure they all stayed safe.

"We will, my darling, make this town rock. Let us first send the Jägers on their way, deal with your sheriff, and then we'll have our nirvana."

"I hate waiting." For a strong woman, Little Wolf could sometimes whine. It wasn't attractive.

She chose to ignore the whining. "It will pay off in the end." It would too, she felt it in her heart. She'd been traveling alone for too long, and it was the right time to stop, at least for a little while. And this was the place to do it. Her way, not Little Wolf's.

"Yeah, if you say so."

She put her arms around Little Wolf and kissed the side of her cheek. "We'll create our perfect world, I promise. Just be patient and trust me."

Little Wolf leaned down and kissed her on the lips. "Funny how much I trust you. Never been around someone I trust more."

This was the Little Wolf who gave her hope. "Good. Now, let's take a trip to town. I need to retrace my steps from the last few days and see if I can find my necklace. I dropped it somewhere when I was out and about."

During the night she'd tried to convince herself it didn't matter if she'd lost that trinket from her old life. But all her rationalizing fell short of accomplishing her goal. She didn't give a damn if the universe was telling her to move on. She had to find her necklace, and that's exactly what she planned to do.

CHAPTER TWENTY-SIX

"He or she is heading to Spokane." Jayne's declaration was logical, based on everything they'd seen this morning. The evidence supported her conclusion. Lily still wasn't buying it. Deep down she sensed that they were being played. Beyond that, something about this scenario rang familiar, and she was searching her memories for what.

Lily hedged. "I don't know. It feels off. What do you think?" She directed her question to Kyle and Ava.

Kyle had already confirmed for them that the woman the deputy found alongside the highway was indeed the same one who'd come to him at the house. He didn't perform any necromancy at the site as he felt she'd given him all she could earlier. Nothing would be gained, and Lily wasn't all that wild about having him use his powers in such a public way. Too many first responders nearby to be able to do anything covertly.

"I'm with Lily," Ava said as she scanned the countryside. "I understand how it looks, particularly with another body in Spokane County, but somehow it feels off. Something isn't ringing true." She shuddered.

Lily got it. The air that kissed her cheeks didn't feel right. "I agree, so let's not jump to the conclusion that the wolf has moved. Maybe he has and maybe he hasn't."

Jayne turned toward her. "You think it's a he?"

Shaking her head, Lily explained. "No, not really. It could just as easily be a woman. Both genders possess great strength and prey drive once they've been turned. Using the word 'he' doesn't really rule out a woman."

"I would actually like it better if you did mean a man. At least then it would cut down my suspect pool."

"Don't do that. We're going to have to look at everyone."

Particularly at the stranger they had yet to track down. That was the only promising lead they'd come across so far, and it wasn't much. They needed to watch this apparent change in killing pattern closely, but she wasn't quite ready to pack up and head south. "I need to make a call."

She walked far enough away from Jayne, Kyle, and Ava to give herself some privacy. It would be early evening back home. Senn picked up on the first ring. "What is it? Have you put the wolf down?"

"Sadly, no."

"I thought you'd have it done by now." There was no accusation in his voice—only a statement.

"So did I."

"What's the problem?" Senn was a true leader. He was great at taking the facts and helping find a solution.

"I can't get a fix on it. Something feels really off here, Senn. Last night two bodies were left miles away from Chewelah, as if the wolf was moving toward Spokane. Going to the city for easier hunting."

"You're not following that path, are you?"

He knew her so well. "No. I still feel its spirit in Chewelah. I get the sense it wants us to believe it's moving south, but it's more of a game. Ring a bell with you?"

For a heartbeat he said nothing, though she could hear the click of keys as he typed into his computer. "Damn," he muttered. "I was afraid of that."

"Afraid of what? Come on, Senn. We'd appreciate a little help here."

Again there was a big pause. "There's something we never told you."

For a second she wasn't sure she heard him correctly. "Not possible. I've been Jägers for too long for there to be any secrets." She wasn't bragging. She had simply been in the order so long that she'd been around for the good, the bad, and the ugly. Her relationship with Senn had been the closest with another person since her two best friends. They didn't have any secrets between them.

"I wish that were true, though I always knew this day would come."

Lily ran a hand through her hair as a pounding began behind her right eye. Yes, something definitely not right here. She was starting to get a bad feeling in the pit of her stomach. "Senn…"

"You understand about the link between the werewolf and their maker."

It wasn't a question, because everyone in the Jägers understood that basic. When a werewolf was near their maker, an invisible bond existed between them, a link only broken when the alpha was dead. What that had to do with her, she had no clue. Her maker had been destroyed centuries ago.

"She must be there."

"She, who? Senn, you're not making any sense and I don't have time for your puzzles."

"Your maker."

For a second she thought she'd heard him wrong. "My maker died the night I was attacked. You told me that yourself."

"I lied."

❖

A surge of energy roared through Kyle. Seeing what the werewolf had done to the woman who'd come to his bedroom asking for help made him want to scream. Even more than that, it spurred him to action. There had to be something more they could do. This son of a bitch had to be stopped today.

What frightened him a little was how ineffectual they'd been so far. Tiny bits of info here and there hadn't gotten them far, and two more had died because of it. If this was the best he could do, the last thing he should be was a Jägers.

Ava took his hand and pulled him back toward the SUV. "Come on," she said as she opened the back door. "We can't do anything more here."

"I haven't done anything at all," he muttered as he climbed into the backseat of the rig right next to Ava. Talk about feeling like a total failure.

With her hands on his face, Ava stared into his eyes. "You've done more than you realize. You've guided lost souls into the light, and you've brought help to these people discarded along the road as though they were garbage. You gave them dignity. That, my very handsome necromancer, is a great deal."

"I'm just so damned frustrated." Again he felt like screaming. There was a lot to be said for childish tantrums. He'd give anything to throw one right now.

"As am I."

He dropped back against the seat and rubbed his hands over his eyes. If only he could come up with something to get them closer to the killer. Then he had a thought. "What if we combine our powers again? We opened one door. Maybe we can open another. We've got to do something to get us ahead of this bastard."

She twisted in her seat and stared at him. "That's an excellent suggestion. You do realize this is new for me too."

"I didn't. I thought you could do just about anything you wanted."

Ava leaned into him and put her head on his shoulder. "I inherited much from the women who came before me. They passed down powers through the blood and, more importantly, passed down the knowledge of how to use those powers. I've been taught how to be one with the universe, to respect the laws of threefold."

"You have an amazing family." He thought about his own grandmother. If not for her, he'd have gone crazy. Unlike Ava, though, those with his kind of power were unique in the family, not the norm. Even his parents didn't really understand. They tried and they were kind, but they simply couldn't relate.

"Yes," she murmured. "I'm blessed, as are you."

His laugh lacked humor. "I never really thought of it as being blessed. I just tried to figure out something to do with it so I didn't lose my mind. People aren't exactly lining up to hang out with the guy who talks to dead people."

"You found a place where you fit in and, even better, you found me. You might not realize it, but I do."

"Realize what?"

She snuggled in closer. "Together we're dynamic."

Now that was something she didn't have to tell him twice. He put an arm around her and let her nearness fill him with peace. Yes, together the two of them were more. The Jägers filled his life with purpose, but Ava filled his heart with love. They were definitely dynamic.

Out the front windshield he could watch what was happening beyond. Lily was off to the side talking on her cell phone, and he had the impression she wasn't crazy about what she was hearing because her face was filled with darkness. Jayne was working with others near the car, where the body of the woman he'd alerted them to was now covered to protect her from the gaze of passing motorists. He and Ava were alone for the time being. No one to see them; no one to overhear their conversation.

He continued to stare out the window as he said, "You know I'm in love with you."

At first she said nothing, and he feared he'd gone too far. Probably should have kept his pining-heart declarations to himself. When he chanced a sideways glance, he was surprised to see a small smile on her lips.

"I know."

"And?"

"And I'm glad."

His chest felt as though a three-hundred-pound man had just rolled off it. "Really?"

"Really. I believe it's the reason we're able to do what we do together. If I'd tried that spell with someone else, I seriously doubt it would have worked. With you, with us together, who knows what we can do."

She was right, and the only thing that bothered him was what she didn't say. By uttering those three words, he'd bared his soul to her. She hadn't turned away or laughed, but she hadn't said she loved him too.

CHAPTER TWENTY-SEVEN

Jayne went on autopilot once they arrived at the crime scene and directed her staff like the professional she was. It was easier than letting herself think about what this could be. What it probably was.

Damn it, but Lily, Kyle, and Ava had made a believer out of her. Instead of being pissed at the council for bringing this team in, she was glad they were here, and she was glad they were in her home. She was glad they all had her back.

Was she losing her mind?

Jayne turned and looked at Lily standing near the trees talking on her phone. No, she wasn't going crazy. Some people were special, and Lily was one of those people. That the attraction was mutual between them was heartwarming. In an odd way she felt as though they'd known each other for a lifetime instead of a few days.

She was trying to concentrate on what was going on around her, and her mind wandered down the path of choices. In her life she'd made many that caused her to wonder at the time why she'd made them. Each one took her down a path that altered her life just a little. As she studied the scene around her and the people who were 27 (all a part of her life today, she realized how each decision had brought her to this place. More importantly, had brought her to this woman. Gave new meaning to the term "big picture."

It was noon before they got back to Colville. By the time she walked into her office she felt as though she'd been at work for days. Five dead and two missing, and if Lily was correct, a full moon to crank things up even more. Great, just fucking great.

For what was beginning to feel like business as usual, Lily joined her in her office. They looked at each other and words weren't necessary. If she were a betting woman, she'd put odds on Lily thinking the same thing she was: they were running out of time.

Lily, it occurred to her, had said very little since she ended her call out at the crime scene. Even since coming into the office, she'd been quiet. Whatever had been said on that call weighed heavy on her mind. This wasn't the woman she woke up next to this morning.

"Are you all right?"

Lily's dark eyes met hers. "Yes."

"You don't seem okay."

"I'd tell you everything is perfect, but I'm relatively certain you wouldn't believe me."

"Tell me how I can help." The shadows in Lily's face concerned her.

Shaking her head, Lily's gaze went somewhere beyond Jayne. "I don't even know how to process what I just found out, let alone tell you how to help."

"Try me. I'm a professional, you know."

A ghost of a smile flitted across Lily's face. "Yes, you are. I like that about you. This, however, will take a professional of a different type."

Jayne took an educated guess. "Your type?"

"Yes, most definitely my type of professional."

"So tell me anyway."

Lily began to finger the lovely ruby necklace at her neck. "I feel like the rug has been pulled out from under my feet. I know it's a stupid saying, but it's how I feel. As it turns out, everything I thought I knew is a lie."

Jayne leaned across the desk and took Lily's hands. "Tell me what you mean."

"You wouldn't believe me."

Twenty-four hours ago that might have been true. Today, she had a completely different mindset. "Try me."

Lily's hands dropped away from her throat, and she folded them in her lap. She studied them so intently Jayne wondered what she was thinking. Finally she looked up and her eyes met Jayne's. Pain filled them, the kind that could tear the heart apart. "I was born in Danzig in 1579. My parents were Prussian royalty."

Jayne wasn't exactly sure what she was expecting Lily to say, but she did know that wasn't it. "Get out of here."

The smile that flickered across Lily's face was not full of warmth. "Oh, I'm not kidding you, Sheriff. You're sitting across from a real-life princess."

"But you look younger than me." She looked not only younger but incredibly attractive. If what she said was true, no fucking way should she be that beautiful.

"What I am now changes all the rules. Once I was as human as you are. I was preparing to be wed to a wealthy nobleman. I was a privileged young woman in a revered family."

That stopped Jayne. Not the part about her royal family. No, given what they'd done last night, hearing that Lily was to marry a man still shocked her. "But I thought…"

"You thought correctly." This time the smile was warm. "It didn't matter how I felt. Not in my time. I was told what to do and who to do it with. Love or desire had nothing to do with the realities of my life. I was pretty, I was young, and I was nobility. A prime catch for any number of high-born."

"That had to suck." So when exactly did she buy into Lily being hundreds of years old?

"Indeed it did. On the eve of my wedding everything changed. My two best friends came to see me, and one of them brought this." She held out the necklace. "One for each of us. We'd grown up together and were like sisters. It was the last time we would be together before our lives changed. Two of us were on our way to becoming dutiful wives. As it turned it out, it was the last time I would ever see either one of my best friends. I've never stopped missing them."

The faraway look that came into Lily's eyes spoke to the truth of her words. "I'm sorry about your friends."

"It is the way of my kind. Until that night, however, I was as human as you. I was attacked by what I thought was a wolf. Only later did I learn it was no ordinary wolf."

"A werewolf."

Lily nodded. "My parents had no idea and were devastated. Not so much by the attack but by what it did to me. The wolf had sliced open my face. The beautiful daughter they had essentially sold off was no longer the highly sought-after darling. Aldrich backed out of the marriage agreement. My family was humiliated. I had become a liability instead of an asset."

"That's so wrong."

She shrugged, remembering the world she'd left behind. "It was the way of our time, good or bad. My family was relieved when I died."

Jayne's head snapped up. Died? She could testify to the fact that Lily was very much flesh-and-blood. "You don't seem very dead to me."

"As I told you before, it was the Jägers who came for me. It was easy enough to convince my family I had expired as a result of my injuries. It was the perfect solution for them. No longer was it whispered that Aldrich turned his back on me. Instead, Aldrich and my family were treated with great sympathy for my too-young demise. Everyone came out a winner in that scenario."

"Doesn't seem right somehow."

"It was the right thing for me. Without the Jägers I would become the very thing we're hunting. They saved my life."

That wasn't much of an explanation, given she'd told her a few minutes ago that everything she knew was a lie. "What part is the lie?"

This time Lily closed her eyes and sighed. When she opened them again, tears glistened. "The Jägers gave me a home. They gave me the serum I need to control what I am. They taught me to be a warrior. They gave me a family to replace the one I'd lost. They were, they are, my everything, yet I just found out they lied to me. All these years. When I had recovered back then, I was terrified of being attacked again. The Jägers assured me the werewolf that attacked me was a rogue they tracked down and destroyed. The knowledge gave me peace and the will to go forward with my altered reality."

"It wasn't true, the part about the werewolf being tracked and killed?"

She shook her head. "No. Some werewolves are born. Some are made. I was made. The one who did that to me was born, only I didn't know that until today. I also didn't know she was one of my best friends."

"What?" She was shocked, and she wasn't the one this had all happened to.

"Pretty much my reaction too when Senn just told me."

"They've known this all along?"

"In their defense, not exactly. They only discovered her true identify about a hundred years after the attack on me. They had known of a family and had spent decades trying to find out who they were, but this family hadn't survived for centuries without developing exceptional skills. In short, they spent much of their time hiding in plain sight." Her fingers drifted to the necklace once more.

"I still don't understand why they're bothering to tell you now if they've kept this information from you all this time. You have enough going on here without being sidetracked by something this huge."

"Because this family was well-known for their tactics."

For a second it didn't hit, and when it did, it was like a lightbulb hitting a hundred watts. "Like those we're seeing here."

"Yes. Senn believes the werewolf that attacked me on the night before my wedding is here in Stevens County."

"Son of a bitch." A knock on her door startled her. "Yes?" It was one of her deputies, Bill Bower.

"Sorry to bother you." He held something in his hand. "My wife was at the grocery store and found this on the ground. She said a lady, someone she'd never seen before, must have dropped it because it was right next to where her car pulled out. You'd mentioned keeping our eyes out for people we didn't know so figured I'd run this by you." He opened his hand.

Lily gasped at the sparkling ruby necklace.

Bellona stood in the open doorway to the barn and wanted to scream. Damn that woman. Out of control didn't even begin to describe what was happening with Little Wolf. Such promise, and it was going down the drain in a hurry. It seemed that if Bellona didn't have her eyes on Little Wolf, she was causing problems.

Excuses for her behavior were no longer viable. It made Bellona sad because she found Little Wolf exciting. She'd had such high hopes for her and for starting a new life in this beautiful place. Adam and Eve were delightful. So many pieces fit into the puzzle that comprised a family, except Little Wolf kept pulling them apart no matter how she tried to rein her in.

The two bodies scattered on the barn floor were beyond help.

Bloody and ravaged, they showed that Little Wolf had enjoyed herself. Her taste for blood was something she hadn't seen in a very long time. Reminded her of her cousin Ralston. He too had been out of control. Fun but totally uncontrollable and fearless. He'd put the entire family at risk, and in the end, she'd dealt with him just as she had the others. Above all else, Bellona protected herself.

"Sorry," Little Wolf said as she came up behind her. She had a chicken breast in one hand and was nibbling on it. She wasn't surprised. Given what she'd been doing night after night, she had to be ravenous. This kind of activity burned calories like crazy. "I went for a little run while you were out on the highway last night. This just sorta happened."

"We've talked about this."

Little Wolf shrugged. "Yeah, but you know a girl's gotta have fun."

"This kind of fun is going to get us all killed."

"Are you kidding me? Who the hell is going to be able to stand up against us?"

The young and the foolish. "The Jägers."

"You sent those dumbasses to Spokane last night, remember?"

"I tried. It's too early to tell if it worked, and this," she waved her hand toward the bloody mess in the barn, "is going to complicate things."

Little Wolf leaned against the open door and considered her handiwork. "You'll take care of it." Was it boredom she heard in her voice?

Rage boiled up inside Bellona. Little Wolf's enthusiasm was morphing into arrogance, and that she wouldn't stand for. In the werewolf world, just as in the canine world, the alpha's word was law. She was the alpha. It was time to bring this to an end. She whirled, fully intending to put Little Wolf down, but as she did, Eve walked up.

"Hi." Her smile was bright and innocent.

If Little Wolf was the worst in them all, then Eve was the best. She wouldn't do this in front of one who retained such a kind and gentle nature. Bellona stepped back and put an arm around Eve's shoulders, turning back in the direction of the house. "Hi, my precious one." She kissed the top of her head. "Let's go have a soda."

She looked back over her shoulder at Little Wolf. "Clean up that mess."

Little Wolf laughed and almost skipped into the barn. "No problem, boss."

Back in the house, she sat Eve at the table and poured her a glass of soda. As a general rule, she abhorred the sugary beverages. In Eve's case she made an exception. The young woman seemed to delight in it, and it became very clear to Bellona, very quickly, that she would indulge Eve her whims. The lightness she brought to their makeshift family was in direct contrast to what Little Wolf was doing to them.

Tonight was the full moon, and she was worried. If Little Wolf was this far out of control now, she was going to be unstoppable in a few hours. It didn't matter which way she came at it, Little Wolf had to be stopped.

That, however, was only part of the problem. She was good at running and could extricate herself from any situation that threatened harm. One couldn't survive as long as she had without superior skills. She was the last in her family, and she intended to stay that way for many more years.

Tonight, she would have to take Little Wolf down, and if that was all she had to do, she could then be on her way. Her plans for a long life here with a new family would be chalked up to a miscalculation in picking a mate. But what should she do with Adam and Eve? Adam had such promise. He was strong and young and smart. She could envision him at her side for years. She could show him the world.

Eve was a more delicate situation. She would be hard to run with and equally hard to leave behind. Her only hope would be to see how Eve did on this full moon. Perhaps it would give her enough strength and power that the three of them could make their way out of this town and on to greener pastures, as the saying went.

"I like you," Eve said as she held her glass of soda. "You're nice and you're pretty." She patted Bellona on the cheek.

No, there would be no leaving Eve behind.

CHAPTER TWENTY-EIGHT

Lily hadn't wanted to believe Senn, hadn't wanted to believe that Taria, her sister of the heart, was the one who took away her life. Even as she'd told the story to Jayne, a voice in the back of her mind had whispered "not true." Now she was face-to-face with a truth she could no longer deny.

In the outstretched palm of the deputy sheriff lay a golden necklace, old and intricately inlaid with sparkling rubies, identical to hers. Slowly she brought her gaze up from the deputy's hand and to Jayne's face. In her eyes she saw the recognition.

"Taria," she whispered. "Dear God, it's Taria's necklace."

Jayne took a small plastic bag out of her desk and held it open for the deputy. He dropped the necklace into the bag. "Thanks, Bill. I'll take care of this." The deputy turned and left.

"I can't believe it." Despite her words, she very much believed it. Taria was here. Only three of these necklaces had ever existed, and she'd personally witnessed Alexia's go to the grave with her. That left only two: the one currently around her neck and Taria's.

"Senn was right. It has to be Taria."

"So you know her?"

"I thought I did." There was a time, and not so distantly, when she'd have sworn she knew Taria as well as she knew herself. Today she'd learned how wrong she was. She didn't know her girlhood friend at all, and maybe she didn't know herself either. Time had allowed her to learn many things. Obviously there wasn't enough time to truly know oneself.

"You know enough to be able to track her down?"

Leave it to Jayne to cut through the self-pitying crap and get to the heart of the matter. "Yes, I do, and I will bring a stop to this. Tonight."

All of a sudden she understood everything she'd been feeling since she came here: the whispers that swirled around her, the prickles that crawled up her spine, the sense of being in touch with another who remained just out of her line of sight. It all made sickening sense.

Her eyes drifted to the window, where snow was beginning to lightly fall outside. The sky was gray and cloudy, the trees swaying in the wind. She thought of another time when she'd watched the snow blanket the landscape. As if it had happened only yesterday, she remembered the cold brought on by the incoming storm and the dread that had filled her for what she was going to have to do. On that night, she'd been thinking about the man she was to marry on the coming day and of the life she would be forced to smile about and endure. On this day, she was thinking about the woman who was once her best friend and of the life she would be forced to end.

As she watched the snow drift to the ground, she realized, with sudden clarity, that she'd come full circle.

❖

"Are you sure about this?" It wasn't that Kyle didn't trust Ava, because he did. He trusted her with his life. It was more the feeling of spiders crawling up his spine that had him questioning whether this was a good idea.

"I believe we can do it." Her earnestness showed in her words and in her eyes as well. She didn't lack confidence at the moment.

So far she hadn't led him down a wrong path. Not in this hunt and not in their previous hunt. "Okay."

He decided to ignore the spiders and the boulder rolling around in the pit of his stomach. He would put his hands in those of the woman he was in love with and pray that the same god or gods that saw fit to give him this gift wouldn't fail him now.

"I'll call on the power of the Old Ones," she said, her eyes intent on his. "We'll see how far we can take this. Together, I believe we can open a window on whatever has been eluding us."

A werewolf had been eluding them, and it was a very much alive werewolf that was exceptionally careful about making sure no one saw his human face. Made it really hard to track him down. Or her.

Ava was certain they could make this work, even if he wasn't. He called to the dead, not to the living, so he wasn't sure how this was even going to help. He shivered as a cold wind kicked up, blowing snow into his face. Too bad they couldn't part the veil inside, but Ava insisted they needed to be surrounded by nature. They stood only a hundred or so yards from the river, its cold waters smooth and glassy, as though the currents below weren't running at all. Like the world around them, the currents were deceptively powerful, not seen by the naked eye and yet there just the same. It was those unseen powers he and Ava were going to tap into now.

Once she had everything in place, they stood face-to-face, and she took his hands in hers. Despite the cold air and the falling snow, her touch was warm, and it sent that warmth right into his heart. Her words were quiet, and he could barely make them out. It only took a few seconds before he no longer heard Ava and the world around them began to waver.

"Come." The woman was tall and painfully thin. Her short black hair was standing up on end, her pale face marred by deep gouges. "She'll be back soon."

"Come," said another voice, and Kyle turned to see a second woman. She too was covered in blood, her shirt ripped and her arm dangling useless at her side. "We don't have much time."

"Who are you?"

Both women ignored him as they turned and hurried out of the tree cover. His only choice was to follow them across a field because they weren't waiting for him. They ducked through a barbed-wire fence and, again, he followed. The field was sizeable, and in the distance he made out a large house as well as a number of outbuildings. The moon overhead was full, and its light was shining down to illuminate the field as though they were in a baseball stadium.

He stumbled on a rock and nearly went down. The two women never lost stride, and, righting himself, he hurried to catch up. A thin layer of snow covered the field, and he stumbled again, unable to see the rocks that poked up from the ground that had been plowed before the cold weather set in. He was the only one having trouble staying on his feet on the nearly frozen ground.

At first he thought they were leading him to the big house. It was huge and beautiful, and he had a vague sense he'd seen it during their travels through the county, either when he and Ava had made their way to Jayne's house or as Jayne took them to various places around Colville. He just couldn't place when or where.

It wasn't the house they hurried to but the big red barn. This wasn't the typical run-down rural barn on a hardworking farm. Rather it was large, with fresh paint and elaborate doors. This barn might be on a working farm, but it was a farm where money wasn't an issue. Not unusual in places like this, where families were here for decades and, if successful in their endeavors, passed it down from generation to generation.

As they neared the side of the massive structure, both women came in close, and each put a finger to her mouth. When he was next to them, the taller woman whispered, "Don't let her see or hear you."

"Who?" Besides the two women, he'd seen no one else.

The shorter woman nodded in the direction of the window. "Her."

He rose on his toes to peer through the high-placed window. Inside a woman in blue jeans and a hoodie paced. She was talking to herself, though he couldn't make out the words. Something about her struck him as familiar. Staring to try to place her, he failed. He couldn't figure out what it was about her that he might have seen before. Besides, he hadn't been here long enough to really know anybody.

He dropped back down flat on his feet. "Who is it?"

"The wolf." The tall woman began to cry.

They might not realize it, but he knew the truth. Both of these women were already dead. It was cruel to make them stand against the barn wall and be frightened when it wasn't necessary. The time was now to release them from the bonds keeping them here. "You have to go," he said in a calm and gentle voice.

The smaller woman reached out to take the other one's hand. Her whole body was trembling. "We have to help you."

He nodded solemnly. "And so you have. I will take it from here. Please, they're waiting for you."

The light that was behind him wasn't something he could see, yet he knew it was there just the same. It was there for these two souls who'd *risked eternity to come to him. Ava was right. He'd have never been able to reach these two without her. Together they could do miraculous things. "Go now," he said softly.*

And they did.

When they were gone, he once more raised himself up on his feet. Inside the barn the woman still had her back to him, but now she was naked, the blue jeans and hoodie tossed carelessly to the side. Her head was back and her howl was loud, even through the barn walls. Again he was struck by a sense of familiarity. When she turned he understood why, and as he gasped, the woman changed.

Chapter Twenty-nine

The sun was starting to fade by the time Jayne pulled into her driveway. Lily was nervous, and Jayne suspected she had a plan she didn't want to share with her. Too bad, because by the time they left the station they had two more missing persons reports. The werewolf might have tried to redirect their efforts to Spokane, but it was a poor job and time was up.

"What do you need me to do?" Jayne felt certain Lily knew exactly what she wanted to do. What she didn't realize was she wasn't going to let her do it alone.

Lily shook her head as she unbuckled her seat belt. "You can't help me with this."

"Bullshit. This is my town. I was born and raised here. I might have left for a while, but that doesn't make it any less my town."

"This isn't about loyalty or whose town it is. This is about a werewolf gone feral."

"That doesn't make sense."

Lily turned in her seat and took Jayne's hand. "For hundreds of years she has traveled the globe and managed to keep her identity secret. Hell, Jayne, she was my best friend, and I had no idea about her and her family's secret. She attacked me and changed me, and still I didn't know. Something had to have changed for her to do the things she's done here. She's sick, she's mental, she's something, and the only one, the only thing, that's going to stop her is me."

"You mean another werewolf." Jayne could read between the lines. This was to be a fight to the death, as though they were two wolves fighting for alpha. "I can just shoot her."

Lily shook her head. "Is your gun loaded with silver bullets?"

"I figured that was a folk legend."

Lily raised a single eyebrow. "Folk legends all have a basis in reality. In this case, it is a very accurate basis. A regular bullet is annoying but not life-threatening. It takes silver to end it."

"I can slow her down at least."

Again she shook her head. "That might be true for a new one, a recently turned werewolf, but not so much for those my age. As we age, our powers grow. We heal incredibly fast from what might kill you."

"So how can you stop her?"

"By tearing out her throat."

Jayne's hand tightened on Lily's, and not because she was repulsed by what she'd just told her. The other possibility that statement suggested sent ice racing up her spine. "She could do the same to you."

"It's a possibility."

"I can't let you risk that." Jesus, she'd just found Lily, and by doing so realized that a piece of her heart had been missing for a long time. She wasn't about to lose her now, and certainly not to some bloodthirsty dog. Although comparing this bloodthirsty killer to a dog was insulting to the species.

"It is not your decision, Jayne."

"It's my county, my investigation."

"And your bosses brought me in specifically for this reason."

"Fuck my bosses."

Lily leaned across the console and put her arms around Jayne. "I know what you're feeling," she said into her ear. "I feel it too."

"Then don't do this."

"It's my destiny."

"It's fucked up."

"Destiny often is."

Before Jayne could argue any more, Ava came racing out the front door. "Hurry." She waved her arms at them, motioning for them to come. "Something's wrong with Kyle."

❖

The day just got better and better. Or, more accurately, worse and worse. She'd made up her mind about Little Wolf. She had to be put down for the safety of the rest of the family. She'd planned to do it after dark and before their run. She didn't want Little Wolf ruining Adam and Eve's first full moon.

What she hadn't anticipated was Little Wolf's almost psychic touch. Bellona had been in the living room thinking through where she'd go next, when Little Wolf came sauntering in. She looked as enticing as ever, which put a little quaver in Bellona's resolve. At least until she opened her mouth.

"You know you're stuck with me."

"Where did that come from?" She hadn't said a word about her plans.

"I know what you're thinking. You want me out. You think I'm dangerous. I'm not, at least not to the pack, but you also have no idea how powerful I am."

"You're a new wolf. All newbies believe they're invincible." She'd seen it a hundred times or more, and they all had the same attitude. She hadn't been an exception, but she'd had plenty of elders around to put her firmly in her place. In time she'd paid them back for those harsh lessons. Little Wolf wasn't going to have the same opportunity.

"You need time. True power comes from experience."

Little Wolf smiled, and for the first time Bellona saw something in her that gave her chills. How had she missed that before? "True power is in the blood. I've always had it. You gave me a boost. Kind of like a steroid injection. It's amazing."

The chill she'd felt earlier went glacial. "What do you mean?"

"My family lineage is long. This farm isn't just the result of years of successful farming. We had a little help." She winked at Bellona.

"I'm not following."

"Nobody else has either, and that's what has made it so fucking awesome. We're witches, you dumb bitch. Black witches."

Bellona thought she might throw up. How could she have made such a colossal mistake? This was a disaster. "You're lying." Good gods, she prayed it was a lie.

"You think your showing up here was an accident? You just picked this stupid little town by accident? I called you here. I called you!"

Bellona closed her eyes. The puzzle pieces that had been eluding her fell into place. The wanderlust that had brought her from the New Orleans condo where she'd made herself a home the last three years, the immediate draw to Little Wolf the moment she laid eyes on her. All of it fell like locking pieces into place.

"Yeah, you've got it now, don't you?"

Bellona stared at her. "Why?"

Little Wolf shrugged. "I was bored. It was time to liven this place up. More important, it was time for me to take over the town. That dumbass Jayne Quarles thought she could waltz back home and be queen of the world. I'm the one who's been here all along. I've done all the hard work. I deserve what she's taken from me, and I'm going to get it back, with your help."

"I'm not helping you."

"You already have." Little Wolf laughed. "You think I did all this because I was out of control? Not even close. I was never out of control. Everything I've done was carefully planned. Everything."

"You're crazy."

Again she laughed. "Not at all. I'm ambitious, and I figured out a way to make it all happen and have a little fun in the bargain. By the way, you're dynamite in bed. Thanks for that. Too bad you're gonna have to die. I'll miss you."

"What about Adam and Eve?"

"Oh, Adam." She sighed. "That boy is fun. I think I'll keep him around for a while. Same with Eve. She makes me smile, and she does whatever I ask her to."

"You're going to kill me."

Little Wolf looked surprised. "No. I'd never kill you. Besides, I won't have to. The Jägers will take care of that."

CHAPTER THIRTY

Lily threw herself out of the car and raced up the front steps. Inside, she found Kyle on the floor. He was ghostly white and soaking wet. "What happened?"

Ava was near tears. "We did another spell together, and now I can't bring him out of it. He's been this way for half an hour. I tried calling you, and you didn't pick up. I don't know what to do."

"Why is he all wet?"

"We were outside and he fell to the ground. I dragged him by the shoulders back into the house."

Lily took a look Ava and marveled that she was able to move this much-larger man all the way into the house. Of course, she'd seen people who were frightened do things they'd never be able to accomplish under normal circumstances. Love had a way of making the impossible happen.

Kneeling beside Kyle, she took his hand. It was cold, yet at the same time she could feel a buzz beneath his skin. "Explain to me exactly what you did."

Jayne had taken one look at Kyle and raced out of the room. She returned now with a blanket in hand and spread it over him. "Thanks," Lily told her. "That was good thinking. Ava?"

Ava's words were rushed as she told them about the magic circle, the candles, and the spell. "I called on the Old Ones, and it appears they answered."

"Have you done this before?"

Ava shook her head and frowned. "It was the first time." Her words were choked. "My mother and grandmother always talked of the power of the Old Ones, and I believed our combined strength would get us to the killer. I think," she choked out on a sob, "it worked."

Unfortunately Lily understood too well what Ava was trying to tell her. Though she'd never seen it, she'd heard of it. Her studies with the Jägers included reviewing the books kept throughout the history of the order, which contained the recording of several similar situations. No one had Kyle's particular brand of necromancy, but enough had similarities to give her an idea of what might have gone sideways.

Once more she was hit with the undeniable sense of time flying by. They had to get to Taria, and soon. First, she had to figure out how to help Kyle. "He's trapped," she told them as she stood. "Jayne, do you know of any witches that live in these parts?"

Jayne shook her head. "A few certifiable bitches, but I've never heard of witchcraft around here. What does that have to do with Kyle? I thought our problem was a werewolf. Where in the hell does a witch come into this?"

"It would take a powerful witch to trap him, particularly when you consider the combined power he and Ava possessed. Someone is very dangerous, and if we don't stop them soon, I'm afraid we're going to lose Kyle."

"Oh, now that's just fucking awesome," Jayne muttered.

Ava's sob made her look down. "Stay with him," Lily told her. "Keep physical contact. I don't know if he's said anything to you, but it's clear that he's in love with you. If anything can throw him a lifeline, it would be love."

"I won't leave him." Ava held his hands and laid her head on his chest.

"Ava," Lily said. "Have you ever heard about any hereditary witches in this part of the country?"

Ava looked up at her thoughtfully and then shook her head. "No, and I would probably know. My family is one of the oldest in the country. I could call my mother, if you think it would help."

"I don't want you to leave Kyle."

"I won't." Ava pulled her phone from her back pocket.

"If you learn anything, tell Jayne." She turned and sprinted toward the front door. The *tick tick tick* of an invisible clock was setting her nerves on fire.

"Wait," Jayne said. "What are you doing? Where are you going?"

"You stay here with Kyle and Ava. I have to stop Taria."

"No way I'm letting you do this alone."

Lily was busy taking off her clothes and tossing them on one of the porch chairs. Cold air battered her skin, raising goose bumps on her arms and legs. It didn't matter if she was cold; it wouldn't last long. "I have to go." She tilted her head toward the buttery moon that was starting its ascent and felt its light whisper over her body. She heard its silent invitation and accepted it.

She called the change.

Kyle wanted to drop back down on his feet and hide. It was too late. Through the dirty window she'd locked eyes with him, and a wicked smile spread across her face. He came back down flat on his feet and pressed against the side of the barn. With concentration he willed himself out of this place and back to the spot where he and Ava sat holding hands inside the safety of the magic circle. It didn't work. His back was still pressed against the side of the barn, and from inside he could hear her deep-throated howl. It was the howl of a bloodthirsty predator. For a flash of a second he stood paralyzed, uncertain what to do. Never before had he been trapped, unable to bring himself fully back into his world. It wasn't working here, and the only thing he could think of to do was run.

He spun on his heel, slipping on the snow-covered earth, and raced toward the protective cover of the trees he and the two women had earlier walked away from. He needed to get back there and to the spot where he'd entered this realm. He had to believe that, in that place, he could find the portal back. This wasn't like anything he'd experienced before. He and the dead usually stood alone together and talked. They remained in their respective worlds and talked across them. He didn't enter the domain of the dead, and the dead didn't really come back to the sphere of the living.

So what the hell was happening here? This wasn't a case of just speaking with the dead. He was here with both the living and the dead, only it wasn't really here either. It all looked real enough, but it couldn't be. It was as if he had jumped ahead in time, and that wasn't something he could do. The wrongness of everything made him want to scream like a warrior preparing for battle.

Outside the barn it was pitch-black, and far more snow lay on the ground than when he and Ava had returned to Jayne's house. Everything was out of sync with what he expected to see. Especially her. His heart was still pounding like a kettledrum as he hauled ass across the slippery field. Behind him he could hear her panting, and the sound grew ever closer no matter how hard he ran.

He risked a glance back over his shoulder and stopped in surprise. She wasn't there. The massive wolf he'd witnessed her change into was no longer behind him. He didn't understand how that could be. He'd just heard her.

God, he had to get back to the spot where he'd entered this place. It was, he felt deeply, his only hope of escaping this place and the most unexpected monster. Through the trees he could see a light, and it was there he focused his effort. Though the moon overhead was bright, it wasn't the moonlight that glowed through the pines. It was Ava, he was sure of it, and she was the one who would bring him back. He started to run again and then stopped abruptly, his feet sliding out from under him. His hands hit the ground hard as he tumbled to the earth.

Standing on all fours at the edge of the trees was the wolf, her teeth bared and her growl filling the night air. Kyle scrambled, trying to get purchase on the wet, slick ground. He managed to right himself and got back up on his feet. She blocked his path to the light, to Ava. Her growl filled the night air.

"No!" he screamed and dodged first right and then left. As she made her lunge to the right, he ran to the left as if his life depended upon it because he feared it did. His feet slid, and he hit cold rocks with the toes of his shoes, sending shards of pain up his legs. His lungs hurt and his quads screamed. He kept pushing, rolling through the barbed-wire fence, feeling the trickle of blood as the barbs tore his shirt and pierced his skin. He didn't slow and didn't look back, certain the wolf cleared the fence in a single bound.

When he made it to the tree line the circle of light was so close, he could almost touch it. Only then did he allow a thread of hope to enter his heart. He was going to make it. Ava was going to bring him back. Throwing out a hand to try, he felt the whisper of warmth on his fingers as they touched the light. He could feel her on the other side even in the tips of his fingers. He was there, he was safe.

And then she hit him, her long powerful body colliding with his and forcing him to the ground. His single thought as her powerful jaw closed on his neck was Ava.

CHAPTER THIRTY-ONE

Jayne wanted to shout. Lily had outwitted her, plain and simple. All Jayne could do was stand in her yard dumbly watching the mighty wolf race away in the night. If she'd ever felt powerless before, it was nothing compared to what she was feeling right at the moment.

Powerless and scared shitless pretty much covered it. She had a horrible feeling that Lily wasn't coming back from this one. She might be the master Jägers hunter, but all the rules seemed to have been thrown out in this one. Things had a way of doing that when it became personal. She had to think. What could she do to help?

First things first. Spinning, she trotted back into the house. Kyle still lay prone on the floor, with Ava holding his hand. Her eyes were closed and she appeared to be chanting something. Her voice was so low, her words were an incomprehensible mumble. Just as she reached her side, Kyle jerked, and Ava's eyes popped open as she screamed.

Jayne dropped to her knees, hitting the hardwood floor with a thud. In the back of her mind was the thought, *That's gonna hurt like hell in the morning*. "Is he coming back?"

Ava's eyes were filled with tears as she glanced up at Jayne. "He's close." Her hands held so tight to his, her knuckles were white.

"Bring him back, Ava."

She nodded and closed her eyes. As she began to whisper once more, she rocked gently back and forth. For a moment, Jayne stayed on her knees staring down at Kyle, who had stilled again. She felt as useless here as she had standing out in the yard watching Lily race away as a wolf. Then a thought struck her and she pushed up to her feet.

"I have to go," she said.

Ava didn't open her eyes or let go of Kyle's hand. "I have to stay here with him. It's the only way I can keep from losing him."

"I'll be back as soon as I can."

"Go," Ava said. "I'll bring him home."

Jayne headed down to the basement. At a closed door, she turned the knob and walked inside, flipping on the light switch as she did. The overhead fluorescent fixture bathed the room in light. A lump rose in her throat, and for a second she thought this was going to be too much. She hadn't been in this room since before her brother's funeral. This had been his workshop, his place to go when he needed to relax or, after the cancer diagnosis, when he needed to forget.

Everything was exactly as he'd left it the last time he was in here, and despite her best intention not to let it get to her, tears slid down her cheeks. It still pissed her off. Nobody should lose their life so young. Not her brother. Not anyone.

Wiping away the tears, she blew out a breath and stepped up to his workbench. It was a long shot and probably wouldn't work. It was, however, the best idea she had, and though the chance it might help was slim, it was still a chance. She looked at all the equipment and supplies spread out. Empty shell casings were lined up in a box waiting for the reloading he'd run out of time to complete.

Jayne grabbed two of the shells from the box and set them on the bench in front of her. Next she reached around her neck to release the chain she always wore. The silver links dropped into her hand. With a sigh, she took it in both hands and yanked. The chain snapped in two. She dropped a piece in each of the empty shell casings. From another box she tipped shot into each shell until both were full and she could close them. She glanced at the gun safe set into the wall. It too had been closed tight since the day her brother made a one-way trip to the hospital. She'd not had the heart to spin the dial and open it.

She did so now. She knew exactly what she wanted and walked inside. The shotgun had been a gift from their father and was a beautiful weapon her brother had cherished. She hoped his spirit was with her now as she took it in her hands and returned to the bench, where she picked up the two shotgun shells. When they were loaded, she left the workshop. "Thank you," she whispered as she turned off the light.

She took the stairs two at a time, wondering how she was going to find Lily, because that was exactly what she needed to do. When she reached the front entry she was relieved to see Kyle sitting up and Ava hugging him. "Are you okay?" He looked pretty damned pale.

He nodded. "I'm going to be fine." He was rubbing his neck as if it was hurt. "But we've got bigger trouble than we thought. I know who the werewolf is."

Her heart leapt. If he knew who it was, she'd be able to figure out where it was. "Who?"

"Your deputy, Dana Landen."

❖

Bellona felt the power of the moon surge through her as it rose high in the black sky. How she loved these nights, and this one would only be better if Little Wolf hadn't turned out to be a colossal bitch. She should have known there was a bigger reason for her intense attraction than simple lust.

It was her own fault. She'd wanted to believe it was love, even though deep down she knew there was ever only one for her, and she'd died so long ago. That too was her fault. She'd been young and full of herself. She'd believed she could make it happen the way she wanted it to, and instead she'd ended up destroying the only person she'd ever really loved. She'd had to live with that knowledge, and guilt, for centuries.

Now she had a huge mess to clean up and very little time to do it. Adam and Eve were pacing and rightfully so. The time was here to let them come into their full strength. It was exciting and should be a time filled with joy. If not for Little Wolf's power play, it would be.

As it stood, she had to take Little Wolf down. Now that she knew what she was up against, she was ready. Little Wolf's arrogance wouldn't be enough to defeat her. She might be a witch and a werewolf, but she was still young, which was to her disadvantage. Bellona had come up against every conceivable threat and had come out victorious every time. It wouldn't be any different tonight.

And as soon as she took out Little Wolf, she would come back for Adam and Eve. They had no choice but to abandon this place, and so they would, together. She would not leave them behind.

Outside, she called the change, and her paws hit the ground with a thud. She was off and running, following Little Wolf's scent. That she could follow her so easily was no surprise. That there was a shaft of light shining like a beacon in the stand of trees to the south of the barn was. Was it Little Wolf calling upon her witchcraft? Or was it something far different?

Even in wolf form she was fully aware that out there somewhere lurked the hunters she'd had to avoid her whole life. They came in all forms and with varying preternatural skills. She intended to approach with a great deal of caution. If it was the Jägers, she would not put herself in jeopardy, nor would she charge in to save Little Wolf. That bitch was on her own from here on out.

As she drew close, a growl rose low in her throat. Little Wolf was in the center of the circle of light, her jaws around the neck of a man. She prepared to charge, to seize the moment while Little Wolf focused on her prey. She started into her run when two things happened at once. The man disappeared, and a third wolf roared into the light.

Bellona skidded to a stop as the third wolf's scent reached her nose. She knew it as well as she knew her own, even though it had been hundreds of years since she'd smelled it last. It was a winter night and snow had been falling just as it was now. She'd been leaning through the window with her long dark hair flowing around her face. The love she'd felt that night had overwhelmed her, and she'd done the only thing she could think of to give love a chance. She'd pulled Lily from the window and pierced her throat with her canines. She'd wanted to turn her so they could be together forever. Instead, she'd killed her, or so she'd believed until this moment.

CHAPTER THIRTY-TWO

Lily caught Taria's scent but she was already in motion, her sights on the wolf with her jaws around Kyle's throat. She didn't stop to wonder how he could be here on the forest floor when she'd seen him only minutes before on the hardwood of Jayne's entryway. It didn't matter how or why. All that mattered was stopping the wolf who was trying to kill him.

She surged, all four paws coming off of the ground, her eyes focused on the wolf that held him down. As she hit her, Kyle disappeared as if he'd never been there at all. It didn't stop her attack. She hit her hard, her own jaws clamping down on the back of her neck. She sank her teeth in with both power and fury. She shook her head, and blood poured from the tearing wounds. Still she didn't stop. The wolf in her roared.

As she battled with the wolf that didn't want to give in to death, she waited to feel Taria's attack. This wolf was no match for the older, stronger, and better-trained Lily. Her life began to fade away beneath her teeth. Lily dropped her body to the ground and raised her head in a massive howl.

When her head came down, she stared across the wolf's lifeless body and into eyes she hadn't seen in five centuries. She remembered them as if the attack had happened only yesterday. Again she raised her head and howled. Fury at what had been done to her and what she had lost filled her with a rage so deep it had to be turning her eyes red.

Taria had been a sister to her, someone she had loved and trusted. Betrayal had been her reward, and now she would repay the favor. She charged, and as she did, Taria came straight for her. Leaping over the body of the wolf, shock almost stopped her as the wolf she thought she'd killed rolled over and bit her hind leg. She yipped in surprise and pain.

How was this possible? She'd killed that wolf, and yet it had buried its teeth deep into her leg. She was held captive as Taria raced toward her with teeth bared. It was all going so wrong, and now she was going to die.

Just as Taria reached her, two shots rang out, the sound deafening in the night air. The pressure on her leg disappeared as Taria dropped, landing hard on the ground. Lily limped away, getting herself out of range of an additional attack. Only then did she notice that neither wolf was moving. She shook her head, trying to clear her vision. It couldn't be. As she watched, both returned to human form.

Taria, blood pouring from a wound in her chest, pushed herself up on her arms. "I'm sorry, Lily. I'm sorry."

Lily dropped to the ground and panted. Pain burned in her leg. Taking a long, deep breath, she too let herself return to human form. The pain didn't go away, and she put pressure on the open wounds. Unlike humans, she wasn't worried about infection. She would heal and quickly. "Why did you do this to me? You were my friend."

"I loved you. I couldn't let you marry Aldrich because I knew you belonged with me. I thought if I made you like me, we could be together forever." Her words grew softer and softer.

"You had no right."

"No, but love doesn't always do what's right. I'm sorry..." She slumped to the ground and didn't move again. Her long-ago friend was gone.

The wind whipped up and Lily shivered. More than the weather was sending chills through her body. She wanted to hate Taria for what she had done to Lily and for what she had robbed her of, except she couldn't. Despite it all, she thought of the days when they had talked and read and shared their inner thoughts. She thought of the friend who'd always been there for her, the friend she hadn't realized was in love with her. It was all wrong and sad and should never have had to end like this.

"Good thing I brought this," Jayne said as she kneeled beside her and put a long, heavy coat over her shoulders. The warmth was immediate and felt like heaven.

"I can't believe you're here. How did you know where to come?"

Jayne wrapped her in a hug that felt fantastic. "Kyle told me who the wolf was."

"Taria." It almost broke her heart to say it.

"Well, yes, Taria. She was the stranger we kept hearing about. The girlfriend she was staying with just happened to be my deputy."

"Oh," Lily breathed, and then took her first good look at the wolf she thought she had killed. "How did you..." She looked over at the two bodies.

Jayne gave her a little smile. "You might not have believed I was paying attention, but I was. I used what you told me about folk legends and what my brother and my father taught me to create a couple of shells loaded with silver."

Lily rested her head against Jayne's shoulder, suddenly very tired. "You didn't have enough time to make silver bullets." Jayne couldn't have melted down silver and had it cool quick enough to be able to use them.

Jayne kissed the top of her head. "No need for bullets when you can load shotgun shells. Bless my brother's heart. He had everything I needed to make the shells quickly. I wasn't sure the silver in my necklace would be enough, though it appears," she nodded toward the bodies of Taria and Dana, "it was."

"Did anyone ever tell you that you're pretty smart?"

"You mean for a small town sheriff?"

"Yes, that too."

Epilogue

L ily couldn't believe how fast the last two weeks had gone by. That night in the woods was a bit of a blur, though she would never truly be able to put it out of her mind. She would forever see Taria, or Bellona, as they learned that she now called herself, as she stood in wolf form staring at her with those familiar eyes. She had grown up with them, and only now did she understand why she had been paralyzed on the night she was attacked. It had been Taria's eyes in the body of the wolf that had shocked her into inaction, and that was when she'd been struck, pulled from the open window, and her life forever altered.

At the time she'd believed a stranger had harmed her, one of the lone werewolves known only to the Jägers to wander the countryside looking for prey. The Jägers had perpetuated that belief and further cemented it by telling her they had tracked the werewolf down and killed it. They had lied to her so she wouldn't be afraid to go into the world as the hunter they deemed her to be.

When Senn had first explained it all to her, she was furious. Where did they get off manipulating her and her life? However, after she calmed down, it all made a weird kind of sense. She had settled into the life of a Jägers hunter and become fearless. That never would have happened if she'd known Taria had attacked her and that she was still out there. Her ability to trust anyone would have been compromised by knowing it was one of those she trusted the most who betrayed her. She would have been fearful to walk outside her door if she'd worried that right outside the wolf might still be waiting. No, she grudgingly admitted, the decision the Jägers made to lie was, in her case, the right one.

Her heart still hurt even as she finally understood what had happened on that long-ago night and how Taria had tried in her own strange way to help the woman she loved. Lily always thought if she knew who had done this to her she would hate them, but the opposite was true. She still loved her friend, misguided as she might have been. She even understood her attraction to Dana. No one, not even a werewolf, really wanted to spend eternity alone. Like Taria, Lily realized she was lonely, and coming here had brought it all home.

Jayne made her feel for the first time in years. She filled something in Lily's heart that had been missing her whole life. Incredibly, Jayne knew exactly what she was and what she did, and it didn't make her turn away. Instead of repulsion, in her eyes she saw love and passion. It was easy to forgive Taria with Jayne by her side. Lily might be powerful, but Jayne gave her a different, and more important, kind of strength.

A car was coming up the driveway, and she smiled. Senn had made it, and it took only two phone calls to get him here. He had left his sanctuary on the other side of the world to make the trek to Northeast Washington. As he had done for her so long ago, he was here now to save two very special souls. Nate and Willa, or Adam and Eve, as Taria called them, were going with Senn to join the Jägers. Lily had no doubt that Nate would turn out to be a fantastic Jägers hunter. Willa, a beautiful, gentle soul, would find a place with Senn. The Jägers would help them control the beast that was forever inside them and give them a job that would suit their now-special nature.

Nate had filled them in on the details behind Dana, and they hadn't been good. Taria had made a rare bad decision in turning Dana. Her rebel nature combined with her dark witchcraft heritage made her a dangerous and out-of-control wolf. If Taria hadn't already figured that out, Lily had no doubt she would have soon enough. It was a shame so many had been harmed before they were able to stop Dana and Taria, but the town could now heal.

Kyle and Ava had left three days ago to make the long journey from Colville to New Haven. Kyle planned to stay with Ava—no big surprise there—to explore the source of magic that had saved him from the jaws of Dana, or as Taria had called her, Little Wolf. What Dana was able to do was something Lily and Senn wanted to explore in more detail too, for it was the first time they had come across someone who could manipulate time and space as Dana had done when she trapped

Kyle in a shadowland. If not for that sliver of light that linked Kyle and Ava, he would be dead now. The necromancer and the witch planned to investigate and strengthen that link, and that would give the Jägers a powerful tool in their battle against the darkness.

Jayne was still having a hard time wrapping her head around the reality that her trusted deputy was not just a homicidal werewolf but a dangerous witch as well. Lily knew it would take time for Jayne to once more trust her instincts when it came to seeing the best and the worst in people. But she would do it, and Lily intended to be there to help her.

The sun was shining today, the blue sky clear though the snow that had begun to fall the day before now covered everything in a clean, white blanket. It was beautiful. Normally, she would be gone as soon as her work was done. This time things were different, and the reason why was no mystery. She leaned against the railing and watched Senn steer his rental car down the long drive. She was glad he was here and glad he would be able to help both Nate and Willa transition to their new lives. They would do well under his tutelage. She knew that from firsthand experience.

Their meeting would be tense, and she wasn't quite sure what he might say when she told him she wasn't leaving with him. Certainly, she expected him to push back. It wouldn't make any difference. She was staying right here.

"You ready for this? Ready to tell him you're staying here with me?" Jayne came up behind her and put her arms around her shoulders, pulling her back against her chest in a warm hug. She didn't think she would ever tire of Jayne's embrace.

Lily nodded and smiled. "I'm ready."

About the Author

Sheri Lewis Wohl grew up in northeast Washington State, and though she always thought she'd move away, never has. Despite traveling throughout the United States, Sheri always finds her way back home. And so she lives, plays, and writes amidst mountains, evergreens, and abundant wildlife.

When not working the day job in federal finance, she writes stories that typically include a bit of the strange and unusual and always a touch of romance. She works to carve out time to run, swim, and bike so she can participate in local triathlons, her latest addiction.

Sheri can be contacted at her websites and her blog:

Website: http://www.sherilewiswohl.com/
Website: https://sherilewiswohl.wordpress.com/
Blog: http://www.sheri26.blogspot.com/